Praise for Georgia

The Do-Over

"You can count on Beers to give you a quality well-paced book each and every time."—*The Romantic Reader Blog*

"*The Do-Over* is a shining example of the brilliance of Georgia Beers as a contemporary romance author."—*Rainbow Reflections*

"[T]he two leads are genuine and likable, their chemistry is palpable… The romance builds up slowly and naturally, and the angst level is just right. The supporting characters are equally well developed. Don't miss this one!"—*Melina Bickard, Librarian, Waterloo Library (UK)*

Calendar Girl

"*Calendar Girl* by Georgia Beers is a well-written sweet workplace romance. It has all the elements of a good contemporary romance… It even has an ice queen for a major character."—*Rainbow Reflections*

"A sweet, sweet romcom of a story…*Calendar Girl* is a nice read, which you may find yourself returning to when you want a hot-chocolate-and-warm-comfort-hug in your life."—*Best Lesbian Erotica*

The Shape of You

"I know I always say this about Georgia Beers's books, but there is no one that writes first kisses like her. They are hot, steamy and all too much!"—*Les Rêveur*

The Shape of You "catches you right in the feels and does not let go. It is a must for every person out there who has struggled with self-esteem, questioned their judgment, and settled for a less than perfect but safe lover. If you've ever been convinced you have to trade passion for emotional safety, this book is for you."—*Writing While Distracted*

Blend

"You know a book is good, first, when you don't want to put it down. Second, you know it's damn good when you're reading it and thinking, I'm totally going to read this one again. Great read and absolutely a 5-star romance."—*The Romantic Reader Blog*

16 Steps
to Forever

"This is a lovely romantic story with relatable characters that have depth and chemistry. A charming easy story that kept me reading until the end. Very enjoyable."—*Kat Adams, Bookseller, QBD (Australia)*

"*Blend* has that classic Georgia Beers feel to it, while giving us another unique setting to enjoy. The pacing is excellent and the chemistry between Piper and Lindsay is palpable."—*The Lesbian Review*

Right Here, Right Now

"The angst was written well, but not overpoweringly so, just enough for you to have the heart-sinking moment of 'will they make it,' and then you realize they have to because they are made for each other."
—*Les Reveur*

"[A] successful and entertaining queer romance novel. The main characters are appealing, and the situations they deal with are realistic and well-managed. I would recommend this book to anyone who enjoys a good queer romance novel, and particularly one grounded in real world situations."—*Books at the End of the Alphabet*

"[A]n engaging odd-couple romance. Beers creates a romance of gentle humor that allows no-nonsense Lacey to relax and easygoing Alicia to find a trusting heart."—*RT Book Reviews*

Lambda Literary Award Winner *Fresh Tracks*

"Georgia Beers pens romances with sparks."—*Just About Write*

"[T]he focus switches each chapter to a different character, allowing for a measured pace and deep, sincere exploration of each protagonist's thoughts. Beers gives a welcome expansion to the romance genre with her clear, sympathetic writing."—*Curve magazine*

Lambda Literary Award Finalist *Finding Home*

"Georgia Beers has proven in her popular novels such as *Too Close to Touch* and *Fresh Tracks* that she has a special way of building romance with suspense that puts the reader on the edge of their seat. *Finding Home*, though more character driven than suspense, will equally keep the reader engaged at each page turn with its sweet romance."—*Lambda Literary Review*

Mine

"From the eye-catching cover, appropriately named title, to the last word, Georgia Beers's *Mine* is captivating, thought-provoking, and satisfying. Like a deep red, smooth-tasting, and expensive merlot, *Mine* goes down easy even though Beers explores tough topics."—*Story Circle Book Reviews*

"Beers does a fine job of capturing the essence of grief in an authentic way. *Mine* is touching, life-affirming, and sweet."—*Lesbian News Book Review*

Too Close to Touch

"This is such a well-written book. The pacing is perfect, the romance is great, the character work strong, and damn, but is the sex writing ever fantastic."—*The Lesbian Review*

"In her third novel, Georgia Beers delivers an immensely satisfying story. Beers knows how to generate sexual tension so taut it could be cut with a knife...Beers weaves a tale of yearning, love, lust, and conflict resolution. She has constructed a believable plot, with strong characters in a charming setting."—*Just About Write*

By the Author

16 STEPS TO FOREVER

by

Georgia Beers

2020

16 STEPS TO FOREVER

ISBN 13: 978-1-63555-762-6

This Trade Paperback Original Is Published By
Bold Strokes Books, Inc.
P.O. Box 249
Valley Falls, NY 12185

First Edition: December 2020

CREDITS
EDITORS: RUTH STERNGLANTZ AND STACIA SEAMAN
PRODUCTION DESIGN: STACIA SEAMAN
COVER DESIGN BY ANN MCMAN

Acknowledgments

Anybody who knows me knows that I'm a pretty orderly person. I'm organized. I like things just so, please don't mess them up, thank you very much. That includes the inanimate objects in my living space as well as the thoughts in my head. Everything in its place. Because of that aspect of my personality, I write a lot of orderly characters, but this time, I wanted to take one a little closer to the extreme. I wanted to give this one many of my own traits but also give her a past that would compound those traits, exacerbate them, so that not only does she neatly box up her home and work stuff, she boxes up her thoughts, her heart, herself. What would that do to a person, especially when she unexpectedly falls for someone? How would she handle something messy and disorganized, being as neat and tidy as she is? What would she be like? Allow me to introduce you to Brooke Sullivan. I hope you like her. I do.

As always, thank you to Radclyffe, Sandy Lowe, and the entire staff at Bold Strokes Books, for making a process that could be tense and stressful neither of those things. I am grateful.

My editor, Ruth Sternglantz, for her patience and her help. She makes me look good, as does Eagle-Eye Stacia Seaman, my copy editor. I have a terrific editing team and I couldn't be happier.

Big thanks to my friends that make up my support team; I don't know what I'd do without them: Melissa (title guru, review filterer, and direction pointer), Carsen (word counts and cheerleading), Rachel (sends periodic "How you doin', Boo?" messages to warm my heart), Nikki (my own personal comic relief and cat story sharer), Kris (chart expert), my family, and more. I am a lucky woman and an even luckier writer to be surrounded by the support system I have. I am forever grateful.

And to my readers: thank you from the bottom of my heart for your undying support and love. I am happily upholding my end of our deal: you keep reading and I'll keep writing.

CHAPTER ONE

C at puke.

She knew it the second she tried to put on her shoe.

"Sweet baby Jesus on a cracker." Macy Carr began to hop on her left foot as Emily's voice sounded from the speaker on her iPhone.

"What? What happened?"

"There's cat puke in my shoe, which I didn't see, so I put my foot in, and it squished through my sock and between my toes and I'm so grossed out and *I don't have time for this*."

Captain Jack sauntered away, head held high, and Macy squinted at him as he went. "I see you, you little punk. It's a good thing you're so cute. And that I love you." The cat looked back at her over his kitty shoulder. "He just winked at me. Swear to God."

"Is it possible to wink when you only have one eye?"

"It has to be because he just did it."

Emily's laugh was musical, like notes on a xylophone. "He's still mad at you for leaving him, huh?"

Macy peeled off her sock, made a face as she walked using just her heel to the downstairs powder room, and lifted her foot high enough to get it into the sink. "I was only gone for two nights." It was a whine. She knew it, and she didn't care. Just washed between her toes. Squirted some soap on her foot. "I explained to him that it was a conference for work. That work stuff helps me make money so I can keep him in catnip."

"Made no difference to him."

"Apparently not." Done washing, she grabbed the hand towel off the rack. "Thank God the dogs are outside, or they'd be trying to lick this off me right now."

"Ew, now *I'm* grossed out," Emily said, and Macy could picture her wrinkling her nose. "Thanks for that."

"Good. Why should I be the only one? You're welcome." Three sets of eyes peered at Macy through the sliding glass door off her small dining room, and she couldn't help but laugh. "All right, let me go. I have to find other shoes and take care of the pack."

"See you soon. I'll have a vanilla latte."

A grin and a shake of her head and Macy hung up, tucked the phone into the back pocket of her jeans. Shoe in hand, she slid the door open and let in the troops, watching as twelve paws brought April into her house, and it marked its territory with wet and brown—the two key elements of March and April, as far as Macy was concerned.

"Damn it, I liked these shoes," she muttered as she dropped the shoe in the sink to be dealt with later. Dog towel in hand, she said, "Hey, come here, dirty doggies."

Pete, an eight-year-old golden retriever and the sweetest boy on the face of the earth, stood obediently next to her as she wiped each of his paws, then kissed him on the head. Priscilla, her twelve-year-old dachshund, was already all comfy on her pink dog bed in the corner of the living room by the fireplace, so Macy went to her, was gentle with the old girl who'd begun to suffer from some joint pain in the past year. From behind her, she heard the telltale *rowr* from Angus, her four-year-old Scottie, whose life revolved around Tennis Ball. Sure enough, when she turned around, he had one in his mouth, the yellow felt muffling his demands, his tail wagging madly, his dark eyes almost impossible to make out under all that black fur.

"Aw, buddy, I don't have time for Tennis Ball now. You can discuss that with Captain Jack, if you want." Angus blinked at her, *rowr*ed again.

On the floor. Macy spent more time there than on her furniture, and she dropped there now. "Let me wipe your feet, and I'll throw it."

Angus seemed to contemplate this deal offering as Macy grabbed the ball. She'd never get it out of his mouth if he didn't want her to, but surprisingly he let her have it. Ball tucked under her thigh, she wiped all four of his paws, then dutifully threw it into the kitchen and grinned as stubby-legged Angus toddled after it.

Back on her feet, Macy turned to the cat tree. Captain Jack sat in the top tier looking out the window, pointedly ignoring her. Jellybean, on the other hand, stood from her perch one level down. Macy bent to eye level and scratched her as the tiny tiger cat bumped heads with her. A sign of affection, and Macy loved it.

A run upstairs to find new shoes, a chewy to all dogs and treats to both cats, and Macy was out the door. A glance at her cozy house as she backed out of the driveway sang of impending spring. Big flowerpots of brown and wilted flowers left over from fall, just waiting to be refilled with color. Lawn peeking through the mud and puddles in patches, trying its hardest to be green. Birds exploring the bird feeder she needed to fill. Macy turned on the heat, slid mirrored sunglasses onto her face, and turned up Lizzo's latest tune as she got on the road.

A quick stop at Starbucks later, Macy parked her car and entered the back entrance of Stage One Property Staging. Located on a shop-lined stretch of Main, the office wasn't large because it didn't need to be. Two desks, a small conference table, a refreshment area. That's all Macy and Emily needed in their office space, as the bread and butter of their business was in a warehouse fifteen minutes away. Emily owned Stage One, but Macy's goal was to become her business partner in the near future, and then take it over once Emily retired.

"One vanilla latte," Macy said and set the cup down with a flourish on Emily's desk. "You look lovely today, Ms. Baxter."

"You say that every day," Emily replied, removing the lid and taking a deep inhale from the coffee cup.

"Because I think it's nice to hear it every day."

"Well, thank you."

"Well, you're welcome."

Emily took a pointed look at Macy's feet, now clad in brown ankle boots rather than the cute wedges she'd planned on.

"Puke-free," Macy told her with a roll of her eyes, then hung her coat on the antique coat tree in the corner and took a seat in her chair.

Having their desks on opposite walls was a good way to make the small space seem larger. Important, as that's what they did: made spaces look a certain way. Bigger. Smaller. Cozier. Roomier. More modern. Less modern. While there wasn't a lot in their office itself, the way it presented to potential clients was important. The walls held framed photos of different properties they'd staged, shots of open concept homes, modern penthouses, lakefront cottages. Both Macy and Emily kept the personal items on their desks to a minimum—which was easier for Emily than for Macy. One framed photo each. Macy had a succulent in a bright purple pot. Emily had a small crystal vase of fresh flowers, while a larger one served as a centerpiece for the table between them.

Tidy and sparse not being huge parts of Macy's regular world, she had to work a little harder than Emily to keep things that way.

"What have we got today?" she asked Emily. An unnecessary question, as their schedule was right in front of her on her computer screen. The phone rang before Emily could reply.

"Stage One, this is Emily."

Macy smiled at the singsong tone of Emily's voice, the way she was able to put clients at ease in an instant. Two clicks and she was scanning the day's appointments. It was a busy one, but that's the way Macy liked it. Full day of work. Full evening with her animals.

It was going to be a good day.

The weather in upstate New York isn't really all that different than in Ohio.

The thought crossed Brooke Sullivan's mind as she glanced out the bedroom window. April in Ohio was kind of…well, brown. With a promise of color by the end. Outside the window of her new rental, the sun was shining, what remained of the snow had melted away, and most of the landscape was…brown.

But the brown meant the green was on its way, and Brooke loved the green so could deal with the brown until it got there. She could be patient. She smiled as a squirrel ran across the yard of the complex toward a tree, his bushy tail like a feather boa trailing behind him.

With a large exhale, she turned back to the full-length mirror and stared at her reflection for several moments. Analyzing. Scrutinizing. Criticizing.

"It'll have to do."

There would be days when she wouldn't have to dress like the CEO of a Fortune 500 company, but it was her first day at Wolfe Realty, and Brooke had way too many emotions rolling through her to worry about changing into yet another outfit. Nerves were coated with excitement. Uncertainty wrestled with positivity. She was a ball of feelings, none of which she really wanted to deal with. No, Brooke wanted to get to her new office, meet the players, and settle into this new life. It was time.

Her reflection showed a woman with purpose. A woman in charge. A no-nonsense woman brimming with confidence. A little snort over that, but then she studied the mirror. Black pantsuit, simple white blouse underneath the jacket, three silver buttons down the front, thick auburn hair in a French braid and tucked under for a professional, streamlined look. Black heels, but not too high. Brooke had learned in her five years as a high-end real estate agent that wealthy clients trusted sales agents who looked put together and neat, but not richer than they were because that would mean the agent was making too much in commission. So she did her best to walk that fine line, and it had seemed to work so far. She looked exactly right for the part.

Satisfied she'd reached as-good-as-it-was-going-to-get status, she headed downstairs to her small kitchen, dodging the occasional unopened box. Two days. That was all she'd been there, and she still had unpacking to do, but she was in no hurry. A nudge with her foot slid a box against the wall and out of her way.

I like this place.

A thought that surprised her, to say the least. She wouldn't be there long. She was a Realtor, after all, and had the resources to find herself the perfect home. But being new to town and needing to start work right away were obstacles that left her little time for house hunting. A rental had become a necessary stopover until she got settled. Getting her license in New York State took longer than she'd expected. That being said, she'd found a nice place. New, well-maintained, and roomy. Her master bedroom had high ceilings, which made the one thousand square foot town house seem airy and bigger than it was. Once her mug was set and her coffee pod was in place and brewing, she leaned her back against the counter and surveyed her kingdom.

Clean lines. Sleek surfaces. That's what Brooke liked. Her black leather couch faced a forty-two-inch flat-screen television perched on a black TV stand. The standard beige carpet didn't thrill her, but she envisioned finding a black-and-white area rug to pull together the living room's design. Maybe this weekend, she'd go shopping. The walls were empty, but she had some art she intended to hang. That would help keep the living space from seeming too cold. Impersonal. Two things her ex had accused her of being.

The Keurig beeped, thank God. Black and strong. That was how she liked her coffee. She took a big inhale, let the delicious scent of it fill her, wake her up, bolster her. Then she transferred it to a black metal travel mug and screwed on the top.

Her weather app said it was fifty-three degrees outside, so she donned her long black coat, shouldered her black messenger bag, and scooped up her coffee cup. A mirror in the hallway by the front door was the only thing she'd hung on the walls so far, and she glanced into it, stared into the dark brown eyes looking back at her.

"This is the first day of the rest of your life," she whispered. A mantra she'd used for years now, and it did the trick. She felt herself stand up straighter and lifted her chin. "Let's do this."

❖

Brooke shifted her Audi into park and sat back in the driver's seat. Wolfe Realty was in what used to be a very large house in an affluent section of town. Two-story, white siding with some brick facing, and two large round columns, it looked warm and inviting, homey, while at the same time held an air of regality, of wealth and success.

Tons of research had given Brooke all the details. Started in 1971 by Robert Wolfe, Wolfe Realty had begun as a small office with two real estate agents selling houses to families. Within ten years, there were eight agents, and Robert had added commercial clients to the residential ones. Another decade went by and Wolfe Realty had become one of the top-selling real estate agencies in the state, with two distinct arms: residential sales and commercial sales. When Robert had finally retired five years ago, his daughter Sasha had taken over as head of the business. Brooke had had three Skype interviews with her, and after the third one, Sasha'd made her an offer she couldn't refuse.

Now, she sat in her car, steadied her breathing, and psyched herself up. She knew she had this. Her résumé had spoken for itself—Sasha Wolfe had literally said so. But even at thirty-one years old, starting fresh in a new town in a new job was hard. Nerve-racking. Made her jittery. She held a trembling hand out in front of her, squeezed it into a tight fist, then opened her fingers again. Three times before the tremors stopped.

Deep breath.

Pull the door handle.

Here we go.

It was 8:45 a.m. In Brooke's experience, real estate offices tended to be busier in the late morning and into the evenings, as residential agents often showed houses and made deals after the normal workday, when clients were free. Commercial real estate was different, though. Working with businesses—unlike families looking to buy a house— took place during business hours, and the offices of Wolfe Realty reflected that reality. While she couldn't see how many people milled about in the heart of the building, the parking lot had been at least half full, thirteen cars, by her count. The lobby was two stories, all glass and sunshine and expensive furniture and lush plants. A large horseshoe desk stood in the center, with waiting areas on either side and a hallway directly behind it leading, she assumed, to the inner sanctum of Wolfe Realty. The woman at the front desk wore an earpiece and spoke in a cheerful, helpful tone. She glanced up at Brooke and smiled, held up one finger. Maybe in her late forties, chestnut hair cut short and stylishly, red manicured fingernails.

"I'll transfer you now." A push of a button and the woman's attention turned to Brooke. "Hi there. How can I help you?"

"Hi. I'm Brooke Sullivan, the—"

"New agent! Oh, hi there!" The woman's excitement was apparent as she stood and held out her hand before Brooke even had time to. "I've heard so much about you. Everybody's excited to meet you. I'm Annie Blue." She shook Brooke's hand firmly, then waved a finger up and down in front of her. "*Love* your suit. Let me tell Sasha you're here."

Brooke's smile appeared with no permission from her. She couldn't help it. Annie was a bundle of sunshine and cheer, and it was obvious why she sat at the front desk. She'd put anybody at ease, that was clear.

"Brooke Sullivan is here…Got it." Annie hit a button and turned her smile back Brooke's way. Brooke had missed it, she realized, glad to have it trained on her again. "She'll be right out. Can I get you anything? Coffee? Tea? Water? Smoothie?"

"Smoothie?" Furrowed brow.

"We have a machine, yes. They're *wonderful*." Annie's face reflected the delight that was apparently the Wolfe Realty smoothie machine.

"I'm good. But thank you."

Brooke heard the clicking of heels coming down a hallway and counted them in her head—twelve of them—for a good five seconds before she actually saw Sasha Wolfe approaching, hand outstretched, welcoming smile on her face.

"You made it. I'm so glad you're here." Sasha was tall. Brooke hadn't expected that, though she wasn't sure why. Five ten, at least. Blond hair pulled partially back, the rest hanging in golden waves around her shoulders. Blue eyes that looked like they didn't miss a thing. And a simultaneously welcoming and intimidating demeanor, as if she was silently announcing *I will be your friend, but also, I will cut you if you cross me.* Sasha's handshake was firm, confident. "Welcome aboard. Ready for the tour?"

"Absolutely." She glanced back at Annie, who wiggled her fingers in a cute little wave, then followed the formidable Sasha Wolfe into the halls of what she hoped would be her new home away from home.

Chapter Two

R ight Up Your Alley was a boutique bowling alley on the edge of town, and Macy loved everything about it. In addition to bowling alleys, it had foosball tables, Ping-Pong, shuffleboard, and air hockey. Soft and inviting couches and love seats were sprinkled throughout the seating areas, the bar made craft cocktails, and the food had been reviewed as some of the best in the city. It was one of Macy's favorite places to hang out.

Also, Macy was a god-awful bowler.

She knew it. She didn't care. She loved to bowl. There was something freeing in hurling the heavy ball down the alley, listening to the rumbling sound of it, the crash as it hit the pins. Or in her case, the small clack or two when it hit a couple of pins. Maybe.

"I love bowling with Charlie," she said as she waited for her ball to return.

"That's because the bumpers make it so you can't get a gutter ball," Tyler said with a snort-laugh that Macy was certain only teenagers could master.

"Hey, be nice to your favorite aunt."

"You're my only aunt. And I'm also kicking your ass."

They both looked up at the monitor where they were in the fourth frame. Macy had a score of twenty and Tyler had thirty-two.

"Yeah, you'll both be on the pro tour before you know it, I'm sure." Eva was older than Macy by ten years, but they were as close as two sisters could be. It was her turn, but toddler Charlie, at just two years old, could fall asleep anytime and anywhere and just had. "Ty, take my turn?"

"Yes," Tyler said, adding a fist pump to punctuate his excitement.

As he grabbed his mother's bowling ball and readied himself, Harlan returned from the bar with three beers in plastic cups.

"I put in a food order. About fifteen minutes, they said." He handed Macy a beer, took a seat, sipped. "You got this, Ty."

Tyler let the ball go, pretty much straight down the alley but with just the right amount of spin, and eight pins dropped. Harlan mimicked his son's fist pump.

Macy dropped to the orange plastic seat next to him, sipped her beer, and took a moment to gaze around and be thankful. Something she'd been working on for a while now—gratitude for what she had, not anger/envy/frustration at what she didn't. She was here with her family. Eva and Harlan and their kids, people she loved more than life. Tyler was shooting for a spare, which he would likely get, and she watched the beauty of his approach. There was very little sports-wise that he couldn't ace. Charlie was out like a light on Eva's lap, his blond hair tousled, orange crumbs from his Goldfish crackers sprinkled along the front of his blue and white striped shirt, thumb in his mouth. He'd been unplanned. Eva was forty, exhausted, her eyes so full of love it often made Macy tear up. She wanted that, wanted kids, wanted to feel that love. There'd been a plan…

No. Stop it. Gratitude. Focus on the gratitude. Be thankful.

Eva met her gaze over the scoring table and smiled. "How was work?"

"Oh my God, so busy." Macy said it like it was a burden, but it wasn't. She loved when work was busy.

As if reading her mind, Harlan said, "But that's good, right? Busy is good. Busy means business and business means money. So busy is good."

"It really is. We had to lay out three different houses today, and then Wolfe Realty set up a meeting to talk to us about some of their commercial properties that are for sale. So that could be big."

"They stage commercial properties?" Eva's brow furrowed.

Macy shrugged as a staff member showed up with a huge tray of food. "I mean, sure, why not? We can make an office look good. And there could be an apartment building or a building of condos, you know? So residential, but also commercial?"

"Ah, okay. That makes sense."

They paused their bowling match to eat dinner, passing different dishes across to those who ordered them.

"Ugh, get this away from me." Harlan made the same face he

always made when faced with Macy's vegetarianism—like he'd smelled something foul. She took her veggie burger out of his hands. Rolled her eyes. Tyler handed her a basket of fries, and his suddenly pink cheeks registered embarrassment, something Macy saw often on her nephew's face lately. She winked at him, hoping to take away some of what looked a lot like stress hanging out in his kind blue eyes.

"How's school?" she asked him. He opened his mouth to speak, but Harlan's voice interrupted him.

"You talk to the coach about football season?" Harlan took a huge bite of his decidedly not-veggie burger.

"He doesn't want to play football anymore, Harlan." Eva's voice was calm but held an edge that told Macy they'd talked about this subject more than once. "He wants to focus on soccer."

"It's okay, Mom." Tyler ate a fry, shrugged.

"He shouldn't just quit. My boy's not a quitter. Right, Ty?" Another bite. Harlan bumped his son with a shoulder.

A grimace from Tyler. A sigh from Eva.

High time for a subject change.

"Ty, you still coming over on Saturday?" Seeing her nephew's face light up the way it did right then was a balm to any bad thing that could ever happen to Macy. He was growing so fast and was currently in the homestretch of that gangly stage where he was often clumsy, like he wasn't sure how to operate his rapidly lengthening arms and legs. His journey from boy to man was happening at an alarmingly fast rate, at least for Macy.

"Hell, yeah," he said, and then his expression turned sheepish at the look Eva shot him. She didn't even have to say *Watch your mouth.* It was unspoken, but crystal clear. A universal talent of moms everywhere.

Charlie picked that moment to wake up, his sleepy face breaking into a smile as he stretched his chubby arms over his head and yawned widely to display the bright rows of teeth in his little mouth.

"Well, hi there," Eva said to her son as she sat him up.

"Who's the happiest baby on the planet?" Macy asked as she reached for him, and he lifted his arms to her. "Is it you? Is it? Come here and see your Aunt Macy."

Charlie pointed to a bowler, and his little lips formed a perfect O as he watched the bright green ball roll down the alley. Then he uttered a small "Whoa." Macy laughed and kissed his dimpled cheek.

Ten more minutes and Harlan clapped his hands together once. "Back at it?"

Nods all around and the bowling resumed. As Harlan took his turn—all power, little skill, lots of pins knocked down—and Eva followed Charlie as he toddled around the bowling alley, Macy sat back next to Tyler and folded her arms over her chest.

"You know, you don't have to play football anymore if you don't want to, right? Doesn't make you a quitter. At all." She didn't look at her nephew as she spoke.

"I know." He stared straight ahead, his sandy hair falling into his eyes, and shrugged but said nothing more on the subject. A beat passed. Two. Then, "Hey, can we watch *Rent* Friday night?"

Macy grinned, didn't bug her eyes out and say *Again?* or remind him how many times they'd already watched it—close to a dozen. "Absolutely. I'll make caramel popcorn."

"Sweet." He got up to take his turn.

Eva dropped into the chair Tyler had vacated with a tired groan.

"I love that boy, you know," Macy said quietly.

"I know."

Macy turned to Charlie and swooped him off his mother's lap and into her own. "And I love this boy, too." She dove at him, kissing the side of his neck with loud smacks as her nephew's gleeful giggles filled the air.

Much of Brooke's job involved adrenaline. Not huge doses, not like she was a firefighter or somebody on the trading floor on Wall Street or an emergency room doctor. But smaller steady doses of it. The thrill of a sale. The anticipation of showing a client something that's exactly right. Knowing she was getting a sizable commission. All those things gave her little shots of adrenaline. Little boosts that kept her running all day.

The downside of running on adrenaline was that you had to come down sooner or later, hopefully as a gentle lowering onto a soft pillow and not as a painful crash onto a concrete floor. She'd experienced both, and she much preferred the gentle lowering. No surprise there.

Tonight, though…tonight, she was just tired. Bone-weary, no-energy-to-stand-up-any-longer exhausted. Wiped the hell out.

Unsurprising, really. She'd been firing on all cylinders since Saturday afternoon when she and the movers had arrived at her town house. Since she'd rented it online, without having actually seen it, she was pleasantly surprised by the spaciousness of the rooms, the privacy of the backyard area, small but mostly fenced. It was a newer build, so her kitchen appliances were all modern. Stainless steel. Black granite countertops. She poured herself a glass of sauvignon blanc, grabbed her tuna salad sandwich, and went into the living room where she dropped to the couch with the sigh of a woman who'd worked nonstop for nearly ten hours. Because she had.

She should have done more unpacking, but her brain didn't even have the capacity left for something mindless on the television, let alone deciding where things should go, so she left the boxes alone, left the TV off, and ate in the silence.

A muffled thump came from the wall behind her. Neighbors. Renting was new for Brooke—she'd owned a house back in Ohio. Small and older, but the first thing she'd purchased on her own. Leaving it had been hard, but until she got to know the various neighborhoods of Northwood, she didn't feel comfortable buying something sight unseen. Renting a town house temporarily had been the solution. What she couldn't really anticipate virtually was how thick or thin the walls separating the houses might be.

Another thump, this time followed by a man's voice. "Goddamn it."

"I'm sorry." A woman. "I didn't think—"

"You *never* think, do you?" He definitely sounded mad.

The voices faded, and Brooke figured they must've moved to another room. She shook her head, sipped her wine. As she did so, she glanced at the sliding glass door off the dining area and jumped in surprise. Two yellow eyes stared back at her, slightly below knee level.

An investigation revealed it to be a cat. Brooke squatted to get a better look. The cat didn't move but simply sat there, watching her. Inky black fur made it hard to see in the dark, those yellow eyes the only pop of color at all. No collar that she could see, and it seemed kind of thin.

"Are you a stray? Lost?" she asked through the glass.

The cat continued to watch her, yawned once, then watched some more. Blinked occasionally.

Brooke pursed her lips. "Not a huge cat fan, not gonna lie. Maybe you should find a different house."

The cat seemed unaffected by her statement, so she stood and went back to the living room to finish her dinner. Maybe tomorrow she wouldn't be quite this tired, and she'd be able to take a walk, explore a little bit, get to know her new city.

By nine fifteen, Brooke was yawning widely. She knew there were a few boxes in her bedroom that needed to be unpacked, so she decided she'd make an attempt at starting at least one of them until she was ready to fall into bed. "Yeah, I'll unpack for five minutes," she muttered with a small chuckle as she put her dishes in the dishwasher. As she hit the light switch in the kitchen, she noticed the cat was still there, still at her door, now lying down. Watching.

They had a little stare down. Five seconds. Ten. Finally Brooke sighed and grabbed the tuna can she hadn't rinsed yet.

"Fine," she said, crossing to the door and sliding it open. "Don't get used to this," she said to the cat as she set the can on the ground and shut the door again, locked it.

She left the vertical blinds open.

Upstairs, she pulled some clothes out of an open box and hung them in the walk-in closet. It wasn't huge, but it was bigger than any closet she'd had in her old house, so she loved it. As she hung a shirt here, a pair of pants there, she reflected on her day, which had been a whirlwind of new faces, meetings, and an influx of information that had her reeling from the potential. She'd been given her own office—many agents were in cubicles—and Sasha had scheduled her to sit in on several meetings during the week.

"Your reputation is stellar." That's what Sasha had said during their first interview, and she'd said it again today, then indicated that she had at least two clients she would introduce Brooke to this week. One of them involved a brand-new build featuring twenty-four luxury apartments. "I want you on this," Sasha had said to her, right there at the conference table in the Wolfe Realty offices in front of fifteen staff members. Sasha's confidence in her was apparent. Not only to Brooke, but to the other agents. Brooke noticed a scowl or two here, a subtle eye roll there, but most of the staff was welcoming.

She hung up one more dress and felt herself hit the figurative wall. She fell onto her bed just as her phone pinged the arrival of a text. She glanced. Eddie.

How was ur first day?

Well, it had only taken all day long and well into the evening for her to hear from her little brother. "Better late than never, I guess," she muttered as she typed a response.

Super busy, but good.

His reply came a few seconds later: *Dope.*

She waited for more, but apparently, that was going to be it. Typical. Back in its place on the nightstand, the phone stayed quiet.

It had been hard to leave her hometown, but moments like this reminded her why she had. Her family really didn't know her, and what they did know, they didn't like. Eddie was three years younger than Brooke, but they'd grown up very close. She'd always been very protective of him, until he grew to his full height of six two. Then the roles had reversed, and Eddie became Brooke's protector.

All that changed the day she'd come out.

"Nope." She said it aloud. Got undressed and ready for bed, continually shaking her head. "Nope. Not going there."

Master of Not Going There.

She needed a degree or at least a certificate of some kind to show people how adept she'd become at it. At avoidance.

Under the covers, she let out a long breath, tried to get herself to relax, to let go of the tension that seemed to be a permanent part of her existence. As usual, she was only able to get partway there.

This was her chance. A new town. A new home. A new job.

A new start.

CHAPTER THREE

How the hell was it Thursday already?

The question ran through Macy's mind as she gathered up her bag, her purse, and the box of Danishes she'd brought with her to the Wolfe Realty offices. She wasn't late, thank God, but she was cutting it close for her nine thirty meeting, thanks to the fact that Priscilla took her good old sweet time doing her business that morning, wandering the small backyard for what felt like hours to Macy. And while she hated to rush the little dachshund—Macy didn't want to be rushed when *she* was that old—she had things to do. Then, there had been an unusually long line at Sweet on You, and her favorite doughnuts had been sold out, so she'd had to settle for Danishes. Which had looked really good, she had to admit.

"Macy!" Annie Blue smiled wide as Macy walked toward the front desk. "Long time no see, girl. How's life? How are all those adorable animals of yours?" And just like that, Macy felt the tiniest bit less frazzled. Annie had that effect on people.

"Priscilla rules the roost, the boys fall in line, Jellybean is a love muffin, and Captain Jack continues to plot my death, I'm sure."

"So same as always then, huh?" Annie stood and held out her hands. "Here, give me that. I'll make 'em look nice." Macy handed over the bakery box without a word. "Gimme two minutes. Sasha's running a little late anyway. You've got time." She indicated the waiting area with her chin, and then disappeared through a door behind her desk.

Macy loved the lobby at Wolfe. It felt so open and spacious, regardless of the weather. Today being sunny only added to that effect, the rays of light pouring through the enormous windows and bathing the floor plants with the giant leaves in sunshine.

"Here you go." Annie had reappeared and held out a plate to Macy, the Danishes arranged in a lovely display.

"You're the best, Annie—you know that, right?" Macy took the plate.

"I was going to just bring them to the conference room, but I thought it would be better if you arrived with them." She gave Macy a wink. "You can go right in."

Another reason Macy adored Annie Blue—she got it. Yes, bringing pastries to a meeting could be construed as a tiny bit of a bribe, a way to ingratiate herself with the staff, and Macy knew that. It also made her look good because what office staff didn't love when somebody brought them food? Annie knew that it made for a better entrance if Macy showed up, pastries in hand.

Wolfe Realty was a not-quite-new, semi-regular client of Stage One, and Emily wanted to lose the *semi* part. While Stage One's bread and butter was residential staging, branching into offices and luxury apartments was something Emily had been working toward for months now. Wolfe was definitely a way toward that goal, and this meeting was a big step. Emily would've come herself if she hadn't had a prior commitment.

Macy smiled and nodded at various staff members as she walked toward the conference room she'd been to probably a dozen times now.

"Hey, Macy," called an agent named Martha from her desk across the open room of cubicles. Macy had staged a condo for her that helped nudge Martha's clients into the *let's make an offer* category. Macy lifted her chin in a salute, the best she could do with full hands as she turned into the doorway of the large conference room…

And walked directly into another person.

Not gently. A full-on body check, complete with *oof*s from both parties and Danishes everywhere. In the air, on the floor, smashed into the beautiful and probably very expensive ivory suit worn by the tall figure that Macy'd collided with.

Time stood still, as if they'd frozen mid-chaos. Everything was everywhere, and Macy was afraid to move. So was the woman in front of her, apparently, because they both stood still, the woman, arms out, looking down at all the icing and—*Oh God!*—raspberry jam smeared all over the chest of what had to be a designer jacket. Macy's gaze was riveted to the same place, the same spot.

As if given a jolt of electricity, action started up again. People already in the room ran over to them. The woman kept her arms out to her sides, and when she looked up—or down, rather, she was taller—at Macy, her large brown eyes were hard. Icy, which seemed like something brown eyes couldn't be, at least to Macy.

"Oh my God, I am *so* sorry," Macy said, looking around for something to help clean the woman up. She grabbed a napkin from a pile on the table and wiped at the stain, unintentionally grazing a breast.

The woman pushed at her hand, eyes going wide. Indignant. "Excuse me?"

Macy felt her own eyes widen as she realized her mistake. "God, I'm sorry. I was just trying to help—"

"Well, don't." The woman took a step back from her, out of her reach, still looking down at the mess on her jacket.

Annie must have heard the collision because she suddenly appeared out of nowhere with paper towels and immediately squatted to pick up the scattered pastries. "No worries. Accidents happen all the time. We'll get this cleaned right up." The reassuring words helped, definitely, and Macy blew out a breath as she watched the woman step over the mess and leave the room without another word, presumably to head to the bathroom.

For the first time, Macy focused on the conference room and the others in it. Not many, thank God. Sasha Wolfe was there—that wasn't good—though she seemed more amused than anything. Two people she'd seen before, but only once or twice, so she didn't know their names off the top of her head. Brennan Templeton, an agent she'd worked with more than once. He was precise, almost too meticulous, a little snarky, but Macy knew how to handle him. He stood at his seat at the large oval conference table and straightened his purple tie but made no move to help.

Between the two of them, Macy and Annie got things cleaned up. Sasha stood near them and held the plate while Annie filled it with sad chunks of squashed and misshapen Danish.

"So much for wooing you with pastries," Macy said, looking up at Sasha with a grimace.

Sasha was the epitome of sophistication as far as Macy was concerned. Tall, blond, beautiful, successful, wealthy, respected. She was practically the poster child for Women to Crush On, and Macy definitely crushed on her. From afar, of course, because this was business, and Sasha Wolfe was so far out of her league they were playing different sports. But Sasha was gorgeous and intimidating and the last person in the world whose floor Macy wanted to throw Danishes all over.

Emily was going to kill her.

"No worries," Sasha said with a warm smile. That was the other thing about Sasha—she could very easily have been hard, was often labeled an ice queen, but she was far from it. She held a hand down to Macy and tugged her to her feet.

Macy glanced over her shoulder in the direction the other woman had gone. "I feel awful. I hope I didn't ruin her outfit."

Sasha waved a hand. "Like I said. No worries." She gestured to the back of the room where a coffee station was set up. "Grab yourself a cup, and as soon as Brooke gets back, I'll introduce you and we'll get started."

Brooke. She must be the new agent Sasha had mentioned in her last email to Emily. She was supposed to be some dynamic salesperson in the commercial market. Came from out of state with a sparkling reputation and Sasha had high hopes.

Macy winced quietly as she doctored her coffee. Her mother's voice echoed through her head from years ago. *You never get a second chance to make a first impression.* Yeah, she'd definitely blown that with this Brooke person. It was an accident, and she sincerely hoped that the woman understood that. Macy leaned a bit toward the klutzy side, but she didn't enjoy showing that to people on her very first meeting with them. Her back still to the table, she measured her breathing and told herself to relax. That accidents happened.

When she turned back to the face the room, it was with a big, confident smile.

❖

"Goddamn it."

Brooke knew she shouldn't have scrubbed. Water and raspberry Danish filling just made for a large pinkish stain on her jacket. Her new BOSS suit she'd splurged and spent an inordinate amount of money on when she'd learned she'd been hired at Wolfe. And now, for some reason, she couldn't get herself to stop scrubbing. Finally forcing herself to let go of the paper towel, lower her arm, and just look in the mirror, she wanted to cry. The dry cleaner would probably laugh at her.

"Goddamn it."

Ripped off the jacket. Tossed it on the floor. Parked her hands on her hips and focused on her breathing. *Get a grip*, she told herself. *It was an accident. Accidents happen. She didn't arrive with the intention of ruining your suit. Just breathe.*

Inhale through the nose.

Hold it.

Count.

Exhale through the mouth.

She heard the instructions for meditating in her brain as she counted. Inhale, two, three, four. Hold it, two, three, four. Exhale, two, three, four. Somehow, counting always seemed to ease her stress levels, and within moments, she felt better. Her heart slowed down, her anger dissipated. Shaking her head with a sigh, she picked up the jacket off the floor, took it to her office to drape it over a chair, and headed back to the conference room in her ivory pants—which had miraculously avoided any and all Danish contact—and black silk top with the white pinstripes.

Laughter came from the conference room as Brooke knocked lightly, then opened the door. The pastry flinger must have been telling a story because her hands were whipping around animatedly, and all four of the other folks in the room seemed enamored with her, including Sasha, who saw Brooke come in and stood.

"Brooke, come on in," Sasha said, holding out an arm. "I know you've unofficially met Macy Carr, but let me introduce you officially. Macy works for Stage One, the property stager we use most often."

"And hopefully exclusively. In the near future." The woman stood and Brooke really looked at her. Average height. Brown hair with a slight wave that just brushed her shoulders—she tucked a hunk behind an ear in what might have been a nervous gesture, as she held out a hand for Brooke to shake. She was dressed business casually in simple black pants and a red sweater. Brown eyes, clear skin, little makeup. Macy Carr was a natural beauty. "I'm so sorry," she said, and those brown eyes held a surprising sincerity. "Please let me pay for the dry cleaning."

Brooke let go of her hand, took a seat, shook her head. "Not necessary," she said. "But I appreciate the offer."

She looked like she might press the issue, but instead, Macy gave one nod, sat, and knocked her pen off the table. With a loud sigh, she bent to retrieve it as Sasha said, "Remind me not to have you carry anything made of glass today."

Macy clunked her head on the underside of the table before

sheepishly sitting back up, pen in hand. "God, right?" she said and shook her head.

Flaky. That was the description Brooke settled on. Macy Carr was a pretty, klutzy flake.

But Sasha trusted her and said Stage One was the best property stager she'd worked with. And since, so far, Sasha had given Brooke no reason not to trust her, Brooke had to sit tight and keep her mouth shut and work with Macy Carr.

Fine. If she had to. Brooke was nothing if not professional.

For the next hour, Sasha talked about the new Whitney Gardens project, a ten-story building of luxury condos with shops on the ground floor, offices on the second, and condos the rest of the way up. Already well into construction, it was scheduled to be ready for occupation by early fall, and Wolfe had been hired to fill it with buyers.

"Brennan, I want you and Brooke on this, both offices and condos." Sasha looked to Brennan first, who looked like he'd smelled something rotten, and Brooke had already gotten the impression that he was not thrilled by her presence. "I know you've got some clients who might be interested. Have Amanda help you." She gestured to one of the women who'd sat quietly this whole time. She was around thirty-five, petite, and gave Brennan a hesitant smile. Then Sasha turned her gaze on the other woman in the room, Jasmine, who Brooke put at about twenty-three, and maybe fresh out of college. "Jazz, I want you to assist Brooke. Get her whatever she needs. Brooke, if you have questions about the city, ask Jasmine. She grew up here."

She grew up here. Brooke kept her expression neutral, stifled a sigh even as she wondered how exactly a kid was going to be able to help her sell high-end condos to wealthy people.

"The second and third floors are going to be ready to show within the month," Sasha went on. "So, Macy, we're going to need you to stage an office and a condo, at least to get us started. We'll probably do a couple more in different styles, but for now, one each. Sit with each agent after they see the place, and get yourselves on the same page, all right?"

And that was it. The meeting was over. People stood. Gathered their things. Sasha had told Brooke during her interview that she didn't like to micromanage her agents. That if she trusted you with a job, she expected you to get it done without her having to hover over you like a drone. Brooke appreciated that.

Jasmine literally bounced over to Brooke's chair like Tigger, all pep and excitement. "I'm so stoked to work with you," she said, her smile wide, revealing teeth way too perfect not to have been helped. Across the table, Brooke thought she saw Brennan smirk in her direction, but she didn't know him well enough—yet—to be sure.

With a nod, Brooke said, "Let's meet tomorrow morning and lay out our plan, yeah?"

"Absolutely." Jasmine continued to smile as she bounced through the door and presumably to her own cubicle.

"Are you sure I can't pay for dry cleaning your jacket?" The voice surprised Brooke, and she turned around to face a sheepish Macy Carr, messenger bag slung over her shoulder, hands clasped in front of her like she was praying. "I want to say again how sorry I am. I'm such a klutz. One of my less charming qualities." She was trying to lighten the mood, Brooke realized, a little late, and forced a smile.

"It's fine. Really."

"As long as you're sure." Macy gave a sort of bow of her head and took a step or two toward the door before she turned back. "Could I buy you a cup of coffee instead?"

Brooke blinked at her, surprised, her hands stilling as she absorbed the offer. "Um." She looked down at the table, at the notes she'd taken, and wondered why the invitation made her uncomfortable. When she glanced back up, Macy's expression said she was hoping the floor would open up and swallow her whole. "I really appreciate that, but it's my first week, and I'm still trying to find my footing…" She let the sentence trail off because was that disappointment in Macy's soft brown eyes? Before she could even think about what she was saying, the words "Can I take a rain check?" were out of her mouth and hanging there in the middle of the room.

Macy's face lit right up. It was a clichéd description, but it was fitting. And something about that change did things to Brooke that she didn't quite understand. The girl was a flake, right? Cute—super cute, really, actually very pretty—but a flake. Brooke had sized her up easily, the way she spoke really fast, the mess that was her bag, the way she'd whipped around the corner and right into Brooke with little regard for where she was going. Flake. But it was okay. No big deal. A rain check was polite. Vague. Easy not to collect on. Brooke was just being nice because there was no reason not to be a nice person.

"Sure," Macy said. "I'd like that." At the door, she stopped, hand on the doorframe. "Welcome to town, Brooke. I hope you like it here." And then she was gone.

Brooke stared after her for a long time. It seemed to take her a while to find her balance again, and it took her a minute to understand why. Hurricane Macy. That was what she'd just experienced, and somehow, someway, with total clarity, she understood that today was only the beginning.

"Terrific," she muttered.

CHAPTER FOUR

"Oh my God, that smells amazing." Macy closed her eyes and inhaled deeply through her nose.

"Please. It's just quiche." Lucas set a large pie plate down in the center of the table, its top a lovely golden brown, peeks of green from the veggies inside sprinkling it with color. "We've been trying to go plant-based a couple nights a week, so it helps to invite our vegetarian friend over for dinner."

"I appreciate that more than you know," Macy said as she took in the lush salad in a bowl next to her plate. With a glance up at Lucas's husband, Sam, who was eyeing the quiche with obvious skepticism, she asked him, "Do you need me to Grubhub you a Quarter Pounder with Cheese?"

"Would you please?" Sam said with a wink from across the table. He squinted as she stared. "What?"

"I'm still getting used to the beard," Macy told him, gesturing around her own chin, and it was true. She'd known Sam for several years now, and this was the first time he'd decided to grow a full beard. It was neatly trimmed and made him look older, more sophisticated.

"I didn't think I'd like it, but I really do," Lucas said. He was clean-shaven, with a head of thick, dark hair most men would kill for, and the kindest blue eyes Macy had ever seen. He sliced the quiche and served it, gestured to his husband with a jerk of his chin. "He's been doing great with the meal change," he said.

"I need a steak," Sam grumbled, then forked his salad with a sigh.

"We'll have steak tomorrow." Lucas kissed the top of Sam's head. The grumbling was exaggerated and meant to be humorous, Macy knew. Whatever Lucas wanted, that's what they did. Sam adored his husband and would give him anything in the world. As always, Macy's heart warmed for them and squeezed for her own situation. "We're just trying this. It'll be good for us."

"Isn't that what he said about kayaking?" Macy asked Sam and arched her brow comically.

"And pottery class." Sam grinned.

"There was the ballroom dancing."

"Hey, I'll have you know the ballroom dancing came in handy at the last wedding we went to." Lucas pointed to each of them with his fork.

"You're not wrong," Sam agreed, and they dug into dinner.

"How are the residents at Macy Carr's Home for Wayward Animals?" Lucas asked. He'd named Macy's house that after she'd adopted Angus, her fifth creature.

"They're good, though Captain Jack horked in my shoe the other morning. That was lovely."

Sam barked a laugh as Lucas said, "He is such a drama queen."

"He really is. Thank God I have Jellybean for contrast."

"She's almost as sweet as Sheba," Lucas said, referring to his shop cat. She was a gorgeous domestic longhair with a coat that was a stunning mix of brown, black, and gray, giving her a sooty look that was truly unique. She had free rein to roam around Lucas's antique shop, making herself comfortable wherever she felt like it, and she'd startled more than one customer.

"The only pussy you'll ever touch." Macy held her arms out, expression expectant.

"Ba-dum-bum," Sam said dutifully and shook his head as Lucas snort-laughed.

"I'm telling you, Sheba's going to give some poor old lady a heart attack one of these days," Macy said, then took another bite. "The way she just hangs out in drawers or on pillows, all staring and creepy?"

Lucas fake gasped, pressed a hand to his chest. "Creepy? How dare you? She's beautiful."

"And creepy," Macy and Sam said in tandem, and all three broke into laughter.

Macy loved these men. They'd gotten her through so much bad. They'd comforted her when Michelle had died, they'd hauled her up to her feet when she didn't think she wanted to stand anymore, they'd given her multiple stern talkings-to when she began to veer in any direction that wasn't actually her own authentic one. She had no idea how she'd be sitting there at that table, eating, drinking, laughing, without Sam and Lucas. She owed them her life. Literally.

She and Lucas got the Irish coffees made, a tradition with the three of them. Dinner, then coffee and dessert—the coffee often containing a little zing of Baileys or something similar.

As Macy entered the dining room carrying two full cups in saucers—Lucas was a stickler for complete sets of dishes: they couldn't have coffee in regular mugs, they had to use cups with saucers—Sam's eyes went wide.

"You're letting *Macy* carry in the coffee?" he asked in feigned horror. "On *saucers*? Have you actually *met* her?"

"Oh no, it's totally okay. I already had my major catastrophe this week." She set the saucers down without incident as Lucas joined them carrying the third cup and saucer and a pan of peach cobbler. "I should be good at least until Monday."

"Uh-oh." Lucas took his seat. "What happened?"

Macy shook her head, still unable to believe what she now referred to as The Danish Incident really happened. "New sales agent at Wolfe. I go in to meet with her and a few others about a new project Sasha's working on. A big deal. Emily is all goofy and excited about it. I, of course, bring pastries, 'cause that's how I roll..."

"Uh-oh," Lucas said again, setting a plate of warm cobbler in front of Macy.

She stopped the story to inhale deeply from the plate. "Oh my God, Lucas. This must be what heaven smells like." When she'd apparently waited too long, Lucas made a rolling gesture with his hand.

"And? You dropped a Danish on the new agent, didn't you."

"Better. I ran right into her, full plate in hand. Smashed Danishes right up against her."

"Please tell us she wasn't wearing white," Sam said.

"Oh, she was. Expensive white, I'm pretty sure."

"And the Danishes were cheese?" Sam asked hopefully.

"Raspberry."

Lucas made a face, clenching his teeth and wincing. "That's bad, even for you."

Macy dropped her head back and groaned. "*I know*. I was so embarrassed. And then I tried to help wipe it off her and..."

"Accidental boob graze?" Lucas's brows rose.

"You know it."

"Oh God." Lucas made the face again, then burst into laughter. Across the table, Sam made the exact same face, then also devolved into laughter.

"Exactly. So. Chortle away." Macy lifted her fork to her mouth while her friends reveled in her klutziness. "I made a fantastic first impression. I'm sure of it. I bet she can't wait to work with me." She chewed the cobbler, and Brooke's face popped into her head. Annoyed expression. Pretty face. Very pretty.

Sam waved a dismissive hand as he got himself under control. "Don't sweat it. It was an accident. If she can't understand that, she's not worth your time. Do your job well, and it'll be fine."

"I hope you're right." Macy wasn't so sure. She didn't know Brooke at all, but something about the way she was, the way the air felt around her...Macy could tell she was a woman used to being in control. Having a handle on things. Running the show. And flying Danishes were not in her plans.

❖

"All you have to do is change the location. Boom. Done."

Lena's words had rung through Brooke's head all morning, in and out, ever since their phone call. Now, as she crossed her fifth intersection on her walk, she thought about it again.

Her online dating profile. That's what Lena meant. Brooke had created one several months ago, before moving was a sure thing. Now that she was in a new city—hell, a new state—she hadn't given it a second thought.

Lies.

She had. She'd thought about it. She just didn't want Lena to know that because she knew what would happen. Lena would get on her, tell her all she had to do was change one thing on her profile, and she'd be good to go. Brooke had been right because that's exactly what had happened.

"Why are you afraid of dating?" Lena had asked, and Brooke had silently cursed her BFF for her inability to leave things alone once in a while.

"I'm not afraid." Had she sounded as weak to Lena as she had to herself? Probably.

"No? Sure seems like it. Is it the bisexual thing?"

Big sigh.

"No," Brooke had replied, indignant. Yes, in fact, it was the bisexual thing. At least a little bit of it was. The rest was just...dating. Dating in general. Online dating in particular. Ugh.

Lena had given her a pep talk, as Lena tended to do, and it was good, as it almost always was. Brooke had not second-guessed her decision to move out of Ohio to this small city in upstate New York, not once, but *man*, she missed having Lena nearby.

Walking was the way Brooke had always cleared her head. Whether in the city, down a street of shops and restaurants, or in a more rural setting, along country roads and through old cemeteries, Brooke walked. When she was upset, when she was confused, when she was elated, she walked. Something about the mindlessness of her stride, the fresh air, any kind of wildlife—from city birds to country deer—all helped her straighten out her thoughts, iron out any wrinkles of worry, logic something that had seemed illogical.

Weather rarely kept her inside when she felt the need to walk something out, and that day was quite beautiful, a crisp and bright late Saturday morning. The sun shone down, adding noticeable warmth and the promise of a spring that was well on its way. The occasional green of a daffodil or crocus was visible, the spring flowers barely peeking above all the brown, as if checking to see if the coast was clear, if winter was gone for good or if hunkering back beneath the soil for another week or two was the best course of action.

The street began to slope upward as Brooke strode along the sidewalk. She'd wanted to wear her Nikes, but April was mostly brown because it was wet and muddy most of the month, and she'd opted for her waterproof ankle boots. Now her feet were hot, but she pressed on because the slope rose significantly to a large hill on the left where a sign for Ridgecrest Park and Reservoir was displayed between two brown posts. Without a second thought, she veered to the left, entered the park, and headed toward the hill.

Deep inhale through the nose. Out through the mouth. She'd learned the value of breathing mindfully not only while meditating but in yoga. In spin class. In any kind of physical activity, and it was startling how much of a difference it made. Plus, the scent of the fresh air always put a spring in her step. Yes, it was chilly—she was glad she'd added a layer of fleece over her long-sleeved T-shirt and under her puffy vest—but it smelled like spring. Earthy and fresh. To her left was a softball diamond. Two young guys tossed a Frisbee back and forth, and farther down, a guy with long hair and a beard used a Chuckit! to throw a tennis ball for his yellow Lab. Off to the right was a playground, a mix of what looked like old equipment and newer equipment dotting the rubberized area. A dome of monkey bars stood alone and looked like they might be older than Brooke, any color they'd ever boasted long gone, just the dull gray of steel left to hang from. Then one of those modular climbing units took up the center of the space—rope bridge, small climbing wall, bright yellow spiral slide. On the other side of it was a swing set, its date of installation likely falling between the other two, featuring four black rubber swings, two baby swings, and a two-person swing all dangling expectantly, only two in use by a couple of college kids.

Brooke liked this Ridgecrest Park. She could tell immediately. It wasn't anything specific. Just a feeling. She imagined it in the thick of the summer heat, the playground peppered with children squealing in delight as their exhausted parents looked on. There was a sign for the spray park and an arrow that pointed farther into the park, beyond the copse of bare trees that would bud soon and burst into green. Brooke could see a path—a little gravel, but mostly just dirt and trampled grass—to her right, and it led up the hill. She followed it through the trees, passed other hikers, joggers, dog walkers, and counted them in her head. At the end of the woods, she was at six joggers, four hikers, and seven dog walkers with nine dogs. The woods opened up at the top of the hill, and an enormous reservoir spread out before her.

"Wow," she said quietly as she stood and took it all in. Brooke wasn't sure what she'd expected, but it hadn't been this. The reservoir was maybe one hundred fifty to two hundred yards around, an oval, with a black iron fence encompassing the whole thing. A cement path circled outside the fence, so you could walk around the water but couldn't get near it. As she approached it, she found a sign that told her the distance around the Ridgecrest Reservoir Loop—or the RRL, as runners apparently called it—was 1.3 miles. It supplied water to the entire city of Northwood, pulling from one of the Finger Lakes thirty miles away. There was an aerial photo on the sign as well. Brooke smiled to herself—from above, the reservoir was shaped like a butternut squash. There was more to read, more info to absorb, and Brooke was usually big on information gathering—it was a huge part of her job—but that day, that bright and sunny April morning, she simply wanted to walk.

After three laps around the water, her head felt better, her feet were tired, and her back wanted a rest. At the opposite end of the water from where she'd exited the woods, there was a stone gatehouse with steps leading down to the wide expanse of hill and then on down to the street and boasting a spectacular view of the city below. Brooke took a seat on the top step, off to the side so as not to be in anybody's way as they climbed or descended.

So far, so good.

It was a thought that had crossed her mind several times over the past week, and it referred to being here in this new city, new home, new job. Moving hadn't been an easy decision, and she missed so many things about her hometown in Ohio, but the truth was, she'd needed to get away. From the town, from her parents, from her old life.

Why can't you just be normal?

That's what her mother had said that caused Brooke to make her final decision. It wasn't the first time she'd said it, but Brooke had decided then and there that it would be the last. And she'd gotten so many different reactions. Proud of her, that was Lena. Utterly conflicted—Eddie, who had no idea who to side with, so he claimed to side with nobody even as he leaned toward their parents. Completely flabbergasted, that had been her mom and dad. They couldn't believe she'd decided to leave. And then they couldn't believe she was leaving. And now, they couldn't believe she'd left.

Enough.

She hadn't come here to relive, she'd come here to clear her head, to set her compass to true north. With a shake of her head, she continued to sit and people watch.

More Frisbee was happening farther down the hill—was that a New York thing? Lots of dog walking. She grinned with sympathy at the woman toward the very bottom near the street who had three dogs on leashes and seemed to be doing her very best to keep them from tangling with her and each other. Couldn't have been easy. Every now and then, a jogger would reach the steps after running up the hill— insanity at its finest, that's what running was to Brooke—and soon she began to count the stairs every time a runner arrived. There were sixteen of them.

A toddler and another child who was maybe five chased after each other as two adults looked on, the toddler's shrieks of delight tugging the corners of Brooke's mouth up. There was nothing better than the laughter of a baby or the squeals of a toddler. Before her brain could take her thoughts in that direction, she was jostled by another runner, this one heading down the stairs.

"Sorry," he called over his shoulder as he continued on his path.

Brooke watched him go, his calf muscles bulging impressively from below his black compression shorts. Her eyes stayed on his red hoodie as he descended and waved to the woman with the three dogs—who was moving at a snail's pace, apparently much to the chagrin of her terrier, who left zero slack in its leash—and when he hit the sidewalk, he took a right and disappeared from view. Brooke watched the triple dog woman for a few more moments, shook her head with a smile, and stood.

Time to unpack the rest of her place.

"Hey, Macy," Jason Carter called and waved as he jogged by.

"It's too cold for shorts, Jay," she teased.

"Never!"

Macy chuckled as he reached the sidewalk and headed down the street. Turning back to the matter at hand, she said through clenched teeth, "Angus. You have *got* to stop pulling me, buddy." The skin of her left hand was red and tight from having three leashes wrapped around it, and Priscilla's lead circled Macy's leg twice. She groaned and untangled herself. Walking all three dogs at once was not her preference, but she'd worked some extra hours this week, and then dinner with Lucas and Sam the night before had taken time away, and she knew Angus was getting a little stir-crazy. He really was the only one of the three who needed outside stimulation. Pete was happy in his yard, and at her advanced age, Priscilla no longer walked, she moseyed. Much to the irritation of Angus, who wanted to go, go, go. Macy vowed to take him for a solo walk tomorrow, when the forecast had it warming up a bit, but right then, she was cold.

"Okay, guys, let's go. Tyler's coming over tonight, remember?" Pete's ears perked up at the mention of her nephew's name, as they always did, and she was once again reminded how incredible dogs were. Angus was very busy sniffing the roots of a tree, so they waited. Once he'd finished—and marked it well—they turned back toward home.

CHAPTER FIVE

*B*eans *& Batter. I like it.*

Brooke sat in an overstuffed chair in a corner of the small café not far from her house and sipped from the best cup of coffee she'd had in a very long time. It was dark, bold, rich. She'd added a touch of cream because she was in the mood to, but no sugar. She wanted to experience this French roast that was said to be the café's signature cup, and it had not disappointed. She took another sip from the heavy black mug, uncrossed her legs, and crossed them the other way.

It might have been the aroma—that heavenly mix of roasting coffee beans and freshly baked anything and everything—that made her so comfortable, Brooke wasn't sure. All she knew was that she instantly loved Beans & Batter. Her new hangout, she was certain of it. The place was busy. Of course it was busy—it was Sunday morning. But she was warm and cozy and could see herself bringing files from work here when the office got too chaotic. Settling down with a cup of coffee and her laptop. She probably wasn't the only one who did that during the week.

Today, however, she had her Kindle with her. She'd spent all day yesterday unpacking the rest of her stuff, and she'd promised herself a day of relaxation. Not something she did often, relax, even when she had the best intentions, but the café was certainly nudging her in the right direction. The big chair was in a perfect spot. Diagonally situated in a little alcove near the door, she could see out the window to the street and had a full view of the small space as well. Coffee area, glass case of pastries, smattering of eight tables, five chairs, counting hers, and two love seats. It was a narrow space, with cream-colored walls and lots of coffee art. Paintings, sketches, photographs. A mishmash of media, but all focused on the same subject, that illustrious cup o' joe.

Dad would love this place.

The thought ran through her head before her brain had time to catch it, edit it, filter it out completely, and it pressed on her shoulders just enough for her to feel it. No. Not here. She wasn't going to let the guilt—which she shouldn't feel, and she knew it—spoil this nice place she'd found. Hoping for a distraction, she picked up her Kindle and swiped to unlock it, let herself become absorbed in the latest Harlan Coben novel. It worked, and soon she was oblivious to the world around her.

Until a loud crash caught her attention.

She glanced up, expecting one of the baristas had dropped a dish or something. What she saw instead caused a mix of emotions to zip through her. Surprise. Dread. Curiosity. Happiness. Confusion.

Happiness? That one was interesting.

Macy Carr, the girl from the staging company. The one who'd effectively ruined Brooke's most expensive suit simply by walking. It was her. She stood at the counter, one hand flat against her forehead, the other out from her side, palm up. Brooke could hear the endless litany of apologies that streamed from her lips, even at the other end of the café. There was a kid standing with her. Tall, kind of gangly, but with a layer of muscle that said he was athletic and would probably fill out nicely in a couple years. Sandy hair. Laughing his ass off in one of those infectious laughs that made everybody else around him smile, too. Including Brooke. An employee with a mop and bucket appeared from the back, and Macy tried to take the mop from her. Good-naturedly, the girl denied Macy, reassuring her that it happened all the time, and the guy behind the counter was making her another drink as they spoke.

For whatever reason, Brooke couldn't look away and watched with amusement as the floor was cleaned, the order was replaced, and the kid and Macy headed in Brooke's direction, presumably toward the only empty table, which just happened to be near Brooke's chair. The second Macy laid eyes on her, she did a stutter step.

"Jesus, don't drop it again," the kid said and pulled out a chair.

"Brooke," Macy said, and it was clear that she wasn't sure what kind of reception to expect. "Hi. It's nice to see you." She gave one nod of her head and gestured to the chair next to the kid's. "Do you mind if we sit here?"

"Not at all." Weird question. It's not like Brooke decided who sat where. But Macy was clearly uncertain, and Brooke knew she should probably fix that. "Is this your son?" she asked, setting her Kindle aside.

The kid snorted, tossed his head, the top of his hair floppy while the rest was shaved close, and took an enormous bite of one of the three chocolate chip muffins on his plate.

"Him?" Macy asked, and then laughed. "Only if I'd had a much different high school experience." At Brooke's questioning look, she said, "He's my nephew. Tyler, this is Ms. Sullivan."

"Brooke, please. Hi, Tyler."

Tyler lifted his chin. "Hey." Then, with a gleam in his eye, he asked, "Did you see her drop her entire mug of chai over there?" It had obviously entertained him, and he mimed the whole thing in slow motion, complete with a long and exaggerated, "*Noooooooooo!*"

Brooke couldn't help but smile at his display. "I didn't actually see it, just heard it. But that's okay because I got to experience something similar firsthand the very first time I ever met your aunt."

Macy's cheeks turned a deep pink, but she grinned and nodded.

Tyler laughed. "She dropped stuff in front of you?"

"Oh no, she dropped stuff *on* me." Brooke smiled, made sure to keep it light because there was something about this kid, this Tyler. Brooke liked him, though she had no idea why. Teenagers weren't really her jam. Something in his eyes, though, something she couldn't quite put a finger on but could identify with somehow. Which made zero sense, since she'd met him a whole three minutes before, but as his eyes went wide and he guffawed, the feeling only intensified.

"Yeah, she does that. It's her thing." Tyler was ribbing Macy, and she clearly knew it. Her angry face was definitely exaggerated.

"It is not my *thing*," she said in what sounded like feigned defensiveness to Brooke.

"It's totally your thing. It's why Grandpa calls you The Dropper."

"The dropper?" Brooke asked.

"Yeah, with capital letters." Tyler tossed his head again, his eyes—were they blue or green?—bright and sparkling.

"Like it's her superhero name," Brooke said, and Tyler guffawed again, which was really the only way to describe his big laugh. And she couldn't help but notice that it made Macy's face light up.

"Yes!" Tyler said. "Exactly. She has the superhuman inability to hold on to things." He finished the first muffin and started in on the second.

"You're both hilarious." Macy turned to Brooke, her brown eyes deep. Warm. "So, you're new to Wolfe Realty. Are you all settled in?" She looked really cute in her weekend clothes. Worn jeans and a black hoodie with a yellow puffy vest. Her hair was down and tousled, likely from the slight breeze outside. She had small hands, Brooke noticed for some reason. Small and fine-boned, with a silver ring on her right ring finger. Pretty.

A question had been asked, hadn't it? Brooke blinked herself back to the present when she realized her silence had gone on a tad too long.

"Just unpacked my last box yesterday. I've been exploring the neighborhood."

"Well, you lucked out finding this place." Macy looked around. "It's fairly new."

"Is it? I walked here. I was just strolling and came across it, so I decided to spend my Sunday morning with coffee and a book." She indicated the Kindle with her eyes.

"Oh, I'm so sorry." Macy's eyes went wide. "Don't let us interrupt." She smiled, revealing a slight dimple in her left cheek. "Go." She waved her hand like she was shooing a fly, though the smile stayed warm. "Read. Don't mind us."

You're not interrupting.

I don't mind you. Either of you.

It's okay. I don't know anybody in this town yet, and it's nice to meet people.

Brooke could've said any of those things. For some reason, not one of them would leave her mouth. Instead, she smiled, gave a small nod, and reached for her Kindle. Unlocked it with a swipe and pretended to read. As she did so, she tried not to think about how much it startled her that she'd rather be talking to Macy and her nephew.

❖

Macy did her best to listen to Tyler as he talked about the new video game he was trying to conquer, but the truth was, most of her energy was going into not spilling or dropping something else in front of Brooke Sullivan. She'd done so twice now. *Third time's the charm,* her father would say. Yeah, the charm that meant she'd be labeled *klutz* forever to Brooke. That's who she'd be.

Why did that matter? Everybody who knew her knew she was kind of clumsy and tended to drop things, spill things, trip for no reason. Why did it matter if Brooke knew that about her?

Simple. It didn't.

And while she didn't venture even a glance in Brooke's direction, her appearance had seared itself into Macy's brain without her permission. Dark jeans. Emerald-green cable-knit sweater. Auburn hair the color of a sunset pulled partially back, the rest down, gold hoops in her ears. Cute little taupe booties.

Macy's phone buzzed with a text.

She's hot.

Macy's focus snapped up to Tyler, who was grinning. "You stop that," she whispered through clenched teeth. That only made him grin wider. "Finish your breakfast."

It never ceased to amaze her just how much food her nephew could put away, and she watched as he devoured the second half of his second muffin and bit into the third.

"Your parents' grocery bill must be astronomical." She watched as he chewed, his hair in his eyes, as usual, and shook her head. The depth of love she felt for him was immeasurable. She'd had no idea on the day Eva announced her pregnancy how very much this new life would matter in her world.

"Well, it's true," Tyler said, voice muffled through the food in his mouth, and it took Macy a moment to realize he was referring to his text.

"Way too old for you," she said and raised an eyebrow.

The kind of overexaggerated eye roll that only teenagers could pull off came next. "I meant for you, dumbass." Eva would've scolded him in a heartbeat for his language, but Macy prided herself on being the cool aunt. Unless he got out of hand with the profanity, she let him say what he wanted.

"Yeah, I don't think so." She sipped her chai, which had gone from hot to barely lukewarm.

"Well, I don't want you to be alone forever." The seriousness of this statement coming from a sixteen-year-old startled Macy, and she blinked at her nephew, who was looking at her with intensity, clearly waiting for some kind of response.

Macy sighed quietly. "It's complicated." He continued to stare, and she finally added, "I know. I know. And I love you for that. But... it's complicated."

Coming in a close second behind the eye roll in the Teenager's Arsenal of Sarcastic Responses was what Macy referred to as the snort-scoff. Not a full scoff, but not quite a snort, the combination was the equivalent of *yeah, okay* or *whatever* or *bye, Felicia.* Whichever nonresponse was appropriate for the conversation.

Thankfully, Tyler let it go, and Macy wondered if Brooke had heard, but she was too afraid to glance to her left and see. Instead, she drank more tea while Tyler finished his third muffin.

"Which was the best?" she asked, referring to his trio of muffins. "The chocolate chip, the chips of chocolate, or the one with morsels of chocolate in it?"

Tyler pursed his lips and made a show of thinking, bringing a finger to his chin, tapping. "Well, Aunt Mace, it was a very tough race with a super tight finish, but I'm gonna have to go with the chips of chocolate."

Macy nodded. "I had a feeling. Ready?"

"Ready."

They gathered their items and Tyler took the mugs and plate up to the return area while Macy slid the strap of her bag over her shoulder. She studiously avoided looking in Brooke's direction until Tyler had rejoined her. When she glanced over, Brooke was watching.

"It was nice to see you again," Macy said.

"You, too." Brooke gave a little wave. "Nice to meet you, Tyler."

"Same."

Could she feel Brooke's eyes on her as she left the café? It certainly seemed like it. What else could've been warming her back like that?

Macy dropped Tyler off at his house, then headed to Everything Old Is New Again, Lucas's antique shop. He'd gotten some new inventory in and texted her to come see. Plus, she loved to hang with him. Normally, she'd go home and spend Sunday with her animals, but having Tyler there for the weekend, all the attention and playing, had wiped them out. When she and Ty had left that morning, all five animals were already napping. Another benefit of her nephew's visits. He lavished her animals with attention, kept them awake at times they'd normally have been sleeping, and left them exercised and tired.

Clouds were starting to drift in, blocking out the April sunshine. A bummer. Winter sunshine was limited in the Northeast, so once the sun started to appear more often, everybody's moods lifted, brightened. But the periodic gloom was part of the process of that transition of seasons, and complaining about it made no difference—which didn't stop people from complaining, of course. Macy slipped off her shades as she hit her turn signal and rolled into Lucas's parking lot.

Everything Old Is New Again was Macy's happy place. No doubt. She loved everything about it. The smells—old wood and furniture polish and paint. The sights—so many different shapes and colors and woods. The history—each piece in the shop had a story, and Lucas knew a lot of them. Macy liked to lose herself in what might have been. One of her favorite things to do was make up a story about a dresser or a sideboard or an armoire, create a history that might have been, wonder how many people had owned the piece, where it had been, where it still might go, what it had seen, and what it would say if it could talk.

Sundays were Lucas's busy days. People went antiquing on Sundays, strolled through Everything Old while dragging fingertips lightly across surfaces. Macy spotted Lucas in a back corner where he displayed random mismatched bedroom pieces. He was talking animatedly with his hands, as he always did, and he waved at her when he noticed her. She waved back just as she heard a startled gasp from her right and grinned. *Sheba strikes again.*

Wandering the shop wasn't a hardship for Macy, even if she already knew everything there. Even if Lucas had gotten nothing new in. She simply loved being surrounded by history. She found an old wingback chair—not necessarily antique, as Macy would guess it was about twenty-five years old. The upholstery had faded considerably to an almost salmon color, but if Macy looked deep into corners, she could see remnants of a dark burgundy, likely the original color. It was the wooden claw-and-ball feet she liked the best, though, and she took a seat to wait until Lucas was free to chat.

Focusing her brain on furniture and design turned out to be harder than usual that day, because other things crowded to the front. Mainly Tyler. She was worried about her nephew. While he'd done his best to be his usual funny, smart-ass self, Macy had noticed something off about him this visit. She couldn't pinpoint what it was exactly, only that he didn't quite seem to be himself. They'd watched *Rent* for the millionth time, and they'd sung along to most of the songs, as they always did, but he seemed slightly less exuberant than usual. Macy had told herself more than once that he was a teenager. Sixteen was a rough age. He was growing. His body was changing—it was all Macy could do not to laugh every time his voice cracked. He was likely thinking about sex *a lot.* All those things they tell you in health class in school—did they even teach that anymore?—but she couldn't get herself to relax. Macy knew Tyler. She *knew* him. And she'd asked more than once if he was okay. His answer was always to smile and nod at her, and she liked to think that if he needed to talk, she'd be the one he'd talk to, but her unease stayed with her the entire visit.

"Hey, gorgeous." Lucas's voice tugged her out of her thoughts and back to the present as he bent to kiss the top of her head. "How's your Sunday so far?"

"I broke a mug in Beans & Batter," she reported with a shrug.

"So a normal day, then." Lucas grinned at her and held out a hand. "Come with me. I want to show you something." He pulled her to her feet and led her to the opposite side of the shop. As they approached a mirrored buffet Macy hadn't seen there before, he held out an arm like Vanna White. "Isn't it stunning?"

"*Ooh,*" she said, drawing the word out as she ran her fingers over it. The wood was a deep brown, rich and grainy. Two drawers were centered, with a cabinet door on either side of them, the handles round and... "Are these brass?"

"I think so," Lucas said. "The label on the back says Empire Furniture Company. I know Empire changed their name to Huntington in 1905, so this has to be older."

Macy tugged one of the doors open to reveal a large empty space, excellent for storing stacks of plates and dishes. She stuck her hand in it, just because, and rubbed her palm along the sides.

"I was thinking about that house you had to stage in Arcadia a couple months ago," Lucas said, referring to a section of Northwood that featured some large and stately older homes. Macy'd gotten frustrated that they didn't have enough antique furniture in their warehouse at Stage One to set the right tone. Emily had shaken her head and told her not to worry about it. The house had sold in a week.

"This would've been perfect in there."

"Happy to rent it to you if another house in that area needs staging. Or Emily is more than welcome to buy it for her inventory."

Macy snorted. "Not a chance." Emily tended to keep more modern furnishings in her inventory, and Macy couldn't really argue with that. People buying residential homes were much more likely to want modern furniture in them than old-timey stuff, as her sister Eva called antiques. Every now and then, though, something more historical would go up for sale, and when a Realtor called on Stage One, Emily almost always let Macy take the lead because she knew her grandma furniture.

"What were you doing at Beans?" Lucas asked as Macy pulled the drawers out, slid them back in place. "Hot date?" The hope in his voice was clear.

"Tyler stayed overnight last night. I took him there for breakfast so he could eat twenty-seven muffins." She turned to Lucas. "Did you eat that much as a teenager? My God, he can put away the food."

Lucas shrugged. "I probably did. I know Bradley did. I didn't play a sport, but he played all of them, so he ate like six horses." Lucas was tall, and his big brother wasn't much taller, but Macy knew he was broad and one solid stack of muscle, even more than fifteen years after playing college football.

"I don't know how my sister keeps up. We ordered a pizza last night. A large. I got two slices. He ate the rest."

"Did he clean out the muffins?"

Macy squatted so she could see herself in the short mirror that ran the length of the buffet. "Not quite." Her brain tossed her a flash of auburn waves. "But guess who was also there?"

Lucas shrugged. "Tell me."

"Brooke Sullivan." At Lucas's furrowed brow, she elaborated. "The new agent at Wolfe? The one I smashed raspberry Danishes into last week?"

"And then grabbed her boob? Her?"

"Shut up, I didn't grab her boob."

"Oh my God, how weird is it that she showed up at your coffee place?" He gasped and his eyes went wide. "What if she's stalking you?"

"She's not stalking me."

"Maybe she is. You don't know. Holy RuPaul, this could be the most amazing love story."

Macy tilted her head. "Love story? I thought she was stalking me."

"What if she is? Because she is so drawn to you and can't get enough but doesn't know you well enough to just launch into conversation yet. She wants to get to know you first. So she goes on social media and looks at all your pages and your photos and figures out what you like and what you don't. And eventually, she makes her move, asks you to something simple and safe. Like coffee. Or lunch. And you guys hit it off, and you fall madly in love and get married, and I am your best man, of course, and you have beautiful babies, and I'm their godfather..." He trailed off, then let out a dreamy sigh.

"You've just described a really awful Lifetime movie. You know that, right?"

Lucas cocked his head. "Is there not one single romantic bone in your body? Just one? That's all I ask. A finger bone. A baby toe. Just one."

Macy ran her hand over the surface of the buffet once more. "That ship has sailed, my friend."

"Well, I call bullshit on that."

"You always do."

"And I will continue to, every time you say it. You gotta have faith, honey."

"I used to." Macy shrugged, not wanting to get into this conversation with Lucas. Again. For the hundred and thirty-fifth time. Or something close to that.

Before they could, a customer approached them and asked Lucas a question about a rolltop desk. Lucas looked at her in apology.

"Go," she said with a smile. "I'm gonna go swim. Text you later." She shouldered her purse and strolled through the store for another couple minutes before exiting and heading to the Y. The second she was out of the shop, the two main subjects that had been on her mind that morning returned to front and center.

Tyler. Always Tyler. And a new one.

Brooke Sullivan.

Macy sighed loudly as she pulled out of the lot. "Yeah..."

Time to clear her head.

CHAPTER SIX

It was almost the end of her second week at Wolfe, and Brooke's brain was overfull. Like she'd made stew in a pot that she thought was the perfect size, but turned out to be too small, and now the stew was right up to the brim, and she couldn't stir it because it would drip all over the stove and make a mess, so she stood there doing nothing, watching it bubble. She needed to separate the veggies from the meat from the juice from the potatoes, and she needed to do it soon.

Compartmentalizing had become a talent of hers at a fairly young age. Maybe sixteen? She'd realized that in order to get through her day, she needed to box up certain topics that weighed on her and put them on shelves until there was ample time to think about them. If she didn't do that, her head ended up a jumble—a stew—and she couldn't concentrate on any one thing at all because everything blended together. Which frustrated her. And nothing did her in faster than a good dose of frustration.

Brooke wasn't a crier. At all. She was a pretty stoic person overall, one who could handle pressure. But frustration? *That* could cause tears to appear out of nowhere. She had the distinct memory of doing chemistry homework one time in her junior year of high school. Science was not really her thing, and chemistry was, like, the worst of science. She didn't understand it. Couldn't grasp it easily. That particular homework assignment frustrated her so much that she'd tossed her notebook and all her papers across her bedroom and burst into tears. Ever since then, she'd done her best to keep frustration at bay. It was the only thing that made her feel like she didn't have control, and she knew that not having control was one of her biggest fears in life.

A knock on her doorframe pulled her attention. "Hey, got a minute?" Jasmine asked and held up her laptop.

Brooke waved her in, and for the next half hour, they went over details of the new building Sasha had assigned them, as well as the list of potential buyers, both commercial and residential. Jasmine's work was impressively thorough, and Brooke didn't hide her surprise.

"This is good work, Jasmine."

"Thanks." The girl grinned, and her cheeks flushed pink. "You can call me Jazz. Everybody does."

"To be honest, Jazz, I was a little worried when you were assigned to me. I need to apologize for that."

Jazz shrugged. Her sleek, almost-black hair was pulled back in a funky twist that Brooke wondered if she could copy. It was simultaneously sophisticated and fun, fastened behind her head, a few strands curling down along her neck. "No worries. Happens all the time."

That surprised Brooke. "Really?"

"It's because I look so young. People think I'm a kid."

"True. How old are you?"

"Twenty-three."

So you are *a kid*, Brooke wanted to say, but didn't. Instead, she nodded and said, "I think we're ready to stage these. What do you think?"

"I agree. Should I call Stage One?"

Brooke's brain tossed her an image of Macy at the café on Sunday, all casually tousled and dropping things on the floor, and the corners of her mouth started to tug upward without her permission. What was it about that girl? "Sure." As Jazz stood, Brooke stopped her with, "Hey, how many people work there? I mean, will they send us…um, that girl from the meeting? Or somebody else?" It wasn't lost on Brooke that she'd slipped right into what she called Protection Mode by pretending not to remember Macy's name. She mentally shook her head, hating that it was so automatic.

"Macy? Yeah, it'll be her. She's the main stager. Emily owns the company, but she tends to stick to residential houses. Macy does most of the design work and directs the on-site setup for offices and apartments in addition to some houses. We work with her most often." Jazz squinted at her. "Is that okay? I mean, I know you had the thing with the pastries, and she can seem clumsy, but I promise you, she's awesome. And really good at her job. Sasha wouldn't use her otherwise."

A dismissive wave of a hand. A *pfft*. "Oh no, no worries. I was just curious."

Jazz gave a nod. "Okay. I'll give them a shout."

Alone again, Brooke did her best to immerse herself in work. She'd made several cold calls this week—something she hadn't done in a very long time, but she needed to build up her clientele in this new city—and she went over her calendar for the next couple of weeks, taking notes on meetings she'd set up. Her cell pinged, and she assumed it was her reminder to hit the grocery store on her lunch break to get tuna. But it wasn't a reminder. It was Eddie.

Hey, Bork. Check in with the 'rents lately?

The text both warmed her heart—because of the nickname, which was the way he said her name when he was little—and made her uneasy because she had *not* checked in lately, and her brother likely knew that. She stared at it for a long time before responding.

Been super busy with the new job and house. Will text them tonight.

The bouncing dots did their dance before Eddie's reply came. *Maybe call them instead. They miss you. Would be good for them to hear your voice.*

Brooke sighed, and that feeling of being conflicted—the one she was becoming alarmingly used to—made its entrance and parked itself heavily on her shoulders like a shawl made of lead.

Okay. She sent that then waited a couple beats before adding, *You good?*

They texted for a few minutes about superficial things. Work. Sports. Movies. Nothing any deeper than that. It's what her relationship with her little brother had become since she'd left, and if she dwelled on it too long, it would pull her all the way down into a lake of depression—a place she worked hard not to swim in. She didn't blame him. He loved her. She knew that. But he loved their parents, too, and he just couldn't choose between them and his big sister, so he claimed he stayed neutral. Which wasn't at all what he did, but Brooke couldn't think about it.

They finished up their meaningless conversation, and Brooke glanced at the time in the corner of the screen. Almost noon.

Good. She could use some fresh air. A quick online search told her there was a small mom-and-pop store within two miles and decided a four-mile walk would do her good. She changed out her heels for socks and Nikes, grabbed her coat and purse, and left her office to clear her head.

❖

"Fantastic. Thank you, Jazz. See you next week." Macy hung up the phone and let out a little squeal of delight. Even after working for Emily for as long as she had, she got a tiny thrill every time somebody set up a staging.

"Sounds like good news," Emily said, not looking up from her keyboard.

"That new build I was telling you about."

"From the Wolfe meeting last week?"

"Yup. They want us to stage a condo and an office, with the possibility of a second condo in the next month." Macy's brain was already racing, thinking about designs, styles, colors. She was going to meet Jasmine and Brooke there next week to see the place, take measurements, brainstorm about styles and colors.

"Your brain is on fire already," Emily said with affectionate amusement. "I can smell the smoke over here."

"It's a *brand-new* building, Em. I have so many thoughts and ideas."

"Your favorite part. The brainstorming."

"It really is." Macy said it on a dreamy sigh, and she knew it. And Emily was right—the brainstorming was her favorite part. Coming up with styles and layouts and themes. She loved every second of it.

Ignoring the fact that Brooke would be there was also happening, but she pretended not to realize it. The truth was, Brooke had been hanging out in Macy's head—sometimes in the forefront, often in the background—since last Sunday when they'd run into each other at the café. She could still see Brooke, dressed casually, which made her look no less gorgeous and sophisticated than that ivory suit had—before The Danish Incident, of course—sitting alone at a table, reading. It was funny—someone sitting alone in a restaurant or a bar, especially somebody who was reading, always gave Macy a little pang of sympathy. She always felt sorry for them, like they had nobody, no choice but to be out in public solo. Seeing Brooke, though? Her thoughts had been completely different. Brooke didn't look lonely or sad. She looked...regal. Utterly content. The fact of the matter was Macy didn't feel sorry for Brooke. Quite the opposite. She wanted to be *invited* to go sit with Brooke. Chosen by Brooke, like being granted a meeting with the queen.

Oh, for God's sake, get a grip, Mace.

A head shake. She was being ridiculous. Some keyboard pokes. *Pull it together.* Macy focused on furniture sites. On artwork sites.

Looked at area rugs. She checked the Stage One inventory. Made notes so she could take a drive to the warehouse, which she had to do anyway to line up stuff for two residential stagings on Sunday. She worked. She focused. Anything, *anything* to keep her mind off this woman who wouldn't stay off her mind.

Mild success was all she could manage, but she tried.

It was what Macy's father would call a middlin' day. It wasn't nice out. It wasn't awful. No rain or snow, but no sunshine either. Not super warm. Not terribly cold. In between. Middlin'. And then she'd make fun of him for sounding like a cattle rancher in an old Western. The drive to the Stage One warehouse took about fifteen minutes. It was on the outskirts of town in a big conglomeration of warehouses that sat on a huge fenced lot. At the entrance, Macy punched in her code, and the fence slid open. To her right was where Dave the Mechanic worked on high-end sports cars. Down from him were a couple of unmarked units that Macy assumed were simply storage. To the left was a unit that housed the various inventory of Hopeless Romantic, a wedding planning service. Down from there was another mechanic and then a warehouse that held the overflow from one of the big furniture stores. There were a few more units, but Macy didn't know who owned them or what was inside. Emily had gotten theirs for a steal when she'd first opened Stage One, and while it wasn't the biggest, not by a long shot, it was large and open and clean. No mice. No mold. No weather or plumbing issues. All very important factors when housing furniture and home decor made out of things like wood, leather, and fabric.

Lucas had said once that the Stage One warehouse inventory was like the paints box for an artist. That Macy had a masterpiece in mind and the items in the warehouse were her colors. She would choose what worked and apply them to her canvas—the property being shown—and the final product would emerge from nothing. At the time, Macy had thought it incredibly dramatic, which wasn't a surprise coming from her dramatic gay bestie. But ever since that day, every time she walked into the warehouse with a new idea in her head, Lucas's description fit. She felt like an artist.

Today was no exception. She used her key, entered the large open space, hit the light switches one by one, which illuminated a section at a time until the whole place was visible. She and Emily did their best to make sure things stayed orderly, and that meant tagging along with the movers when they brought things back from a staging. Couches and chairs were in one corner. End tables and coffee tables were together.

They had five different dining room sets, which might seem excessive to an outsider, but they were all different styles and from different eras, so Emily deemed them necessary. Bedroom sets had their own section and took up nearly a quarter of the space. Area rugs hung from a rack like clothing so Macy could flip through them to see which she needed. Industrial shelving lined one wall and held all kinds of knickknacks and small items of decor that Macy called cherries, as they were cherries on top of a finished design—vases, artificial plants, picture frames, and such. Other shelves held bedding and towels, all wrapped in plastic, washed and repacked every time she was done using it. Another area held artwork of various sizes and styles and color schemes.

Macy loved it here. Her favorite thing to do was to flop down on one of the couches, pull out her laptop with the layout program on it, and design different rooms. Not even just for clients. She liked to do it for fun, see what she could come up with. Every now and then, she'd design something incredible. She saved those.

The next weekend, she had two homes to stage for open houses. When the property was residential and folks currently lived there, Macy usually used their stuff. Their furniture. Sometimes, their knickknacks. The key to staging a home for sale was making sure potential buyers could see themselves there. That meant the sellers needed to remove their personal items—family photos, trinkets they loved, proof of their pets, things like that. And that suggestion didn't always go over well. Nobody liked to be told to scrub a room of their existence, but Macy had been doing this for a while. She did her best to explain to her clients that a potential buyer would have a hard time seeing themselves in a living room if it was filled with photos of somebody else's kids. You could have a potential buyer with a fear of dogs or an allergy to cats, so the dog bed in the corner and the cat tree by the window could be a deterrent for them, even an unconscious one.

Both homes were average. Nothing fancy. Not super modern, not historical. Basic family homes. Macy pulled out a notebook as she walked through the different room sections and marked down which pieces she needed. Both homes already had furniture that would work, but she'd add a few touches—an end table here, an artificial floor plant there. One was home to a family of five, and their dining room set was gouged and stained and old. Macy would have it removed for the open house, replace it with a newer, updated set that did a better job at showing off the potential of the dining room. The second home had a sectional that was older than Macy, or at least looked it. She chose a gray microfiber couch, which would make the room look bigger, then jotted notes. She'd get in touch with Regina, their part-timer, who would handle setting up one open house while Macy did the other.

What Macy was really excited about, though, was the new build. It wasn't often she got to completely furnish an empty space. It let the creative interior designer in her completely loose, let her shake off the reins and run wild. She couldn't wait to see the space, get a feel for it, for what furniture would make it most inviting, and a part of her—a large part that she was once again trying hard to ignore—was crazy jittery with the nervous anticipation of seeing Brooke there tomorrow. She didn't really understand where this was coming from. It was new. Intimidating. Weird. She didn't know Brooke. Brooke didn't know her, and Macy certainly hadn't made a terrific first impression, or even a decent second one. Still, she found herself so drawn to Brooke, wanted to learn more about her, listen to her talk, and what the hell was that about?

"Okay," she breathed out into the echoing silence of the warehouse. "Stop it. Get your shit together and do your job, Macy. Enough of this lusting after the new chick."

Lusting.

That's exactly what she was doing.

And goddamn, it had been a long time.

CHAPTER SEVEN

I should be in church.

Brooke hadn't been to church in over six months, but still, every Sunday morning, the same thought ran through her head. It wasn't just an obligation, either. She missed it. More than she cared to admit. Her faith was a part of her and had been since she'd been old enough to understand what it was. She still prayed, still had some kind of a relationship with God, but it wasn't the same. Part of her wanted to look into churches here, see what she might find, but another part of her was afraid. Ashamed. Felt unwelcome. Never wanted to set foot in a house of worship ever again.

Her loud sigh left her mouth in a visible puff as she climbed the stairs to the reservoir, counting quietly as she went. "Thirteen, fourteen, fifteen, and sixteen." A half turn and she sat on the top step, the same place she'd sat the first time she'd come.

It was cold this morning, and Brooke had smartly stepped into her fleece-lined workout pants. On top, she wore a thermal undershirt, then a fleece, then her puffy royal blue coat with the hood. White hat, white mittens, low boots. It was a good walking outfit, if she did say so. She was comfortable enough to move freely, and plenty warm, and this earlier hour at the reservoir was perfect because it was much less populated than Saturday mornings. She'd started out in the dark, remembering the big, curved lampposts bent over the walking path like stooped elderly men, and she'd watched the sun rise up over the horizon as she strode along, only a handful of other folks there with her. It had been peaceful and beautiful, and Brooke had forgotten how much she loved the sunrise.

She'd forgotten a lot of things.

Much as she loved solitary moments like this, solitary activities, that was the drawback, wasn't it? Too much quiet, too much time for thinking. For recalling. For regretting. Sometimes, when she walked to clear her head, her head actually ended up more crowded than when she'd started out. Just as she began to worry that today was going to be one of those instances, she was startled by a small, four-legged black creature who literally jumped into her lap.

"What the—?" Brooke flinched and the creature—a dog, she could see now, a terrier—turned to look at her with the most soulful brown eyes she'd ever seen in something that wasn't human. "Well. Hello there," she said quietly. "You scared me."

To its credit, the dog tilted its furry black head in a move that looked almost apologetic, then swiped its tongue across her chin.

"Aw, that was nice. Thanks."

The dog—she craned her neck down to look at its undercarriage—was a he and had no collar. Out of breath, he did a little bit of adjusting and lay right down in her lap, his front paws hanging over Brooke's knees like that was a regular position for him, and he lay there all the time.

"No, seriously, make yourself comfortable." How could she not smile at this guy? He was adorable, all scruffy and cute. Remembering the inkblot of a stray cat on her patio, who had made another appearance last night, she muttered, "Am I the lady all the lost black animals come to? Am I wearing a sign? Is there a Lost Black Animals network with my name on a list?" The dog was panting like he'd run a marathon, and Brooke swiveled her head, looking around for a panicked dog owner. "Why don't you have a collar, buddy? Hmm? Did you run away?" He was well-groomed, if not due for a haircut, and well-fed, and Brooke figured somebody was probably missing him. Just as she slid her cell phone out of her pocket to do a search on local shelters, she heard a voice calling out in a frantic pitch.

"Angus! Angus! Here, boy!"

The dog's ears pricked up.

"Oh, is that you?" Brooke asked. "Are you Angus?"

He sat up and looked at her.

"Angus," she said again, and he tilted his head in the cutest display of listening she'd ever seen.

"Angus!"

"I think your mommy is looking for you." Brooke and the dog

both looked to the right where the voice came from. And Brooke's eyes went so wide, she could feel them.

Macy.

She stopped, and they looked at each other. Macy wore light-colored jeans that looked so soft, Brooke wondered if they were her favorites. A red hoodie under a Carhartt jacket, a navy-blue hat, black gloves, boots. She was the epitome of mismatched, and the first word that came to mind for Brooke was *adorable*. Macy looked adorable. In her hand were three leashes. One led to a large golden retriever who was apparently trying hard to get to Brooke without pulling Macy off her feet. The second was attached to a small dachshund who didn't seem at all interested in Brooke. Or anybody, for that matter. The third dangled from Macy's hand, a red-and-black plaid collar attached to the end of it.

"What are you doing here?" Macy asked, then seemed to almost wince, as if she'd heard her words and realized how they sounded.

"Being a seat for your dog, apparently. Hi."

Brooke's voice seemed to spur Macy into motion, finally. She came closer, reached for Angus. "Dude, you can't run away from me like that. You're going to give me a stroke."

"Slipped his collar?"

Macy sighed. "I should've used his harness, but I was in a hurry and thought we could just do a quick walk." A bitter chuckle. "I didn't expect it would turn into a full-out sprint." As she talked, the golden sniffed every inch of Brooke he could reach.

Brooke petted his head and rubbed his velvety ears between her fingers. "Hi," she said quietly. "I'm Brooke. It's nice to meet you."

"That's Pete," Macy said, and the note of pride that crept into her voice was clear to Brooke. "He's a big lug and my love." She pointed to the dachshund. "This is Priscilla, but you may call her Your Highness because that's what she prefers." Then she bent down to Angus, who still sat on Brooke's lap. She took his rectangular head between her gloved hands and brought her face to his. Which meant it was also close to Brooke's. It was the closest they'd ever been, and Brooke tried not to stare at the smooth skin of Macy's face or how rosy her cheeks were in the cold. At the warmth and kindness in her rich brown eyes. At how very full her bottom lip was… "And this is Angus." Macy's voice snapped Brooke out of her dreamy observations. "He is a terrier through and through. He's a handful, and I adore him."

"I can see why," Brooke said, pulling herself together and trying to hide her disappointment when Macy stood back up, and Angus hopped off her lap. "He just came running over and jumped right into my lap. Almost gave me a heart attack."

"I'm sorry about that." Macy's expression went serious, and it bothered Brooke to see the light and pride that had been there a moment ago fade away.

"No, no. No need to be sorry. I'm glad he came to me instead of sprinting down the hill or into traffic or something."

"God, me, too." Now Macy's face registered horror. She was *so* expressive. Everything—emotions, fears, thoughtfulness—was right there in her expression for anybody to see, and Brooke wondered if that was a blessing and a curse for Macy.

There was a moment of quiet, a little awkward, but not unbearable, as the two of them hung there at the top of the steps and looked out onto the open field as it sloped down to the street. Only a handful of people milled about. Dog walkers and joggers. Too early for families.

"Do you always walk this early?" Brooke asked. She wanted to keep Macy nearby, didn't want her to leave just yet. She also didn't want to think about that.

One shoulder lifted in a half-shrug as Macy spoke, looking down at her dogs. Pete was sniffing Brooke's boots. Priscilla had lain down, and damn if she didn't look like royalty. Angus was looking down the hill at another dog in the distance, ears pricked up, back rigid. Macy gave a tug on his leash. "Don't even think about it, mister." She turned to Brooke. "Once in a while, yes, but mostly on days like today when I'm going to be busy."

It was Sunday morning, and Brooke knew what that meant in the real estate business. "Open house?"

Macy held up two fingers.

"Oh, you *are* going to have a busy day. Will you oversee them both?" She didn't really care—she just wanted to listen to Macy talk some more, a fact that made her suddenly clear her throat, give her head a subtle shake, and quickly stand up.

"We have a part-timer who helps on days when we have more than one. But I do the layouts, the design if needed. Stuff like that." Macy's eyes followed Brooke's movements—Brooke could feel them on her, she swore it.

"I see." She had to get out of there. The feeling was sudden and strong and made her antsy. "Well, good luck. I hope it goes well." She took a step to leave, but Macy's voice stopped her.

"Do you think it's weird that we keep running into each other like this?" Her smile was tentative, but open. Her eyes kind and curious. "I mean, we meet at work—and I'm ignoring The Danish Incident—then we run into each other at the café. Now here. It's…interesting. I mean, considering you just moved here. Three times? It's like the Universe is, I don't know, trying to tell us something."

The Universe, huh? Brooke hadn't gotten that far, but Macy wasn't wrong about the strangeness of their meetings. And then a thought occurred to her as she looked at the three dogs. "It's actually four times." At Macy's furrowed brow, she explained. "I was here last week. I went for a walk, exploring the area, and I ended up here. I sat right here on this step and just people-watched for a bit. Way down there by the street, I saw a woman walking three dogs and remember thinking that it must be hard to wrangle them all. It just occurred to me that it was you."

A smile that had been uncertain widened before Brooke's eyes, and it only made all the non-matching clothes cuter on Macy. "Really?"

Brooke nodded. "So. Four times."

"In what? Two weeks?"

Another nod. "Definitely weird."

"But kinda cool."

Macy's words stayed with Brooke as she walked back to her place. They sat in her head and replayed periodically as she scrambled herself some eggs and sipped coffee. "The Universe, huh?" she said for the second time, quietly to her empty kitchen as she ate standing up. It was the phrase some people used when they didn't believe in God. Or weren't sure. Brooke had no problem with that. She had never been one to think her belief system was the right one. Or the only one. Unlike her parents, she'd never expect somebody to convert to her way of thinking.

Was the Universe trying to tell them something?

It was probably a good thing that the rather loud *meow* tickled her ears and stopped that train of thought because she could ride that thing for hours. Instead, she set down her plate and walked into the living room. There at the sliding glass door sat the cat, looking like an expectant inkblot. The wind had picked up since she got back from the park, and the temperature had dipped, the forecast including a possible ice storm.

It wasn't much of an internal debate, but Brooke was sure she'd regret the decision as she slid the door open. There weren't even any tentative steps or hesitation on the part of the cat. He waltzed right in, headed straight for the couch, and hopped up.

"Um, hang on there, bossypants." A towel from the kitchen in her hands, Brooke was surprised when the cat let her pick him up and give him a good rubdown, hoping to make him clean enough to not leave a mess on her couch. Holding him made it painfully clear just how thin he was, scrawny, and Brooke wondered how long he'd been outside on his own. No collar, a couple of small mats near his stomach. She rubbed carefully around them, thinking they might hurt up against his skin like that. A cursory inspection didn't show any sign of fleas, thanks to the time of year, though they'd be hard to see in all his black fur. When he looked up at her with those big yellow-green eyes and started to purr, her heart went all soft and mushy. "Oh, you are working it, aren't you, mister?" The cat brought his nose to hers, sniffed gently. It was all over. Brooke knew it.

With a soft sigh, she set the cat on the couch and watched him curl up on the fleece throw she'd left in a pile at one end. Once he was settled and his eyes became heavy, she put on her coat and boots and grabbed her car keys. On her phone, she searched for the nearest pet store.

She knew when to admit defeat.

Chapter Eight

L ooking at empty spaces and discussing how best to stage them was Macy's favorite part of her job. She loved it. She lived for this part. She was never nervous about it, never weirdly anticipatory. Excited, sure. Creative, absolutely. But nervous? Never.

Until today.

She knew why. That wasn't in question. It was because of Brooke, and Macy hated to admit that. *Hated* it. She didn't want her demeanor, her mood, her overall emotional well-being to depend on who was in the room with her when she was doing her job. In fact, the whole thing was pissing her off a little bit. As she sat in her car in the parking lot and tried to pull herself together, she took stock. Her hands on the steering wheel had a small tremor. What had started as butterflies had become hornets and now careened around in her stomach, bouncing off the sides and making her slightly nauseous. Her palms felt a little clammy, and her mouth felt like she'd eaten some chalk dust.

What the hell?

How was it possible that the mere presence of somebody could have this effect on her? Actually, not even her presence, as Macy hadn't seen her yet. It was the *idea* of her presence. Which was even worse.

Macy dropped her forehead to the steering wheel with a loud groan. Rose, dropped again. Three more times. Finally, she sat up and gazed out the windshield.

This was all so weird.

She wished more than anything in that moment that she could jam the car into reverse, head to the YMCA, and dive into the pool. Swim until her head cleared and her body was too exhausted to dwell.

With a deep and what she hoped was a fortifying breath, she pushed out of her car, gathered her things, and headed to the main entrance of what was shaping up quickly to be Whitney Gardens.

Macy hadn't been in many new builds when they were still in the being built stage, but there had been a few. It was the smell that always caught her interest. Drywall dust and spackle combined with fresh paint and new wood. Macy was pretty sure she'd been a contractor or a construction worker of some sort in another life. In this one, she didn't have the patience or the talent to deal with angles and measurements, but she loved the idea of building something from the ground up.

The lobby was finished, open in concept, with windows and doors on either side and straight back for what would eventually be shops. A grand stairway stretched up in the center, and Macy had been given instructions to go up one flight to the second floor where office space would be, as well as elevators to the apartments.

Residential living space began on the third floor, and she took the elevator up. As she stepped out, she tried to picture living there, what it would feel like, smell like, sound like. This would help her get a better handle on design. Her footsteps echoed, as the hallway had yet to be carpeted, and she could hear voices coming from an open door down the hall and to her left. She inhaled, put on her game face, and headed toward the conversation.

And there she was.

Today's suit was black with subtle silver pinstripes. Pants and a jacket, sleeves rolled halfway up her forearms, black heels, ivory top, hair in a ponytail, and the mix of professional and casual reached right into Macy's lungs and stole her breath.

Jesus Christ, Macy, get a grip.

"There she is." Brooke's gaze turned to meet Macy's, and Brooke smiled widely as she held out an arm in greeting. There was a guy with her, Macy just then noticed. He was tall and bald and wore a navy-blue suit. "Macy Carr, this is Drew Whitney, contractor and builder extraordinaire."

Macy took Whitney's outstretched hand. His handshake was a bit too firm, but his smile seemed nice enough.

"Macy's company has staged countless properties for us, and they do a terrific job. Let's discuss the look and feel of what you're going for, so we can get these apartments sold in a timely manner."

For the next ninety minutes, they walked around empty apartments and discussed possible floor plans, as well as Whitney's target demographic. Not surprisingly, he hoped to sell to thirtysomethings, business types, probably singles or young couples just starting out. The look Whitney was going for was modern. Black, glass, chrome. Macy mentally grinned and shook her head. Guys almost always wanted black, glass, and chrome. She was usually able to temper that a bit by adding some softer touches. Leather. Light grays. Pops of color here and there that kept the spaces from screaming *man cave*.

Macy took notes, made some suggestions, and did a whole lot of listening as they walked through three apartments, each slightly different from the last in either square footage or layout. Then they took the elevator down to the second floor where the offices would be and did the same thing. By the time the meeting was over and Whitney had left, Macy had filled nearly five pages with notes and bookmarked several sites on her tablet. Her brain was filled to capacity. And she was excited. More excited than she'd been about a project in a long time. It was a feeling she loved. It got her adrenaline pumping and her mind whirring and—

"You look revved up." Brooke. She stood with her arms folded across her chest, amusement on her face.

"I have so many ideas." Macy stopped as Brooke's words sank in. "Revved up? What does that mean?"

"Your eyes are all bright and…" She squinted at Macy. "And you've been smiling for the past half hour, and your eyebrows are high."

"My eyebrows are high?"

"Yes. Like you've been expecting something."

"I've been expecting that guy to leave, so I can play with my layout app." Macy grinned.

"Well, that sounds like fun."

"It is. Wanna see?" Macy didn't wait for an answer. She sidled up closer to Brooke, tablet in hand, and punched in the right things. Her app opened, and she began talking about how it worked, how she could put in the measurements of a space, and it would lay it out for her so she could then add various pieces of furniture to see how things would look. Nonstop talking. A little showing off. Lots of ignoring how good Brooke smelled. Like almonds with a hint of vanilla.

"So, what happens now?" Brooke asked, her voice close enough to tickle Macy's ear. "My old company didn't really work with stagers that much, so I'm unfamiliar."

"Well," Macy said and took a subtle step away. She had to. Being that close to Brooke was incredibly distracting. It made words tumble out of her mouth in a steady stream. Too steady. She took a breath. Dropped a pen. Picked it up. Took another breath. "I'll come up with a few different suggested layouts based on talking to Mr. Whitney. I'll send them to you and Sasha, and we'll go from there."

"Sounds simple enough."

They were walking slowly toward the large staircase, Macy noticed. A good thing. It was time for her to put some space between her and Brooke before she said or did something stupid. Like fall down the stairs, which would be just her luck. "Sure, simple for you. I'm doing all the work." She glanced up at Brooke to make it clear she was being a smart-ass.

Brooke laughed softly, and Macy realized that might have been the first time she'd heard it, and she liked it. A lot.

"Then I will let you get to it." They hit the bottom of the stairs and headed toward the front doors. Brooke suddenly turned to her and said, "Unless you feel like grabbing some lunch…" The way she let the sentence dangle made it clear she was unsure for whatever reason. And Macy felt the same way, but she also felt other things. Freaked. Nervous. Terrified. Yeah, that last one was the big one.

"You know, I would, but I really need to get started on this." Lies. She had time. But her fear was ruling her in that moment, and she was letting it.

"Oh. Okay. No worries." There was a split second of disappointment—Macy was sure she saw it—but Brooke recovered in an instant. "I'll talk to you soon, then." And with that, she turned and headed off to her car, leaving Macy standing there wondering if she should've said yes. *Knowing* she should've said yes. Annoyed now that she hadn't said yes.

But then she remembered that she'd already done this dance, had already been through it all and had lost brutally and had zero desire to do it again.

Right?

Nibbling on the inside of her cheek, she stepped off the curb and headed to her own car. Work. That's what she needed now. The one thing in her life that had remained steady.

Work. Yeah.

That's what she needed.

❖

Ugh. That was stupid.

Brooke had been kicking herself all day. Ever since she'd left Macy standing in the parking lot of the unfinished Whitney Gardens building. She could still see her in the rearview mirror, standing there looking both more put together than Brooke had seen her before, in dark jeans, a white top, a navy-blue plaid blazer, and brown booties, and even more attractive.

"Unless you feel like grabbing some lunch…" Brooke sat at her desk and repeated what she'd said to Macy using a high-pitched, really unflattering voice, then dropped her head back against her chair and groaned. It must've been louder than she thought because a voice cut through the room, startling her.

"Everything okay?" It was Sasha, and she came in and took a seat without waiting for an invitation. Which was fine with Brooke because she needed a distraction.

Work talk. Yes. Let's do that. She sat up straighter. "Yeah, I'm fine."

"That groan didn't sound like an *I'm fine* groan." Sasha's gentle smile was kind and…knowing? Was it knowing? What did she know? What *could* she know?

Brooke closed her eyes and told herself to get a goddamn grip.

"Is it your personal life?" Sasha asked. "Please say yes so I don't feel so alone in my own disaster of one."

That surprised Brooke. Sasha's personal life was a disaster? How could that be? "You? But you're so…" She waved a hand in front of Sasha. "Perfect." Brooke couldn't believe she'd let the words slip out, had actually said them, and she nearly winced along with the grimace she made.

Sasha surprised her again, this time by barking a laugh so loud it made Brooke flinch in her seat. "Oh, God bless you, Brooke. I really needed a laugh."

Brooke shook her head, confused.

"I am so far from perfect. We're not only in different zip codes, me and perfect, we're in different states. Different countries, probably. We might even be on different planets."

"You just seem to have it all together."

"Yeah? Well, good. That's the image I'd like to project." Sasha leaned in closer, her blue eyes sparkling, her blond hair pulled back in a complicated twist, and lowered her voice to a whisper. "You're looking at a woman who has been telling her mother all about her new girlfriend. Except there isn't one. She's fake."

Brooke wasn't following. "You have a girlfriend?" Is that what Sasha was saying? That she was gay?

"I don't. But my mother thinks I do."

"Ah, I see. You have a pretend girlfriend." She hesitated, then decided *screw it*, and she dove right in. "So you're gay?"

"Yup." Sasha sat back, as if affirming her sexuality was no big deal, and pointed at Brooke. "*That's* how perfect I am. I talk to my mother once a week and tell her all about the nonexistent Ms. Right I've been seeing simply so she'll stop bugging me about it and worrying that I'm going to be alone for the rest of my life." Something almost sad passed across Sasha's face, paused at her eyes, and darkened them for just a fleeting moment before moving on. Then she squinted at Brooke. "I hope that's not a problem for you. My being gay. Not that it would matter because I'm the boss around here." Her tone was light, but there was something in it that dared Brooke to challenge her.

"Not at all. I'm bisexual." *Oh my God.* Had she said that out loud? How? What was happening?

An amused grin spread across Sasha's face. "I take it, judging by the look on your face right now, that you don't tell a lot of people that."

What was it about Sasha Wolfe that made Brooke feel safe? There was clearly something. "No. I don't. At all. It's not something that has been"—she raised her eyes to the ceiling as if the right words were scrawled up there—"well-received by my family."

Sasha sat up and leaned her forearms on the front of Brooke's desk. "I'm sorry about that. I know that can be rough. Just know there is no judgment here. Okay? I won't go all corny-ass sisterhood talk on you, but…" She left it there, and Brooke felt not only grateful and relieved, but more at ease than she had in a very long time. "If you ever need to talk."

"I appreciate that. Thank you."

Sasha sat back. "Is that why you were groaning? Dating problems? Do you have a girl? A boy?" Then she stood up. So fast, Brooke wondered for a second if she had slipped off the chair, and she blinked at her in surprise. Sasha held out a hand like a traffic cop. "No, wait.

Have you eaten? I haven't. Let's scoot next door, grab a sandwich, and you can tell me all about it." Her tone left no room for declining. Or even for debate. And Brooke didn't mind, really. She felt the corners of her mouth tug upward and was pretty sure she understood why.

She'd made a friend.

CHAPTER NINE

Macy had decided that the range of temperatures she sat through to watch Tyler's soccer games was directly proportional to how much she loved him. Macy had been surprised to learn that Tyler could actually play soccer all year long. Indoor in the winter. Rec in the spring and summer. School in the fall. Deciding rec was her least favorite, at least today, she pulled the fleece blanket more tightly around herself against an icy wind and glanced up at the sky, gray as a dull nickel and spitting a cold drizzle onto the players and spectators alike. Why couldn't he have excelled in swimming? Where it was warm and toasty for onlookers. Or basketball? Something played inside during things like rain and monsoons…

Not a damn thing. That was what Macy knew about soccer. Aside from the ball needing to go into the goal, of course. She didn't know the positions. She didn't understand the plays. More than that, she didn't care. She only went there for Tyler. Many of her friends were huge soccer fans who watched the women's games with rabid intensity and enthusiasm. And Macy would go to some of those gatherings and eat the snacks and drink the beer and cheer when others cheered, but the truth was, she couldn't care less. She found soccer to be mind-numbingly boring. A very unpopular opinion that she kept to herself, lest she have her lesbian card stripped right out of her wallet.

Eva unfolded a chair and set it next to Macy. "Sorry I'm late. Last-minute patient with a lost crown." Eva's dental practice was a successful one, and she rarely turned away patients, even if that meant she missed some of her son's game.

"Lucky you. It's just fifteen minutes' less bone-chilling cold you have to sit through."

"Here." A silver Thermos in her hand, Eva poured coffee from it into a cup.

"Gimme." Steam wafted up from the cup in white tendrils, and Macy reached for it like it was gold. She took a sip, felt the warmth travel down her throat and settle in her belly, and she moaned happily. "You're forgiven for being late."

The crowd cheered, and they looked up at the field. Tyler had his arms up in the air in victory, as did his teammates.

"Was that him? Did he score?" Eva asked.

"I have no idea, but I'm going to pretend he did." Macy threw a fist in the air and cheered for her nephew, who had his arm around his teammate, a boy with dark skin and limbs that seemed almost too long. "Which boy is that?" she asked Eva.

"Jeremy. He and Ty are buds."

Macy nodded. She loved seeing her nephew smile, and he was smiling big right then.

"You guys had fun over the weekend." Eva's eyes were on the game as she pulled out a Ziploc baggie of smoked almonds and held it out to Macy.

"We always have fun. Also, I don't know how you can afford to feed that kid." She turned to look at Eva, kept a straight face. "I think he might have a tapeworm."

"Right? I swear to God, three-quarters of my grocery bill is due to him. And look at him." Eva held a hand out toward Tyler, who was sprinting down the field. "He's a beanpole. Where does he put it?"

"I don't know, but last weekend, if I hadn't grabbed myself a second slice of pizza when I did, I'd have been out of luck. He ate pretty much the whole pie." She tossed a couple almonds into her mouth. "And then at Beans & Batter? Not one. Not two. Three muffins. *Three.* You've seen those muffins. They're enormous."

"Who was the *hot chick?*" Eva made air quotes.

"What *hot chick?*" Macy made them back.

"Ty said there was a hot chick at breakfast. Somebody you knew and were talking with. He liked her."

Realization hit then. Brooke. She was talking about Brooke.

"Oh, her." Macy made a show of shrugging, of being less than interested in the subject of Brooke Sullivan. "She's just a new agent working for Wolfe. She happened to be at the café when we were there, and we sat near her." Another shrug.

"You should shrug one more time, just to drive it home." Eva had that look on her face, the one Macy hated, the one that said she knew Macy better than Macy knew herself. Damn her. "Is she nice?"

Macy took a deep breath, remembered Brooke's lunch invitation, still felt irritated that she hadn't said yes to it. "Yeah, she seems to be. I haven't spent much time with her." Not quite a lie, but not exactly the truth. Between the first meeting, the time in the café, the park, and the walk-through of Whitney Gardens earlier in the week, they'd actually spent a few hours together.

"Well, Tyler seemed to really like her."

"They bonded over my klutziness, yeah."

"I heard." Eva's grin was warm as Macy shook her head. A gust of wind kicked up and reminded them how cold it was. "Ugh. I hate spring games." Eva zipped her coat up higher and pulled the hood over her head.

"Seriously. I'm gonna tell Ty he owes me big-time." April could be fickle in upstate New York, that was for sure. And you could be a person who'd lived there all your life, but you would still complain about the weather. Macy tucked the fleece blanket around her legs and thanked her lucky stars that she'd remembered to toss it in her car. "How the hell are these boys running around in shorts and not freezing to death?"

Eva shook her head, and they watched for a few moments, cheering when necessary, groaning when the rest of the considerable crowd did. Another goal was scored just as the game ended, this time by Tyler's gangly friend Jeremy, and Ty jumped into his arms as the team celebrated.

"Thank God," Macy said as she jumped up and started packing her things.

"Is the hot chick dating material?" Eva asked suddenly as she folded her chair, making Macy blink at her.

"What?"

"Ty said he felt like there was something there between you two."

"Ty is sixteen," was Macy's defense, though she was well aware that Tyler was much more observant and wiser than most kids his age.

Eva shrugged and studied her, clearly waiting for an answer.

Macy sighed. "I have no idea."

"That's not a no."

It wasn't. Eva was right. "Yeah, but…" Macy shook her head,

at a loss. She used the same explanation she'd given to Ty. "It's complicated."

"Is it, though?" Eva's tone said *It absolutely is not.*

Macy shot her a look of warning.

Eva held up her hands like a robbery victim. "Okay, okay. Fine. But I'm with Ty. I don't want you to be alone forever. And I don't think Michelle would have wanted that either."

The mention of Michelle's name always felt like a small zap of electricity through Macy's system, and not in a good way. It wasn't that she didn't ever want to talk about her late partner, the person she'd thought of as the love of her life. But somehow, even after all that time, the sound of Michelle's name still felt like somebody had poked her with some kind of a live wire, jolting her to attention.

Tyler ran up to them then, covered in mud and smelling of sweat and the outdoors, and Macy sent up a thank-you as she was rescued from the subject, at least for now. He hugged his mother tightly, making her shriek about how gross and sweaty he was as she squirmed in his grasp.

He let her go. "I'm going to Jeremy's for dinner. That okay?"

"I love how you tell me what you're doing and then ask if you can." Eva waved down the line of spectators at a woman Macy assumed was Jeremy's mom, since he was standing next to her. She waved back, clearly letting Eva know it had been cleared with her. "Sure. Go ahead."

Tyler bounced on the balls of his cleats, clearly happy, and leaned over to kiss Macy's cheek. "Thanks for coming."

"Order better weather next time, will you?"

"On it," he called over his shoulder as he left them.

"And do your homework!" Eva called after him. She watched as he met up with Jeremy and a small group of kids that had joined in. "See that girl?" she asked Macy. "The little blonde?"

Macy stood on tiptoe. "In the purple coat?"

"Yes. That's Kelsey. She's always at the games, and she cheers Tyler on specifically and always hangs out afterward."

"Think she likes our little Tyler?" Macy watched the kids all interact. Interesting.

"I do. And he seems to like her back, I think. He's nice to her." Eva glanced at her. "I'm watching from afar."

"I don't know—I'm thinking he likes Jeremy." Macy hadn't

intended to give voice to her suspicions, and it just kind of slid out of her mouth before she realized it.

Eva's head snapped around. "Do you?" She was more surprised than horrified or disappointed, thank God, and she looked back in the direction of her son, who still had an arm around his buddy, who had an arm around his back. "Huh. I never thought about that."

Macy shrugged. "Just an observation."

Eva nodded but said nothing more.

Chapter Ten

Friday had been crazy busy, and that's the way Brooke used to like them. Busy days went by faster, and then she had time to be with her family, her friends. Now she was in a completely different city with no family and very few friends. The weekend stretched out before her, and she had no idea what she'd do for the next two days. If she could skip them entirely and just keep working, she would. Absolutely.

She'd just left a meeting with a client Sasha had introduced her to via email. He owned several buildings in the business district and was looking for help finding tenants. He'd been promising. Might end up a good, steady source for her. As she drove, she slid on her sunglasses and shook her head at how changeable the weather seemed lately, but she would take sunshine any day of the week. Just as she turned up the new Billie Eilish song on the radio, she realized she was about to drive past Whitney Gardens. She could see the back parking lot where there was a large moving truck, and she recognized Macy's Honda SUV in the corner.

Before she understood what she was actually doing, Brooke turned the wheel and pulled through the entrance and drove around to the back lot, then parked right next to Macy's car. Two burly men were carrying a gorgeous black leather sofa through the large back entrance, and she stayed out of their way while following them until they got to the enormous freight elevator. Brooke took the hallway next to it until she got to a door that spat her into the sunlit lobby of Whitney Gardens. There was nobody in sight, but she could hear lots of activity from the second floor as she took the grand staircase up one flight.

Contractors and construction workers and the like all had the same look, and Brooke nodded at one as he smiled and walked past her.

Jeans, work boots, flannel shirt, tool belt slung low across his hips, a jangling sound with each step, as if he was wearing spurs. Her dad was a contractor, and she'd been around guys like this her entire adolescent life. Plumbers and electricians and builders. Men with callused hands and muscular shoulders and a knowledge of angles and measurements that made Brooke's head spin. She knew these men, knew how hard they worked, was completely comfortable around them. And they made her miss her father so much her chest ached.

A quick tour around the floor showed no signs of furniture or of Macy, so Brooke hopped the elevator and went up one floor. As soon as the doors slid open, she could hear it.

"Okay, that needs to go here." Macy. "But don't go anywhere yet, 'cause it might not work."

Brooke turned left out of the elevator and followed the sound of Macy's voice until she reached the open door of one of the new apartments.

"I think…" Macy's back was to her, hands on her hips as she studied the black leather couch Brooke had seen in the parking lot. It now sat under a bank of windows. The sunlight streaming into the apartment was so inviting that Brooke had a split-second thought of plopping onto the couch and taking a nap in the warmth of the rays. "Put it over there for a second, would you, guys?" Macy pointed to her left at an open wall.

Brooke folded her arms across her chest, leaned against the doorjamb, and simply watched. Macy was in her element, that much was clear. She wore jeans, low black boots that had a motorcycle feel to them, and a black-and-white striped long-sleeved shirt. Her hair was down, slightly disheveled, and Brooke was beginning to understand that it usually was. Instead of looking frazzled, though, she just looked cutely tousled, like she'd been picked up, given a tight bear hug, rocked back and forth, and set back down again. As Macy pointed and directed, Brooke noticed a silver ring on her right hand and dark polish on her nails. The entire look was… Brooke swallowed. This version of Macy was not the cute, clumsy girl she'd seen so far. Not by a long shot. This one was confident. In control. Commanding. And really, really sexy. Unexpectedly so. Brooke tried to ignore the fluttering in her stomach. Unsuccessfully.

What is happening here?

The question echoed through her head, and Brooke ignored it because the truth? She was enjoying the view. Very, very much.

"No, back over here," Macy said now, and the guys slid the couch back under the windows. They didn't look at all annoyed or impatient with Macy's indecision. In fact, the opposite seemed true, judging by their expressions. They liked Macy. Respected her. "And then that end table." Macy turned and pointed to a square table with a gray wood surface and black legs. As she did so, she saw Brooke, and a quick mix of things danced across her face: surprise, uncertainty, happiness. Brooke saw them all. "Well, hi there."

"Hey," Brooke said, pushing off the doorjamb, and stepped farther into the apartment. "This looks fun."

"It really is," Macy said. To the guys she said, as she pointed to the left of the couch, "This table on that side. Let's see how it looks there." One of the guys moved the table, and then everybody stood and looked. Macy tipped her head one way, then the other, then finally gave a nod. "Yeah. I like it. That works."

"We've got a little bit more," the taller guy said. "Bistro table and chairs, chair and ottoman, and I think that might be it." He looked to his partner, who nodded.

"Great. We're almost done, guys." She slapped one on the arm as they passed her and walked out the door. When it was just her and Brooke left, Macy crossed the room to a cardboard box that sat on the floor. "So, what brings you by?"

"I was in the neighborhood."

Macy looked up at her with a black vase in her hand. "You know, I don't think I've ever heard anybody use that line in person. I've seen it in movies and on TV. Read it in books. But nobody has ever actually said it to me."

Brooke laughed softly. "Well, it's true. I was just up in the business district at a meeting and was driving right past here. Thought I'd pop in and see how it was looking." Not the entire truth, but not exactly a lie.

"And? How's it looking?"

Brooke kept her eyes on Macy, as she took some artificial vegetation out of the box, then forced herself to look around the apartment. "It looks amazing. I'd live here."

It was the absolute truth. The space looked so different with furniture in it. Inviting. Lived in. Comfortable. The furniture and the art on the walls meshed perfectly, seamlessly, all clean lines and dark colors, but as Macy had mentioned during their initial meeting with Whitney, there were enough pops of color and bits of softness to keep it from looking too masculine. Macy set the vase on the end table, then pulled out a couple of throw pillows—lavender with gray polka dots—and tossed them in one corner of the black leather couch. Brooke wanted to go lounge there immediately. Put her feet up. Have a beer.

"Well, that's pretty high praise." Macy shot her a grin. "Thank you."

"Can I wander?" Brooke asked, curious to see the bedroom and bath.

"Absolutely." Macy waved her toward the bedroom while she continued with smaller touches.

It didn't take long, as the apartment wasn't bigger than twelve hundred square feet. But it looked incredible. Macy was fantastic at her job, and while Brooke wasn't surprised, she was inexplicably pleased at the fact. She also chose not to think about why. Back out in the living area, the guys were back with a bistro table and one of the chairs that matched.

"It looks fantastic," Brooke said as she gave the guys a wide berth and crossed to the door.

"Thank you," Macy said again. She held Brooke's gaze as if she had more to say. Brooke waited. "Hey, um…" Macy looked down at her boots for a moment, then back up. "It's Friday and it's been a busy day and I could use a drink. Care to join me?"

"I'd love to." The words were out, blurted, no chance to think about them first. What the hell? But then Macy's face lit up like one of those sparklers kids play with on the Fourth of July, and Brooke's uncertainty vanished.

"Great. There's a place called Finn's over on East Main. Meet me there in…" She looked back at the guys, surveyed the room, seemed to calculate. "An hour?"

"I'll see you then."

Macy lifted one hand in a wave as Brooke turned and left, headed for the elevator. Once inside, the doors shut, and she was faced with her reflection—which showed her a goofy grin and a light in her eyes she hadn't seen in a long time.

Was this a date?

❖

"It's just a drink."

Macy said it aloud into the emptiness of her car. Apparently, she had used up every last ounce of courage she possessed when asking

Brooke to meet her. Because now? Now she could barely manage to get her seat belt clipped. She fought with it. Dropped a few swear words. Yanked on it too hard, so it locked up on her.

"Okay, Mace, relax. Take a breath." She followed her own advice, inhaled through her nose, exhaled out her mouth, and willed herself to calm down. Then she pulled gently on the seat belt, tugged it slowly across her body, and fastened it with a click. Sigh of relief. "There we go."

The nerves ratcheted up again during the seven-minute drive to Finn's because once she'd found a parking spot next to a black Audi, her stomach was filled with butterflies. A flock of them. The idea of bailing entered her brain, made itself a cozy little home, and sat there.

"It's just a drink," she whispered again. But her car was warm now. She could just stay in the driver's seat indefinitely, right? "No. Wrong." With a groan of frustration, she punched in a number on her phone.

"Hey, gorgeous." Lucas's voice came over the speaker above her rearview mirror.

"Help me, I did something stupid."

"Some of my favorite words from you. Tell me."

"I asked Brooke to meet me for a drink and she said yes, and now I'm in the parking lot of Finn's and I'm freaking out."

"Brooke, the new agent at Wolfe? Oh my God, that's awesome! I'm so proud of you, Mace." The tone of his voice echoed that pride. "This is great."

"No. No, it's not great because I'm losing my mind over here."

Lucas took a beat. He knew how to help her, how to calm her down. That's why she'd called him. "Okay. Listen." He let another beat go by. "You listening?"

"Yes."

"Is this a date?"

Macy clenched her teeth, made a face. "I don't know. Kinda? Maybe? I mean, we work together, so it doesn't have to be. It can just be two work colleagues grabbing a drink together."

"There you go."

And just like that, her nerves calmed. Lucas was right.

"Just go in, have a drink with this woman you find interesting, and see what happens. Okay? No labels necessary."

Macy nodded. "Yeah. Okay. I can do that."

"Mace?"

"Yeah?"

"Everything is going to be just fine. I promise."

More nodding. Anybody looking in her car window might think she was having neck issues. "Okay. Thanks, Lucas."

"Anytime. Call me later."

Macy hung up, unhooked her phone, and slid it into her purse. A glance in the visor mirror, a swipe of lip gloss, and she was ready. She yanked the door open and headed in.

Finn's was large and open and could be kind of loud. But it was popular, it had fun craft cocktails, and was almost always busy. The front door was in the center of the building, and Macy stood in front of the hostess podium. To the left was the restaurant, to the right, the big, rectangular bar. She smiled at the hostess and took a right.

Friday happy hour was busy. No surprise. The bar was large and you could walk all the way around it, with two bartenders inside the rectangle working hard, pulling beers and shaking martinis. Macy scanned the crowd, looked through the men in suits, obviously having an after-work drink. She looked around the gang of women standing at one end, maybe eight of them, laughing and holding up their glasses in a toast she couldn't quite decipher. And at the far corner of the bar, sitting alone, gaze on the television on the wall above the high-top tables, was Brooke Sullivan.

Macy took a moment to simply look at her when she didn't know she was being looked at. Dressed for work in the same black suit she'd had on earlier, she looked like she'd just put it on. It was sleek, unwrinkled, her hair shiny and falling in gentle waves over her shoulders. A new accessory had appeared—she now wore black-rimmed glasses. Macy hadn't thought it was possible for Brooke to be any more attractive. She'd been wrong.

Okay. Here we go.

Macy finger-combed her hair, smoothed a hand down her hip, and headed toward the far corner of the bar. She grinned and shook her head as she passed a table of three guys.

"What's amusing you?" Brooke asked as Macy took the stool next to her.

"Don't look, but those three guys at the table over there? Are *so* checking you out."

Brooke turned, leaned around Macy.

"What part of *don't look* did you not get?" Macy asked through clenched teeth. But she laughed.

"I wanted to see," Brooke said. When she smiled, a tiny scar on her right cheekbone became visible. "What can I get you?"

"No, no. I invited you. I buy." She glanced at Brooke's glass of what looked to be a gin and tonic. "I see you started without me."

"Listen, it's happy hour and you were late. I was a woman alone at a bar with no drink. It was very sad."

Macy jerked a thumb over her shoulder. "I'm sure those guys would've taken care of you."

"I mean, the one in the black sweater *is* pretty cute..."

Not sure what to do with that remark, Macy made eye contact with a bartender and ordered herself an extra, extra dirty martini with extra, extra olives. So Brooke was probably straight. Not really a surprise, but definitely a disappointment. And Macy hadn't even taken a moment to wonder about Brooke's sexuality—she was that rusty. *Ah, well. Work colleagues at happy hour it is.*

"Not dirty. Not even extra dirty. Extra, *extra* dirty. I'm learning so much about you already." Brooke grinned over the rim of her glass.

But wait. That was kind of flirty, wasn't it?

"Don't forget the extra, extra olives. Those are important." On cue, the bartender set down the martini, and Macy handed over her credit card. "The ones they have here are stuffed with bleu cheese. Worth it to ask for extra."

"Are you planning to share?" Again with the flirty. There was no way around it. Macy might have been out of the dating pool for a very long time, but she was pretty sure she could still recognize flirting. Couldn't she? This was definitely it. Wasn't it?

"These?" Macy reached for the swizzle stick that had been stabbed through four fat, cheese-filled olives and swirled it around in the glass. "I don't know. They're pretty delicious. What do I get out of the deal?"

"What do you want?"

Gazes held. Sexual tension crazy thick. Macy swallowed hard, opened her mouth to answer—

"Macy! You *are* here."

Macy snapped her head around to the voice. Emily, her boss. *Flirtus interruptus.* "Emily. Hey."

"I wanted to know how things went at the Gardens today, but you didn't answer my text, so I stalked you on Find My Friends. It said you were in this vicinity, so I took a chance." Emily was a fast talker, so her words came out in one long, endless stream, and then she turned to Brooke, stuck out a hand. "Hi. I'm Emily Baxter."

"Em, this is Brooke Sullivan." Macy caught Brooke's eye, hoped she was telegraphing her disappointment over this intrusion. "She works for Sasha and is the agent for the Gardens."

"Oh," Emily said, clearly surprised. "I've heard about you."

Brooke's big brown eyes went wide for a moment. "All good, I hope."

"Very."

Without waiting for an invitation, Emily raised a hand to the bartender and ordered herself a glass of white wine. As she leaned forward on the bar between Macy and Brooke, Macy mouthed an apology to Brooke. Brooke smiled, shrugged, and winked.

She winked at Macy, who could feel the heat flood her cheeks.

Wine in hand, Emily repositioned herself so she could see them both. "So? Tell me about the Gardens. How did it go?"

❖

It was over an hour before Emily finally sounded like she was getting ready to go. Brooke felt bad about the relief that flooded her system when Emily slid her arms into her dark blue peacoat and pulled a pair of lightweight gloves out of her pockets. Emily was nice. She was interesting and funny. Chatting with her hadn't been a hardship at all, not even close. But Brooke had spent the past seventy-five or so minutes trying not to be obvious about looking past Emily so she could see Macy.

And poor Macy. A poker face she did *not* have, and it made Brooke smile to think about it. Macy nodded and chuckled and interjected a few words when it was called for, but the frustrated disappointment was pretty clear on her face, even though Brooke was the only one who saw it. Macy had wanted more time, just the two of them, as Brooke had.

That was a good thing.

"This was great," Emily was saying. "Thanks for letting me crash your party." She was completely oblivious to having interrupted anything, but that was okay. Brooke didn't want her to feel bad or embarrassed about it, so she smiled and said all the right things and watched as Emily made her way toward the door through a crowd that had grown much thicker.

"Does it make me an awful person if I say I thought she'd never leave?" Brooke asked Macy with a grimace.

"Oh my God, no. I felt the same way." Then Macy sighed and

pressed her lips together in a straight line. "Unfortunately, I have to go, too." She motioned to the bartender to close out her tab.

"Oh." Defeat settled on Brooke's shoulders before she had a chance to school her expression. What was happening to her? What was the deal here? Brooke didn't understand how she'd gone from one extreme to the other when it came to Macy. But she had, quickly, and it had her off-balance.

Macy covered Brooke's hand with hers. It was warm and soft. "No, I don't *want* to, believe me. I *have* to. I have three dogs at home, remember? And I have a dog walker who comes by every weekday, but she was there about six hours ago, and my old girl needs medication."

The things Brooke wanted to say surprised her so much that she actually sat there, speechless for a moment.

This is the best evening I've had in longer than I can remember...

I was hoping to spend more time with you...

I am super attracted to you and it's freaking me the hell out...

Until Macy's expression changed to concern, and Brooke snapped to attention. "No problem," she finally said, then grinned and nodded. "I completely understand." And she did.

Macy signed the check, put her card away, then turned to Brooke. "Do you think..." She seemed to study her for a beat before starting again. "Can we do this again? Soon?"

Brooke didn't hesitate. "I'd like that." So much truth in those three words. "Very much."

"Good." Macy put on her coat, shouldered her purse. Then, without warning, she wrapped her arms around Brooke and hugged her tightly. Brooke felt her warm body, smelled the coconut scent of her hair, felt the softness of Macy's cheek as it slid against hers. "Bye," Macy whispered, then turned and left without looking back.

Brooke could do nothing but sit there. Count Macy's steps until she couldn't see her feet any longer: twenty-three. Swallow. Stare.

Yeah, this was going to be a whole thing, wasn't it?

CHAPTER ELEVEN

Yes, it is I," Macy announced loudly as she and Pete breezed into her parents' kitchen. "I and my trusty sidekick, Peter the Magnificent. We have arrived. You may all rest easy now." She unclipped Pete's leash, and he instantly bounded across the room to Macy's mom.

"There's my boy," her mother said happily and squatted down to lavish attention on the golden retriever. His big, furry tail swept from side to side and had been known to clear an entire coffee table in one swish. Macy's mom opened the lower cupboard door where she kept the dog treats. "You want a treat?" she asked him.

Macy grinned and shook her head. It was always this way. Her dogs got attention first. Then, only after treats were dispensed, her mother would meet her gaze, smile, greet her.

"Hi, honey."

"Hi, Mom." Macy crossed the room and kissed her mom on the cheek. She could hear activity and voices coming from the living room. Pete left to investigate. "Who do we have today?" She pulled a mug from the cupboard, a blue one with *Jamaica* scrawled across it in neon pink lettering, and filled it from the fresh pot of coffee.

"Your sister and the baby. Aunt Barb and Aunt Carol. Your father is wandering around here somewhere."

"Tyler?"

"Not today. He spent the night at his buddy's."

Macy doctored up her coffee and headed into the dining room. Smiles and hellos greeted her, and she went to the far side of the table and kissed each of her twin aunts on the cheek.

"There's my gorgeous niece," Aunt Barb said.

"Hey," came Eva's feigned protest.

"She meant her *other* gorgeous niece," Aunt Carol corrected.

"Better." Eva had Charlie in her lap. On the tablecloth in front of him were pieces of banana. He held one up for Macy.

"Oh, squished banana bits. My favorite!" Macy dutifully bent down to her nephew and took the bite from him, nibbling his fingers gently as she did so, causing him to giggle. "God, I love that sound."

"And here's our other gorgeous great-nephew." Aunt Carol made kissy faces at Pete, whose big gold head peeked out from under the table.

On more Saturdays than not, this was the scene at Macy's parents' house. Sometimes, it was her and Eva and the aunts. Sometimes, her grandmother would come by or a cousin here or there. Other times, members of her dad's side of the family would pop in. Some days, there were three people. Some days, there were more than a dozen. Macy's mom wouldn't have it any other way. Her door was always open, her house always welcoming. There was always a fresh pot of coffee on the counter and some sort of pastry for sharing. Today, it was scones—cranberry-orange and blueberry—and Macy snagged one as she sat.

Her aunts, at sixty-one, were three years younger than Macy's mom, but they looked younger than that—midfifties, tops—and super fashionable. Macy had always envied their style. Today, they each wore faded jeans and a cozy-looking sweater, and while they rarely purposely dressed alike, they often showed up to a gathering wearing eerily similar outfits. *The twin thing*, they called it. Both had been married. Both were divorced. Each had two kids, a boy and a girl. If she didn't love them and their big hearts so very much, Macy would find *the twin thing* a little bit creepy.

"I was in your neighborhood last night and stopped by your place, but your car wasn't in the driveway." Aunt Carol sipped her coffee and reached for a scone.

"Did you work late?" her mom asked, bringing her cup to her lips.

If anybody else had asked her that, Macy could have fibbed and said yes. But she could never lie to her mother. Even when she wanted to, she found it impossible. "No, I was out at happy hour at Finn's."

"With friends?" Her mom again.

"With a friend, yes." Not a lie. She considered Brooke a friend at this point.

Eva caught her eye and asked, "What friend?"

At the same moment, Aunt Barb gave a delighted little squeal and asked, "Was this a date? Is our little Macy finally dating?"

Ugh. Here we go.

Macy closed her eyes briefly and took a slow sip of her coffee. Stalling. Yep. That's what she was doing. Totally stalling.

Aunt Carol, always the tiniest bit more sensitive than the others, grabbed Macy's hand and squeezed it. "I'm sorry we're prying, sweetie. It's just been a really long time since you've even entertained the idea, and we want you to be happy. That's all."

Macy flashed back to Tyler at the café telling her he didn't want her to be alone forever, and a lump parked itself in her esophagus. She had to clear her throat twice to get rid of it. "Just a woman I met recently. We're working on a project together and decided to go out for drinks."

The disappointment on the faces of her mother and aunts was obvious, but Eva wasn't that easy to throw off a scent. "Wait." Her eyes lit up as she handed Charlie his sippy cup, because she had clearly made the connection. "Were you out with the chick from Wolfe Realty? The one Tyler met?"

"Tyler met the woman you're dating?" That was her mother, whose eyes had gone wide with what looked to be a combination of excitement and disbelief. Macy would swear to God that everybody at the table leaned forward.

"We're not dating," she said, trying not to feel put on the spot, even though she absolutely was. She shot Eva a look. Eva smirked and didn't seem even a tiny bit sorry she'd brought it up. Big sisters loved to make things difficult on their little sisters, which apparently didn't stop when they were adults.

"You were just on a date." Eva. Not a question.

"I mean..." Had it been a date? Lucas had assured her that it didn't need to be, but God, it had sure felt like one. She blew out a huge breath. "I don't know." And that was the absolute truth. She really didn't know.

They all started talking at once. Macy sat, amused even in her embarrassment, as every other woman at the table began talking at the same time. To each other. To Macy. To nobody. She took a bite of scone and felt large hands drop to her shoulders from behind.

"What on earth has you all so riled up?" Her dad stood behind her, and she craned her neck to find an angle where she could look up at his ruddy, kind face. "Hi, honey," he said and dropped a kiss on her head.

"Hi, Pop."

"What's all the ruckus about?" he asked.

"Your daughter had a date last night," her mom said.

"Mom. I didn't say that." Macy shot her a look.

"She had something that seemed an awful lot like a date last night," her mother amended.

"*Really?*" Her father drew out the word in comedic fashion.

"Listen, I don't even know if she plays on my team." Which was true, because *technically*, she didn't know that. Deep down, she absolutely did. No straight woman flirted with another woman like that unless they were both joking around. And there had been no joking around as far as Macy had been able to tell.

"Ask her." Aunt Barb. Her innocent, matter-of-fact expression told Macy that she really thought it was just that easy.

Was it?

Macy shrugged. "I can probably find out." She wondered if Sasha might know. Then she wondered if it would be weird to ask her.

"Yes, do that!" Her mother was excited, and while Macy wanted to be annoyed at all this interference and assumption, she couldn't be. She knew her family just wanted her to be happy. Macy wished it was that simple. As the hum of conversation continued on to other subjects, thank almighty God, Macy's eyes were drawn to a small table against the wall behind where her mother sat. Several framed photographs were displayed on it, including a black-and-white five-by-seven of Macy and Michelle. It had been taken at Macy's parents' thirty-fifth wedding anniversary party several years ago. They were dancing, looking into each other's eyes, and smiling so big. They'd been ridiculously happy that day. It had been a day full of laughter and joy and family, and it was easily one of Macy's happiest memories. Now? Now she could barely remember what it had been like to feel that content in her life, to have things be that perfect.

Not wanting to let herself get pulled down into that particular mire, she blinked several times and refocused on the table. Eva was looking at her, gave her a wink and a smile. Macy returned the smile and reached out for Charlie, who looked about ready to conk out. Then she sat back, rocked him gently back and forth, and listened as the topic finally shifted, and her family began arguing about which pizzeria had the best crust.

Macy let herself smile. Relax.

She wondered what Brooke was doing with her Saturday.

❖

Saturdays were a mixed bag for Brooke. It was the weekend, obviously, and who didn't love the weekend? While she'd been known to spend too much of her free time working, scanning the real estate ads, looking for both clients and properties, she also very much enjoyed just chilling out with a good book or a movie or a walk. Saturdays were good.

Saturdays were also the day she'd always called her parents. No matter where she'd been—college, vacation, whatever—she'd always touched base at some point on Saturday. It was a hard-and-fast rule, though how it had originated, she couldn't remember. It just *was*.

It was gloomy and rainy out. Typical mid-April weather. So much for a walk, but it was perfect for lounging on the couch with a cup of tea and a good book. She flopped onto the couch, cell phone in hand, and sighed. No, it was more of a groan. The cat sauntered in, hopped up, and made himself comfortable on her chest.

"You'd think you've lived here forever," she said as she scratched his head and his eyes closed in pleasure. His motor kicked on, a sound Brooke was growing to love. When he opened his eyes again and focused on her, she said, "I have to make this call now. Your job is to not let me get sucked into an argument, okay?" He gave her a slow blink, then yawned. "Yeah, that doesn't instill a lot of confidence, mister."

A clear of her throat and she dialed.

"Well, hello there." The voice was warm, happy to hear from her.

"Hi, Dad. How are you?" They'd always been close, Brooke and her father. She was Daddy's little girl, and he was so clearly proud of everything she did. Until that day he'd walked into her room without knocking first…

"I'm fine. More importantly, how are *you*? How's the new digs?"

They fell into an easy banter. That was the thing with her dad—it was so simple to just talk to him. To just discuss work and the house and things she was thinking of doing to it. Surface things. It's what they'd been reduced to. It was better than nothing, though. Brooke reminded herself of that every time.

Stroking the cat's head proved to be a bit of a calming action, she discovered, so she kept doing it, especially when, after about twenty minutes, her father told her he'd hand the phone to her mother.

Her mother was *so* much harder.

"Hi, honey."

"Hi, Mom."

"Are you unpacked? You've been there a couple weeks now. Everything all settled?"

The conversation was normal to anybody outside looking in. Typical mother-daughter talk. But there was always an underlying tone there—Brooke could hear it because she knew her mother. It was a tone of disapproval. Disappointment. A little sadness. A lot of judgment.

"Have you found a church there?"

Brooke swallowed. "Not yet, no. But I'm looking." Not exactly a lie. She had looked. Once.

"I will ask Father Tom tomorrow. I'm sure he can give me a couple suggestions."

"Okay."

"I don't like that you haven't been going." Disapproval. Again.

"I know. Me neither." That was the truth. Brooke did miss going to church. She missed the warmth and the feeling of community that had always radiated from her old congregation. Well, until she started to see things more clearly. Until the unspoken rules became obvious. Until she started to feel unwelcome in a place that had always opened its arms to her.

"Have you made any new friends yet?" That was an oddly touching question coming from her mother.

"A few. Through work. I went out for drinks with a woman who works for a staging company last night. Went to a cool bar and restaurant. That was fun."

"Any potential suitors? I see a couple of good-looking men on the Wolfe website." Her mother said it in a teasing tone, the way one high school girl would say it to her BFF who she's trying to hook up with a date. She'd completely ignored the fact that Brooke said she'd been out with a woman the night before.

"There are. Good-looking women, too." It was out before Brooke thought better of it, but her mother always did this. Always acted like her bisexuality wasn't real and would evaporate if she was with a guy.

"Do you remember the Longs?" her mother asked, as if Brooke hadn't spoken. "Their son is recently divorced. Nice boy. A lawyer. I gave them your number."

"Mom, I don't—"

"Did Eddie tell you he got promoted?" Her mother went on talking as if whatever Brooke had to say didn't really matter. That was how Brooke had felt with her mother for more than five years now, and it was exhausting. It was demoralizing. And it made Brooke so very sad.

She sighed quietly and listened as her mother went on about her brother's promotion at work, apparently a big deal that he hadn't thought to tell her about. She knew Eddie was in a tough position, caught between her and her parents, and she also knew that she was just as much to blame for their lack of communication as he was.

While things with her mother didn't stay quite as surface-level as with her dad, they still didn't delve deep. That was a recipe for disaster. She rarely tried talking to her about anything personal anymore. Not politics. Certainly not religion.

"I have a cat," she blurted. As if understanding her, the cat turned to look at her from his perch still on her chest. Yawned widely, unfurling his pink tongue.

"What? You do?" Her mother's surprise was apparent, but she was an animal lover, so her happiness was also clear.

"You should have seen him. He kept coming to sit at my back door. I thought he was probably a neighborhood cat. I left a little tuna out for him a few times. Some water."

"Well, that did it," her mom said. And then she laughed. It was a sound Brooke didn't hear often enough anymore, and she let it wash over her until it actually brought tears to her eyes.

"I think you're right. I finally let him in, and he was so scrawny and matted that I'm pretty sure he was just a stray. I've kept my eyes open for ads or notices about a missing cat, and I called the shelters, but so far, nothing."

"What does he look like?"

"Hang on." Brooke snapped a photo of the cat where he lay and sent it. "There. He's on my chest right now. He walks around like he's the king."

A beat went by. Two. "Oh, my, he's *gorgeous*. Such deep, dark fur, and those eyes! Have you named him?"

Brooke smiled. "I was actually thinking of calling him Rorschach. He looked like an inkblot sitting outside my door."

More peals of laughter, and then Brooke heard her mother telling her father all about her new cat. She finally came back on the line. "Make sure you take him to the vet so he's up on all his shots and such."

"I will." It was a subject she'd thought about earlier that day, and she wondered if Sasha might have a vet suggestion. And then she remembered that she knew somebody with multiple pets who probably had a vet she trusted very much...

Not that she needed a reason to text Macy. She'd intended to at some point. But now, she had an excuse.

❖

As usually happened when she stopped by her parents' on a Saturday, Macy was sitting back in her chair and watching her family as they talked. Her cousin Tina, Aunt Carol's daughter, had popped in with an apple pie and had joined the crowd. Pete had collapsed on the family room floor next to her dad's chair. Golf was on the television, and Macy shook her head with a smile, noting her napping dog. *I feel the same way about golf, buddy.*

Her phone, which she'd set on the table next to her now-tepid second cup of coffee, lit up with a text notification.

Brooke.

Macy could feel the change in her body. The warm flush of excitement. The smile as she remembered flirting at the bar last night. The tightening of her thighs as her brain recalled how deliciously female Brooke smelled and wondered what perfume she wore. She swallowed hard as she picked up the phone.

Hi. Wanted to thank you for last night. I had a great time.

That warm flush turned to heat and rushed through Macy's blood as she typed back, *Me, too! How is your Saturday?* When she glanced up at the table, nobody was paying her any attention.

Except Eva, who arched one eyebrow and shot her a knowing smile.

It's not bad. Chilling at home. Hey, can you recommend a vet? I have taken in a stray cat, or more accurately he's decided he lives here now, and I should probably get him checked. I've never had a cat before...

More smiling. Macy couldn't seem to stop.

He's decided he lives there now? Then she added a laughing emoji.

Well, I made the mistake of opening my door. So, yeah.

A chuckle. *And now you have a roommate.*

Apparently.

"Who are you talking to?" Eva finally had to ask. It must've been killing her.

"A friend," Macy said as she typed out, *I have a great vet.*

"*That* friend?" Nobody else seemed to be listening, thank God, but Macy shot her sister a look. Eva's satisfied grin said Macy's look had told her all she needed to know.

"You know what? Shut up."

That made Eva laugh, but to her credit, she didn't share the reason with the rest of the table. Macy's phone buzzed.

What are you doing right now?

Seemed like Brooke wanted to keep the conversation going. Macy found herself totally okay with that, though she reflexively turned slightly in her seat and realized it was so the photo of her and Michelle wasn't right in her sight line. *At my parents'. Visiting with family. You?*

Several moments went by without a response, and Macy started to think maybe Brooke was busy and her question had just been polite. Then the dots started to bounce, indicating Brooke was typing. Then they stopped. A moment went by. More bouncing. They stopped. Macy waited. The bouncing started up again, and finally, a text came. *Oh. Okay. I was going to ask if you wanted to come over and meet this cat. You said you have a cat, right?*

The warm flush was back. Come over? Like, to her house? *I have two.* She hesitated, several thoughts rolling around in her head before she continued to move her thumbs over the keyboard. *It's just informal here. I can leave anytime. I'm happy to come over.*

Yeah?

Brooke was stepping carefully, it seemed. Macy typed, *Absolutely. I'd love to meet this confident cat.*

This time, barely two seconds passed before the reply came. *Great! Come anytime. I'm here all day.* And there was an address. Right there on her screen. Brooke's address and a friendly invitation.

Friendly. Friends. They were friends. That's what this was. She looked up at the photo one more time, felt an unfamiliar guilt settle in her lap as she stared. A warm hand closing over hers brought her back to the table.

Eva.

Her sister held her gaze for what felt like a long time. Then she squeezed Macy's hand. She said nothing, but her tender smile spoke volumes. Macy swallowed hard, cleared her throat.

"Hey, Mom, can I leave Pete here for a little bit? I have some running around to do."

Her mother was in the midst of a conversation with the rest of the table, but without missing a beat, she said, "You can leave Pete here forever. He's no trouble. You know that."

Excitement got the better of her for a second, and Macy popped out of her chair. The conversation tapered off as the table turned to look at her, expectant.

"Okay, heading out!" Plastered smile. Wave. A kiss on her mother's cheek. A look from Eva that was so many things: proud, worried, happy. Macy didn't bother waking Pete up. He was fine, and she'd be back. She grabbed her bag and her coat and headed out the door before anybody could ask any questions.

She was going to Brooke's place.

It wasn't until she was in her car, text sent to Brooke that she was on her way, address plugged into her GPS, and backing out of the driveway that she started to obsess about everything she should've thought about *before* accepting the invite. Her clothes, her hair, her makeup. Her breath. God. She fumbled in the console until she found gum, shoved two pieces in her mouth, and chewed like a cow with its cud.

It occurred to her that she hadn't been this excited to go someplace—to go anyplace—in longer than she could remember, and that kicked her adrenaline into overdrive, made her nerves rattle in her body. Still, she followed the directions with a smile.

She was going to Brooke's place.

CHAPTER TWELVE

O h my God, what did I do?"
Rorschach had zero answers for Brooke, even though she'd asked him the question numerous times.

"She's coming here. Here." She pointed at the floor. "You realize that, right?"

The cat was stretched out along the back of the couch like he'd lived there forever, licking his paw and watching her intently. Still no answers from him.

"You're no help at all, Rorsh. None. Zero."

He yawned.

It wasn't like Brooke had blurted out the invitation. Not at all. She'd taken her time. Thought about it. Typed, deleted, retyped. Checked her wording. Considered what she was doing.

"I mean, we're friends. Right? There nothing wrong with inviting a friend over on a Saturday afternoon. Not a thing. Plus, I need a vet. So there's actually a *reason* for this visit. See? It's fine. It's totally fine."

Rorschach stared at her, seemingly unamused.

"Are you judging me? I feel like you're judging me." Brooke nibbled on the inside of her cheek as she stood in the center of her living room and took a good look. It was clean. Hell, she'd been living there less than a month, it oughta be. "Do I have snacks? Anything to offer? Wine? Soda?" She turned on her heel and speed-walked into the kitchen, checked to see what she had to offer a visitor. Cheese and crackers were practically a food group for her, so she had those. She'd just bought some grapes, and she quickly tossed the bunch into a strainer in the sink and ran cold water over it. She had no chips, dip, or salsa, damn it. A six-pack of Diet Coke in the fridge. A small bottle of vodka in the freezer. That was about it.

"It'll have to do," as her mother would say. Her mother would also shake her head in quiet disapproval at the lack of food in her house right then, but whatever.

A quick pop into the downstairs powder room told her she needed to spray her hair and repair her eyeliner, so she sprinted up the stairs to her bedroom and took care of those things, but then stood in front of her full-length mirror and pursed her lips. She hadn't planned on company today, so she was wearing weekend clothes. Leggings, a royal-blue long-sleeved top long enough to cover her ass, big chunky socks. Her hair was in a messy bun, strands escaping around her face. Her entire look was super casual and not at all visitor ready. She grabbed the hem of her shirt to pull it over her head, but the doorbell rang.

Her wide-eyed reflection stared back at her.

"Shit."

Arms dropped to her sides. A huge sigh. Shrug.

"It'll have to do," she said for a second time and headed for the stairs. Once in front of the door, hand on the knob, she inhaled through her nose, blew it out slowly through her mouth, and pulled the door open.

"Hi." Macy stood there, every bit as casual as Brooke, but so much cuter. Brooke's smile burst across her face before she even realized it.

"Hi," she said back and stepped aside. "Come on in." Macy did, and as she walked past, Brooke inhaled the scents of fresh outdoors and…apple pie? Confusing, but not unpleasant. "Here, let me take your coat."

Macy slid out of her coat to reveal a long-sleeved black T-shirt with a happy looking cartoon bear on the front. The tee looked like it had been washed to the perfect softness. Jeans and Nikes finished off the outfit, and Macy toed politely out of her sneakers.

"This is nice," Macy said as she turned and walked toward the living area.

"Thanks. It's just a rental until I'm ready to buy, but I like it." Brooke watched as Macy's gaze landed on Rorschach, still lounging across the back of the couch.

"Well, hello there, handsome." She zeroed right in, crossed the room, and was on the couch nuzzling the cat in about 2.7 seconds flat. "Have you given him a name?"

"Rorschach."

Macy laughed. "I love it. He does have inkblot qualities."

Rorschach soaked up the attention like a little black sponge, turning his head so Macy could scratch just the right spot under his chin. "He's gorgeous," Macy said as she turned to look at Brooke. "Skinny. But so handsome."

"Yeah, I think he's been on his own awhile—he's got some mats he won't let me cut off—but I'll make sure to have the vet check for a microchip, just to be sure." Brooke sat on the couch next to Macy, watched her lavish attention on the cat. "I don't want to steal anybody's cat, but I've been checking animal shelters and Facebook groups for days. Nobody seems to be looking for him."

Rorschach had turned on his little motor and was purring away under Macy's fingers. "He's so sweet for being a stray. He's certainly made himself comfortable."

"You should've seen him when I finally let him in." She told Macy the story of the cat peering in through the sliding glass door for several nights in a row, how she began leaving tuna cans out for him, how he wore her down until she finally opened the door. "He waltzed in here like he owned the place. Hopped right up on the couch as if he belonged there and had just been away for a little while."

"Is he active at night?" Macy had moved her scratching to his ears.

"At night?"

"Cats are nocturnal."

"Oh. Right. Actually, no. He curls right up in bed with me and turns on the purring, and I fall right to sleep." Brooke wrinkled her nose. "But I also sleep like the dead, so he could be up and having a party down here, and I probably wouldn't know it."

Macy grinned at her, and the way it transformed her face from very pretty to stunning almost made Brooke's breath catch. How had she not seen this attractiveness right away? *Because I was busy wearing Danishes, that's how.* "Was there any glitter on the floor this morning? That's always a good sign that there's been a party."

"Not that I noticed. And I *do* think I would've heard the vacuum cleaner."

"Good point." Macy kept scratching Rorschach, who was obviously in heaven, judging by his purring, his closed eyes, and the tiny drop of drool on his bottom lip. Brooke sat there and watched, and the silence was so weirdly *not* uncomfortable that it actually started to *make* her uncomfortable, but before she started to squirm in her seat, Macy said, "So, you need a vet."

"Yes, please."

"Well, I have a terrific one. She's a friend of mine. We actually went to kindergarten together."

"Really?"

"Mm-hmm." Macy took out her phone, scrolled and touched and did some things, and then Brooke's phone pinged. "There. I sent you her info. Just tell the office there that I gave you her number."

"I will. Thank you." Brooke settled into the cushions and propped her elbow on the back of the couch, her head on her fist. She wanted to know more about this woman. So much more. "So, you've lived here your whole life?"

"I have. And my parents were both born and raised here. What about you? Were you born in Ohio?"

"No, I was actually born in Texas, but we only lived there until I was three. My dad works for an insurance company and got transferred to Tennessee and then again to Ohio when I was twelve. So I've moved around a bit."

"And now you're here in upstate New York."

"And now I'm here."

"And now you have a cat."

Brooke looked at Rorschach, ran her hand along his spine, scratched the base of his tail. "And now I have a cat." He was in utter bliss as they both petted him, scratched him, loved on him. Brooke's fingers brushed Macy's, and a jolt of something nearly electrical shot up her arm. She pulled back her hand and swallowed hard. With a clear of her throat, she said, "How do you feel about cheese and crackers?"

Macy tipped her head. "I feel very fondly about them."

"Good." Brooke bounced up from the couch like she'd been sitting on an ejector seat and went to the kitchen. She needed a moment. Away from Macy. Away from being in any sort of proximity to Macy because being near Macy was...doing things to her. Things she didn't expect. Things she wasn't ready for.

Cheese sliced into twelve little squares and laid out on the cheese board, crackers in a bowl, Brooke set them on the small table in the dining area that was too small to be called an actual dining room.

"Here we go," she said, then looked up and met Macy's gaze. "What would you like to drink? Wine? Diet Coke? Water? Something stronger?"

Macy's smile hadn't left since she'd come in the door, and Brooke was glad. It really was a great smile. "Diet Coke would be great."

"You got it."

❖

Thank God for cheese and crackers.

Because…was there something in the air at Brooke's place? An odd sense of *anticipation* was the only word Macy could come up with that even remotely fit how she'd been feeling since she'd arrived. She felt wide awake. On alert. Crazy aware. There was a subtle fluttering low in her body—one that became less subtle the closer Brooke was to her. It had been a long time since she'd been that affected by somebody, and she was trying hard not to dwell on that.

So. She wasn't terribly hungry after munching at her mom's, but cheese and crackers were a good distraction, and she was glad about that. She grabbed a slice of an orange cheese that looked like some sort of cheddar, topped a cracker with it, and popped it into her mouth.

Brooke returned from the kitchen with two glasses of Diet Coke. She slid Macy's toward her, then quickly took it back. "You're not going to spill this, are you? Should I put it in a plastic cup?"

"Oh, a funny girl, I see. Listen, I can't make any promises. I have no control over that kind of thing."

Brooke relinquished the soda with a grin. "I guess I'll have to take my chances."

They stood there quietly, both admiring the cat. After a moment or two, Macy said, "He's gonna get a complex if we keep staring at him like this, you know. I would."

"Me, too." Brooke pulled out one of the chairs and sat. Macy followed suit.

"What made you leave Ohio? I mean, I know you got a job here, but why? I assume your family is still in Ohio?"

Something passed over Brooke's eyes then. Those big, dark, sparkling eyes went dull for just a split second, and then she seemed to mentally shake herself. "Yes, they are. I was ready for a change." She glanced down at her glass, turned it in her fingers before adding, "I needed a change."

Macy wanted to delve deeper. What was that phrase her grandma used to use? Something about still waters running deep. Macy never understood it until she got older, and now, she sat next to somebody who she just knew was the epitome of that phrase. Brooke was calm and still and peaceful on the outside. But in that moment, somehow, Macy knew there was so much more beneath the surface. And good God, did she want to dive in. Headfirst. But she also got the distinct impression that Brooke had lines, limits.

"That was really nosy of me," Macy said, waving a hand. "I'm sorry. Ignore me."

"No, no, it's fine. I don't mind." Brooke's lack of eye contact said otherwise, so Macy went in another direction.

"And how have you been settling in? Okay?"

Brooke's manner eased, which made Macy relax a bit. This was, apparently, a safer topic of conversation. "I'm doing pretty well," Brooke said, reaching for a hunk of cheese. She nibbled a corner. "I mean, I'm all unpacked. I have a new cat, for God's sake. Lotta progress happening here."

A sense of humor. Macy didn't expect one based on the first time she'd met Brooke, but it was there, lingering just under the surface of her very put-together exterior. "Tons of progress," Macy agreed. "Have you met many new people? Outside of work, I mean."

Brooke tipped her head one way, then the other. "That's a little harder when you're over thirty, you know?" She gave a slight shrug and sipped her Diet Coke. "While I do love a good night of dancing, I'm not really a go-out-to-the-bars kind of girl."

An idea struck then, like a tap on Macy's shoulder. She shoved a piece of cheese on a cracker in her mouth and nodded to give herself a little time to absorb what she was thinking. She chewed slowly, swallowed, then sipped her soda. Finally, she looked up at Brooke, and the question slipped from her lips. "What are you doing tonight?"

Eyes that were no longer dull widened slightly. "Me? Tonight? Nothing." She shook her head. "Why?"

"Well, I was thinking."

"Uh-oh."

"Oh, more funny stuff. You're on a roll."

A blush. A mischievous grin. What was Macy going to do with this girl?

"I was thinking that a good way for you to meet new people without going out to a bar is to attend a dinner party."

"*Okay.*" Brooke drew the word out, clearly not sure where this was going.

"My friend Lucas and his husband Sam are throwing one tonight, and I'm going. I'd love it if you came with me." She cleared her throat. Was she really doing this? "They're super nice guys. Lucas has been my bestie for years, and I love him to bits. And I'm not sure how often you've been to dinner parties thrown by gay men, but there's nothing quite like them." She smiled, but it felt a little weird on her face. She hoped that didn't show. Did she sound uncertain and a little bit freaked out? Because she absolutely was.

She didn't need to be.

Brooke's face lit up like the sun had suddenly come out. "Oh my God, I'd love that. I have a weird mental aversion to sitting home alone on a Saturday night." She held up a hand. "Not that there's anything wrong with that. There's not. But…"

"I get it. Totally." And while that was true, that she did understand not wanting to be home on Saturday night, Macy didn't subscribe to that. In fact, she kind of loved being home on a Saturday night. A good movie. Animals surrounding her. It was her idea of bliss. But not tonight. Tonight, she was going to a dinner party with a beautiful woman.

What in the world was happening?

They ironed out details of what time Macy would pick Brooke up before she gathered her things and crossed the room to bid Rorschach good-bye. "I hope I see you again soon," she whispered so only he could hear. Then she kissed the top of his head and turned to Brooke. "Okay, well, I guess I'll see you in a little while."

"You will." Brooke opened the front door for her, and Macy tried to take in the sight without looking like that was what she was doing. She was used to Brooke in suits—not a bad thing at all—and the jeans on the day of the café. But Saturday-at-home Brooke might be her favorite. The leggings. The oversized shirt. The messy bun. Barely any makeup. She looked cozy and inviting, and she smelled amazing, like almonds and vanilla and everything inviting, and she silently called to Macy like some kind of siren. It was weird and unexpected and freaky and all kinds of sexy. *God.*

She had to get out of there.

A quick good-bye, a wave, and she all but fled Brooke's town house.

Once in her car and out of the driveway, she called up the phone app. "Call Lucas," she ordered. She barely let him finish his greeting before she blurted, "Help me. I did something crazy."

"Again?" She could almost see him rub his hands together in anticipation, picture his face as he smiled with glee. "Excellent. Tell Uncle Lucas all about it."

CHAPTER THIRTEEN

Inhale through the nose…Exhale through the mouth…
Brooke seemed to be using that same mantra a lot lately. She'd taken yoga once for about five minutes. Despite it being deceptively hard and an unexpectedly good workout, it just wasn't her thing, and she gave it up after only a handful of classes. The breathing regulation, though, had stayed with her, and she used it often, finding it the best way to calm a racing heart or jangling nerves.

A thud came from the other side of the wall, muffled words, then a louder, "Why can't you just listen to me?" Brooke stopped and looked at the wall, but nothing more came, and she found herself letting go of a relieved breath. She had yet to officially meet her neighbors, and she honestly wasn't sure she wanted to, but she'd seen them a few times coming or going. The guy was tall. Handsome. Apparently some sort of a businessman, judging by the suit and tie he wore each day. He certainly didn't look like somebody who constantly yelled, but Brooke knew that old saying about not judging a book by its cover was alarmingly accurate.

Turning to her reflection in the mirror, she ran her hands slowly over her hips and did the breathing thing again. When she felt better, calmer, she tipped her head to one side and studied her outfit.

"What do you think?" she asked Rorschach, who lounged on her bed and watched her with his big yellow eyes. He blinked slowly. Said nothing.

It had been a long time—a very long time—since she'd been to any type of gathering where there were people she didn't know. It surprised her that she was actually looking forward to tonight, despite also being nervous, and she examined why as she ran a critical eye over the little black cocktail dress. It was a tiny bit looser than she remembered, but her move had been stressful, which led to her not eating as often or as well as she should, and she'd dropped a few pounds. But overall, it still fit nicely. Simple black with a V-neck, three-quarter-length sleeves, the hem just above her knees. She rummaged in her jewelry box for the simple silver necklace with the tiny lighthouse charm that she'd purchased for herself one weekend a few months ago when she'd felt particularly lost. It lay just between her collarbones and sparkled in the light. Her hair was pulled back and fastened low at the base of her neck. She added dangling silver earrings, and a silver bangle bracelet that her mother gave her for her birthday. Stepped into heels. Studied her reflection again.

Not bad.

Before she could get back to how she was actually excited to meet some new people or ponder what Macy might think of her outfit—because that was exactly what she'd been trying *not* to think about—the doorbell rang.

"Wish me luck," she said to Rorschach, then kissed his furry black head and headed downstairs.

"Wow." It was the first word out of Macy's mouth as she stood on the front stoop, and the widening of her soft brown eyes only accentuated it. "You look...amazing." Then she flushed an adorable pink and looked slightly embarrassed, like she'd said something she hadn't meant to.

"Thank you," Brooke said as she ran her eyes over Macy. "I could say the same." And it was true. Macy wore black pants that were tight at the ankle, making her strappy black heels a focal point. A simple red V-neck sweater looked anything but simple on her, the pop of color creating interest and also showcasing a peek of cleavage. She looked sexy and sophisticated—two words Brooke hadn't expected to associate with Macy Carr. She shook the thought away and reached into the closet for her coat. The weather wasn't freezing, but it was still cool, and she hoped Macy's car was warm so her toes wouldn't turn to ice cubes. *The drawbacks of wearing heels when it's not summer.* Keys in her purse, bottle of wine from her wine rack in hand, she met Macy's gaze. "Shall we?"

And they were off. On their non-date date, which was how Brooke looked at it. It wasn't a technical date really, as neither of them had ever touched on the idea of taking the other out. At the same time, they were two women going to a dinner party together, and there was a definite spark between them. So date-ish? Date-like?

With a small smile, she shook that thought away.

"What are you grinning at?" Macy glanced at her from the driver's seat of her Honda CR-V. While it was obvious from a quick look in the back seat that Macy had dogs and that they definitely traveled in this vehicle, the front seat was tidy. She absently wondered if Macy had cleaned it for her.

Brooke shook her head slightly. "Nothing. Just happy to be going someplace new. Thank you for inviting me. I hope your friends don't mind."

"Are you kidding me? Lucas would throw dinner parties every weekend if Sam would let him. He loves to entertain. He was thrilled when I told him I was bringing a date." And then her mouth clamped shut, red shot up her neck and colored her cheeks as her eyes went hilariously wide, and Brooke couldn't help it. She burst out laughing.

"Oh my God, you should see your face right now." Mortified. That's how she looked. That was the best way to describe her expression.

"I'm sorry. That was presumptuous. And weird. And wrong. I'm sorry."

Brooke went from laughing to reassuring. "It's okay, Macy. Really." She laid a hand on Macy's thigh, patted it. "No big deal. Okay?" Despite wanting to make her feel better, letting Macy in on the fact that she, too, was trying to qualify exactly what it was they were doing felt too intimate somehow, so she left it alone. It didn't need a label, right?

Less than five minutes later, they pulled into a double-wide driveway that already had four cars in it. The house itself was beautiful, an interesting combination of classic and modern, and Brooke was already looking forward to seeing the inside.

Macy turned off the ignition. "Ready?"

"As I'll ever be. Lead the way."

Macy didn't knock, just pushed through the front door and shouted, "I'm here. The party can start now."

An impossibly handsome man, tall, with carefully disheveled dark hair, appeared from the back of the house, what Brooke figured was likely the kitchen. His arms were wide, his smile wider. "Macy Lou Freebush!" he called out and then wrapped Macy in a hug that made it obvious how much he cared about her. Without missing a beat—and before Macy could say another word—he looked at Brooke, waved a finger from her face down to her feet and back up again, and said, "And you must be Brooke. Love your dress. I have heard so much about you. More than you're probably comfortable with." Macy slapped his arm and he laughed. "I'm kidding," he said, then shook his head and mouthed, *Not kidding.*

Brooke liked him instantly.

"Brooke Sullivan," Macy said. "This is our host for the evening and my very best friend in all the land, Lucas Chapman. Lucas, this is Brooke."

They shook hands. "It's a pleasure to meet you." He waved a hand to his right. "The others are here. Cocktails and wine are set up in the dining room. Help yourself and I'll be in momentarily." He glanced at Brooke again, and she was stunned by the deep blue of his eyes. "I'm really glad you're here. Welcome." And with what had to be an exaggerated flourish, he went back to the kitchen.

Brooke turned to Macy. "Macy Lou Freebush?"

Macy shook her head and laughed. "From *Miss Congeniality.*"

"I know what it's from. I just find it amusing. I may have to call you that from now on."

Macy groaned good-naturedly and led the way into the dining room.

Brooke took in the house as they went. Like the outside, the inside was a mix of old and new, classic and modern, and the combination was somehow seamless. She'd seen a lot of houses in her line of work. *A lot* of houses. And she'd seen a lot of houses where the owners had tried to combine two different styles and had ended up with a mishmash of confusion and things that just didn't go. Not this house. Everything flowed smoothly, from the furniture to the artwork to the colors on the walls. It was a warm home, intriguing and inviting.

In the dining room, four people sat at the table, and there were gorgeously laid out places for four more. Greetings rose up, and Macy's smile widened as she went around hugging each of the guests. Then she looked up at Brooke and made introductions, starting with the two men sitting side by side, one bearded, one clean-shaven.

"Everybody, this is my friend, Brooke. Brooke, this is Matt and his husband, Shane." The men smiled, nodded. "And over here"—she gestured to the other two folks—"this is Harlow, and this is Rick." Harlow waved. Rick gave her a smile. "And this..." Macy gestured toward the bearded guy manning the makeshift bar. "This is Sam, Lucas's husband."

The corners of Sam's eyes crinkled when he smiled, and he held out a hand toward Brooke. "It's a pleasure to meet you. Can I offer you a drink?" The bar had almost every bottle Brooke could think of that should be on a standard bar, and she silently counted them until she reached seventeen, plus five bottles of wine. While she was pretty well-versed in cocktails, this was a group of new people, and she didn't want to risk being overserved.

"I'd love a glass of wine," she said and pointed toward an Argentinian Malbec she was familiar with.

"You got it," Sam said. "Grab a seat and I will deliver."

Macy gave him a big hug, and then they took their seats at the table. A moment later, a generously poured glass of wine was set in front of her, and Sam was asking Macy what she wanted. Brooke marveled at the place settings—black chargers held white plates, the linen napkins were black and white stripes, the utensils hammered silver. In the center of the table was a beautiful bouquet of red and white tulips, the red giving the table a joyful pop of color.

Though Brooke had started off a little bit nervous, as she always did when being dropped into a group of people she didn't know, she enjoyed herself way more than she'd expected to. Everybody at the table was incredibly interesting, and at one point, Brooke leaned toward Macy and told her so. In response, Macy laid a hand on her thigh under the table and squeezed. Brooke's stomach fluttered wildly.

It was also a super interesting mix of people, and Brooke listened raptly as she ate the most delicious salmon dish she'd ever had.

Harlow was a wedding photographer whose husband would normally have come to dinner but was out of town on business. Matt was a teacher, and he looked at Shane with such love in his eyes that it made Brooke's heart swell in her chest. Rick owned a microbrewery outside the city, and Brooke was pleasantly surprised to realize she'd had his beer before. Sam was an orthodontist with his own practice. Lucas ran an antique shop that Brooke remembered driving past on one of her first exploratory trips after she'd moved to town.

"I love Lucas's shop," Macy said to her at one point when conversations had split into several individual ones. "It's called Everything Old Is New Again, and I could wander around it for hours."

"I think I know where it is, but I haven't gone inside. I'd like to." Once again, the words were out before Brooke even realized she was going to say them. Any kind of understanding about Macy's effect on her was elusive, no matter how hard she searched for it.

"Let's do it. He's always getting new items in. He goes to estate sales and flea markets, and lots of times, he finds incredible things. Wanna go tomorrow?"

"I absolutely do." Just like that. No thinking. No hesitation. No stopping to check her schedule.

What in the world was happening to her? Because whatever it was, she liked it.

❖

Did I just set up another non-date date with her?

The question rocketed through Macy's head, echoing loudly. What was she doing? When she looked up from her plate, she caught Lucas's eye. He was sporting a subtle grin, and Macy wondered, not for the first time, if he could hear her thoughts. He knew her well. Too well. It was almost creepy.

She loved this group. It was Lucas and Sam's regular dinner party crew. Sometimes, they added a new person or two or somebody brought along a friend, like she had with Brooke, but the base was always Macy, Harlow and her husband Rashid, and Matt and Shane. Rick was an addition tonight, not a regular, but Macy thought of him as a recurring character.

"What do you do, Brooke?" Harlow asked, yanking Macy out of her musings.

"I'm a real estate agent for Wolfe," Brooke said.

"Oh, you work for Sasha?" Matt turned to his husband. "We've met her at the wine bar a few times. Tall, blond, pretty, plays on our team?"

"Piper's friend." Shane nodded. "I remember."

He put a forkful of quinoa into his mouth as Matt asked, "Have you worked for her long?"

"No, I'm new. Very new, in fact."

"Brooke's only been here a few weeks. She moved from…" Macy looked to Brooke for confirmation. "Ohio, right?"

"Yes." Brooke pointed her fork at Macy and smiled.

"Oh, wow. What do you think of our fair city?" Rick asked.

Brooke dabbed her mouth with her napkin, then answered. "Well, I haven't had a huge amount of free time yet that hasn't been spent on unpacking, so I haven't been able to do a ton of exploring. But I've found the reservoir, which is great for walking."

"And she found Beans & Batter," Macy added, to nods and happy sounds all around. Popularity was something that café did not struggle for.

"So, did you two meet through work?" Harlow moved a finger between Macy and Brooke.

"We did. Macy is staging some properties we're selling in a new build downtown." Brooke turned to her then, her face smiling, radiant, and it nearly took Macy's breath away.

"Well, it's been a super long time since Macy dated anybody, so this is nice to see." Matt said it so matter-of-factly that Macy almost didn't register the words, but she thought she felt Brooke stiffen next to her.

"Oh, we're, um…No, we're not…" Why were words so hard? How difficult was it to form a complete sentence? Macy could feel the heat in her face, absently wondering just how red she'd actually become as she noticed many pairs of eyes turn to her.

"We're friends," Brooke said. Her tone was light. Breezy. No big deal. Maybe Macy had imagined the stiffening?

"Oh," Matt said, and he held Macy's gaze for a beat before giving her a shrug and returning his focus to his meal. "Sorry. Just assumed."

The rest of the evening was wonderful. Fun, humorous, delicious. Stories were told, or repeated for the benefit of those who weren't always present. Endless food. Endless wine. Macy tried to be surreptitious in monitoring Brooke's fun meter, but aside from that one bump, she seemed to be really enjoying herself. Maybe Macy had been projecting? A mental shrug and she did her best to just have fun.

It was nearly eleven before people started to casually talk about heading home. Some tried taking dishes into the kitchen, only to be scolded by Lucas. "I am the host and my guests do *not* help clean. Understand?"

Coats and purses were gathered and everybody kind of left en masse.

"Oh, it's a gorgeous night," Brooke said as their heels clicked on the driveway. Her breath came out in visible white puffs, but the chill wasn't uncomfortable. The sky was clear, the moon big and full and bright. "Don't you think so?" Brooke shifted her gaze to Macy, who felt it all the way down to her toes. Brooke's big eyes were slightly glassy—an effect of the wine, Macy was sure—and her smile lit up her entire beautiful face. Macy had never seen her smile that big, and she loved it. Realized she wanted to make her smile like that all the time. She gave herself a mental shake. "I do. That moon is something."

They got in the car. Macy had switched to coffee, then water, a couple hours before, so she was fine to drive. She backed out of the driveway and pointed them toward Brooke's place. A few moments went by before Brooke broke the silence in the car.

"That was so much fun." There was a dreamy quality to her voice, and Macy didn't know her well enough to decide if she was drunk, just tipsy, none of the above.

"It was. I'm glad you came."

"I'm glad you asked me to came. Come. Yeah." A tinkling laugh. "I've had wine."

"I'm sorry, did you just *giggle*?"

"I think I did."

"You totally did. I never would have pegged you as a giggler." Macy found this incredibly entertaining. In the handful of times she'd been around Brooke, from their initial meeting to the café to the reservoir to the apartment, she'd always given off an air of put-together. Professional. A little stoic. Giggling was not something Macy would've ever expected her to do. Yet here she sat, in Macy's car, soft giggles that sounded like the super high keys on a piano.

"Did I mention that I had wine?"

"I believe you did, yes."

Brooke's face went suddenly serious. "Do you think less of me now?"

"God, no. In fact, I think more of you." It was the absolute truth. Brooke had been a draw, yes, a magnetic pull of sorts for Macy. But it had mostly been physical. *Hell, who wouldn't be drawn to that?* she thought as she glanced at her passenger. But now? It was as if, in the beginning, she'd been a paint-by-numbers portrait with only some of the colors filled in. And tonight, the rest of them had been added, and now Brooke was a full-fledged human with layers and elements and depth that Macy hadn't seen at first.

"How come you haven't dated in so long?" Brooke didn't look at her when she asked, just kind of gazed out the window. There was no accusation or judgment in her tone. Just a simple question that was so *not* simple.

"It's kind of a long story." Not a lie, that. "And our ride is almost over."

Brooke didn't so much turn to her as let her head roll the other way against the headrest of her seat so their eyes met. "Give me the SparkNotes version."

She couldn't help but smile. Efficiency. Even when a bit intoxicated, Brooke knew how to secure it.

Macy turned the car into Brooke's driveway, slid the gearshift into park, and shifted her body to face her. "Okay. The abridged version." She took a deep breath, swallowed, tried not to wonder why this was so hard to do. "I was with somebody for a long time. Like, from high school. We went to the same college, then we got jobs here, bought a house together—not the one I'm in now, a different one. And we made a life. A good one."

"Did she leave you?" There was sympathy there, in both Brooke's voice and in her eyes, which had gone soft.

"In a way." Macy gave a bitter chuckle. "She died."

Brooke sat up slightly. "Oh God. Macy. That's terrible. I'm so sorry."

"Thanks."

"What happened? Can I ask?" Brooke sat up even straighter. "I mean, if you don't want to talk about it, I get it. I'm not trying to be nosy or anything. I just—"

Macy held up a hand. "No, it's okay. No worries. Really." The change had been instant. Talking had been hard and now it wasn't. She suddenly found she didn't mind talking to Brooke about the subject. Why didn't she mind?

"Was she sick?"

"Not at all. Perfectly healthy." Macy took another deep breath, as if to fortify herself, suck in some strength. She didn't give the details to a lot of people. "She was home with a really bad cold one day. I was at work. She was doing laundry and carrying the laundry basket down the basement steps when she must've gotten dizzy or light-headed or taken a misstep or something. She fell down the stairs, cracked her skull when she landed." A soft gasp. "And that was it."

"Oh God, Macy." Instantly sober, that's what Brooke was then, clearly. She reached across the console, laid her hand over Macy's. "I'm so, so sorry."

"Thanks." Silence reigned for a moment. "That was more than three years ago." She turned to look at Brooke and immediately fell into those eyes. "You know what's ironic about the whole thing?"

"Tell me."

"I'm the clumsy one. I'm the one who drops things, spills things, slips, falls." A bitter chuckle. "You know. You've been a victim."

Brooke gave a small smile.

"So if one of us was going to die in a freak accident of clumsiness, it should've been me."

"You say that like you have some kind of control over those details in life."

It wasn't the first time Macy had heard that. Her sister said it all the time, but it wasn't something she had been able to reconcile in her own head. She knew it but couldn't seem to change it, to put away the guilt. It was a thing for her, definitely.

"Anyway. That's my story, sad but true." An attempt to lighten the mood. "I bet your buzz is gone now." A half grin.

Brooke snorted. "I'm definitely more alert, that's for sure." She paused for a moment, then added, "Thank you for sharing that with me." As if sensing that was all Macy could give right then, she put her hand on the door handle. "I had a really nice time tonight, Macy. Thank you for that, too."

I love the way she says my name. That thought didn't bounce through her head. Rather, it floated gently, as if on a cloud in her brain. "Me, too."

"If you're up for showing me Lucas's shop tomorrow, text me and let me know. And if you change your mind, no hard feelings, okay?"

A smile. A nod. Brooke had given her an out, which Macy simultaneously found classy and was also bummed about. She waited as Brooke exited the car, dug her keys out of her purse, and opened her front door. When she turned back and waved, Macy put her car in reverse and headed home. To her guilt, and to wonderful memories of the evening.

Yeah, her head was a mess. Thank God she had her animals to take up her attention because she had no energy left to sort things out. Not tonight.

Maybe tomorrow.

CHAPTER FOURTEEN

D id they use a giant round brush? Or a flat one? How did they make the circular designs on the ceiling when they built a house?

The questions floated through Brooke's mind slowly, gently, as if on a light breeze as she lay in her bed. Not sleeping, but not quite awake, she studied the swirls and drips—*hangy-downies*, she used to call such things when she was a kid—on the ceiling above her bed, tried to imagine just the right twist of her wrist in order to create them.

A thump from the wall behind her headboard caught her attention. Rorschach lifted his head from where he'd been lying next to her hip and blinked sleepy eyes. Muffled voices could be heard.

"I don't give a shit what you think I said." The guy.

"I don't think it's what you said—I know it's what you said. I'm not deaf." The girl.

Another thump. Maybe a drawer being slammed. His voice lowered, calmed, but he must have been standing right near the wall because Brooke could hear him as clearly as if he was standing next to her. And honestly, the sudden calm of it made her squirm uncomfortably. "You should think twice before you talk to me like that."

Either the woman didn't respond at all, or she did so too quietly for Brooke to hear. A shiver ran through her body as she recalled the parents of a girl she'd gone to junior high with. Julia Jacobs. Brooke had stayed for dinner a few times when they'd worked on a science project together, and the same shiver would run through her whenever she heard Julia's dad talk to Julia's mom. There was never anything physical, but his words were cutting. He would belittle her, mock her clothes, her body, her cooking. All in front of Brooke. She didn't know it then, but retrospectively as an adult she understood that she'd been a witness to emotional abuse.

"Well, that was fun to wake up to, huh, Rorsh?" She scratched his head and he began to purr as she lowered her voice to a whisper. "Probably less fun for her, though."

But it had distracted her for a bit, and that was good. Because she hadn't slept well. A combination of slightly too much wine and recapping the evening and remembering Macy's story…it all kept her brain whirring and sleep at a distance. A glance at the clock told her it was going on eight—later than she would normally be up—but she felt like her limbs were filled with heavy liquid and she just didn't want to move. A roll onto her side, Rorschach shifting to curl up against her stomach, apparently agreeing with her decision not to get out of bed quite yet, and she began to drift off.

She had reached that blissful place where you were warm, relaxed, and *almost* asleep when her phone pinged.

A sigh. Even the cat looked annoyed.

Reaching behind her back, she felt around until her fingers hit the phone, and she brought it to her face.

A text. From Macy. Brooke perked up.

Good morning! Still up for a little visit to Lucas's shop? He hit an estate sale last week and has some cool new stuff.

Brooke could feel her body waking up all of a sudden.

And if you're not up for it, that's totally fine. No worries.

"I am absolutely up for it," she said to nobody, then started typing.

Yes! I'd love to. Still need to shower, though. Meet you there? She didn't want to keep Macy waiting for her if she was ready to go.

Perfect. I'll bring the coffee. Then a smiley, a coffee mug, a car.

Try not to spill it on yourself, Brooke texted back, then added a splat emoji. Two could play at the emoji game.

Oh, funny girl is back.

Brooke laughed.

A little more than an hour and a half later, she was turning into the parking lot of Everything Old Is New Again, surprised by how busy it already was at ten in the morning on a Sunday. Slipping her gearshift into park, she scanned the lot, counting. Four sedans, Macy's SUV, two two-door coupes, twelve trucks. *Those must be the folks planning on taking some furniture home today.* Her mother loved antique shops and yard sales and flea markets, and Brooke had spent many a day of her childhood following her through one or another of them. As a youngster, she'd hated it, been bored, until she learned how to explore on her own, find fun stuff like old toys or books. When she looked back now, she realized all that time spent with her mother on the weekends was time she'd likely never repeat. Their relationship had changed so drastically over the years, and she just couldn't make herself imagine what it might be like to have her mom by her side right now as she walked toward the double front door.

Antique shops had such a unique smell. She remembered that from her trips with her mom as well. Wood, paint, stain, there was always a mustiness, and the scent of history. Which made no sense, she knew, but she'd always sworn that's what she smelled in among the other scents. The past.

Lucas had a spacious location. It had been ages since she'd been in an antique shop or anything similar, and Brooke had to take a moment to simply absorb it all. The smells, the sights, the sounds of people milling about. Holding things up to each other and discussing things like origin, possible uses, worth. A quick scan did not reward her with a Macy sighting, but she knew she'd find her eventually so decided to start to her left and move around the outside walls before easing in toward the items more in the center.

The left-hand wall was apparently where Lucas had decided to display all his tables. While Brooke wasn't familiar with all the proper names for different styles, there were a few things she recognized. Like the claw-feet on one table, and that another was a monastery table, which she knew because her parents had one. There were also three different styles of drop leaf tables like the one that used to be in her grandparents' kitchen.

"See anything you like?" Macy's voice came from behind her, but rather than startle her, it felt like warm syrup had been poured over her, sweet and gentle.

Brooke turned, tried not to show how much *yes!* she did see something she liked. Macy stood there in jeans, a white long-sleeved T-shirt, and a navy-blue full-zip hoodie, pink and black Nikes on her feet. She was completely casual, hair slightly tousled, virtually no makeup aside from some mascara. Rosy cheeks, a big grin, and a cardboard coffee cup with the Beans & Batter logo on it topped off the look. Brooke swallowed, forced her eyes to the cup.

"As a matter of fact, I do. Is that for me?"

"It is." Macy held the cup toward her. "It's the French roast. I hope that's okay. I wasn't sure what you were drinking when I saw you there, but this is the coffee they're known for, so..." She reached into the pocket of her hoodie and pulled out a handful of sugar packets and little creamer cups. From the back pocket of her jeans, a wooden stir stick.

"Wow, you came prepared." Brooke emptied two of the creamers into the cup, passed on the sugar, and used the stir stick. She took a sip, and the warmth, the light roasted taste of the coffee, the blast of caffeine, all of it made her hum in appreciation. When she glanced up, Macy was watching her. "Thank you so much. This is amazing."

"You're welcome." There was a beat of silence, and then Macy seemed to shake herself. "I noticed you were looking at the drop leafs."

"My grandma had one. It was in her kitchen, and she'd always lift the leaves when we were going to play cards." Brooke smiled at the memory of simpler times.

"Is she still around?" By unspoken agreement, they'd begun to stroll.

"She passed away about five years ago."

"I'm sorry."

"Thanks." They strolled some more. "So, do you know antiques? I kind of assume you do, but I'm not sure why." It was the truth and Macy smiled at the words.

"I know some, mostly from my boss and Lucas. They're both really well-versed in furnishings, both old and new." She pointed to a round table with a marble top and a wooden three-point pedestal base. "This is Continental. I think this one's from the eighteen hundreds." She reached for the tag that hung off it. "Yup—eighteen twenty."

"I'm impressed."

"Don't be." Macy pointed to another table, this one rectangular and very simple in its angles. "I have no idea what this one is."

Brooke grinned as Lucas appeared out of nowhere.

"That's a farm table, Macy Lou. You should know that."

"Why? Am I being graded?"

He gave her a quick kiss, then surprised Brooke with a hug. "If you were, you'd be in trouble. How are you guys?"

"Good. Brooke had mentioned last night that she'd never been here, and I was popping by anyway, so here we are. Surprise."

"You come every Sunday. I'm not surprised."

"Yes, but this time, I brought a sacrifi—er—guest."

Brooke almost choked on her coffee when she laughed. "Are there candles and robes and a very old, creepy-ass altar of some kind in the back of the store?"

"Of course not," Lucas said, waving her away with a dismissive hand. "They're in the basement." As she and Macy laughed, he noticed a customer trying to get his attention and went to help.

"He's fun," Brooke said. "I like him." It was true. She didn't really have any gay guy friends, and Brennan Templeton, that other agent in her office, wasn't exactly sunshine and roses. He hadn't been at all welcoming. Or even nice.

"He's the best." Macy continued to wander, and Brooke followed, and they spent the next forty-five minutes looking at different pieces, Brooke asking questions and being endlessly impressed with Macy's knowledge of furniture and layout.

"You should be an interior designer," she said at one point.

Macy sighed, a dreamy quality to it. "I know. I'd love to. But it's a cutthroat business, and this city isn't that big and…" Her words kind of drifted away, but Brooke got the gist.

"It could be tough to break in, I'm sure." With a shrug, she added, "Might be worth a shot, though. You're very good. I'd hire you."

"You would?"

"Absolutely."

Macy seemed to take that information and pocket it, and it was like she visibly lightened on her feet. They perused for a few more minutes before she turned to Brooke and said, "How do you feel about milkshakes?"

"I hear they bring all the girls to the yard."

"Ha-ha. Very funny. Seriously, though."

Brooke squinted at the randomness of the question, but answered honestly. "I mean, is it even a possibility to feel any way toward milkshakes other than intense love and devotion?"

"It's really not, no."

"Well, then, I have intense love and devotion for milkshakes. Why?"

Macy's smile blossomed across her face like the sun revealing itself from behind clouds. She grasped Brooke's hand, and Brooke felt the contact all the way up her arm. Through her body. Down. "Come with me."

❖

The Cold Shoulder held so many memories for Macy. It was where her father took her almost every weekend when she was a kid.

Hand in hand, they'd walk in and marvel at the new flavors, taking samples every time they were offered by Mr. Walton, the owner. Her dad would get an ice cream cone, always mint chocolate chip, despite oohing and aahing over the new options. They'd bring a six-pack of ice cream sandwiches home for her mother. And Macy always, always got a milkshake.

It was a very small shop, long and narrow, yet there were eight customers in line. In the late morning. On a Sunday. In April. Two more came through the front door.

Brooke was surprised. Macy could tell by the wide-eyed look on her face as they sat at one of the handful of tiny round tables, a huge milkshake in front of each of them.

"I love this place," Brooke said, and there was reverence in her tone. And a wistfulness. When her eyes had roved the whole of the place and her focus returned to Macy, she said, "I bet it gets packed in here in the summer."

"Line out the door and around the corner." Macy sipped her peanut butter brownie shake. A sound came up from her throat that she had zero control over. A delighted growl of sorts. Kind of.

Brooke laughed. "Well, that was an interesting groan of yum."

"Can't help it." She drank some more, made the same sound.

Brooke tasted her own shake, and Macy watched as her eyes fluttered closed. "Oh my God," she said quietly.

"See?" Watching Brooke enjoy her shake was almost erotic, and Macy tried not to let that idea very far into her head. She failed. Miserably. "I would like to point out what an unexpected choice of flavor you made."

"Me? What do you mean?"

"Fruity Pebbles? Really? Sophisticated, put-together, always in control Brooke Sullivan, when given a list of more than a dozen deliciously creative milkshakes to choose from, picks Fruity Pebbles. Like a five-year-old." Macy grinned wide, making sure to let Brooke know she was teasing her. *Keep it light, Mace. Keep it light. Friendly. That's all.*

"Listen, don't judge."

Macy held up her hands. "Oh, no judgment. Only amusement."

"I'm amusing, am I?" Brooke took another sip of her shake, and Macy tried hard not to stare at her mouth, at the glossy fullness of her pursed lips, as she did.

"You have no idea." It came out soft. Softer than intended. Macy felt herself blush, so she changed the subject. "I've been coming here since I was a kid." She glanced over her shoulder at the man behind the counter. "Mr. Walton was the owner then. That's his son, Greg. He runs it now."

"I can almost see little tiny Macy trying to peek over the counter. What was your favorite as a kid?"

"Always a milkshake." She smiled as she spoke. "I've had every flavor on the menu, multiple times over, and I always sample the new ones. 'Cause you have to, right? But I always come back to this one." She sipped her peanut butter brownie shake to punctuate her point. "It is easily one of my very favorite things on the planet. This shake has gotten me through so many important moments in life: tests, dances, dates, job interviews, graduations, births, deaths. Each one in my life is marked by a peanut butter brownie milkshake." She stopped talking, wondering if she was coming across as way over the top about a little ice cream shop, but she couldn't help it. This place meant something to her.

"I think that's really sweet. Things like that end up being big slices of our lives, make us who we are, you know? You, my friend, will now forever be defined in my head by a peanut butter brownie milkshake."

"You know what? I am totally okay with that, Fruity Pebbles."

They laughed together, then did that thing where they stopped. Held eye contact. Everything in Macy's body tightened in the moment.

Brooke said nothing, which was a blessing. She simply smiled and blushed a little bit and held Macy's gaze as a couple, a man and a woman, passed their table.

"Did you really need a large?" the man said. "I mean, Jesus. Rein it in once in a while. You're busting out of your pants."

The woman was doing no such thing, but the effect of the man's words was clear, even in the six seconds it took to witness the exchange as they walked by. The woman's eyes cast downward. Her neck and cheeks blossomed into a bright pink. The ice cream cone that had been halfway to her mouth stopped, and she pressed her lips together in a tight line.

The door closed behind them, and Brooke met Macy's eyes. "God, that was brutal."

Macy shook her head, her heart aching for the woman. "I don't understand talking to somebody like that." She swallowed hard, her appetite for her milkshake waning a bit. "Especially somebody you're supposed to care about."

"My neighbors do that." Brooke looked a bit...ashamed? Chagrined? Something about mentioning that made her feel weird. Macy could see it on her face.

"Really?"

A grimace paired with a slight nod. "A man and a woman. I can hear them through the wall sometimes. He's not nice to her and seems to raise his voice a lot."

"Does he hit her?"

Brooke lifted one shoulder. "I don't know. I haven't heard that. Just him being critical." She sipped, and then her light brows met above her nose. "She does stand up for herself sometimes. Not often. She did this morning, though it seemed to make him angrier. He did that thing where his voice went all low and cold?"

Macy gritted her teeth, made a face. "Yikes."

"Yeah. I'm not used to raised voices—my parents just didn't do that. But that quiet thing gave me the creeps."

"I can imagine."

They sat quietly, watched the other customers placing orders and eating ice cream with happy smiles on their faces.

"I like this place," Brooke said after a beat, in an obvious attempt to bring them back to lightheartedness. "Thanks for bringing me here."

For some reason, Macy went all warm and gooey inside. "You're welcome."

"I have a question, though."

"Okay. Shoot."

"Is there a rule about sampling each other's flavors? Because we've been sitting here for almost twenty minutes and you have yet to offer me a taste of your shake."

A laugh burst out of Macy. Another unexpected trait of Brooke's— she was funny. When you first met her, that wasn't something that came to mind. Sophisticated? Yes. Professional? Without a doubt. Hot? Oh my God, absolutely. Hilarious? Um...

"Allow me to apologize," Macy said, sliding her glass across the table. "Please, sample away." Again, she tried but was unable to pry her eyes away from the sight of Brooke's lips closing around the straw. *Her* straw. And how did they stay that glossy all the time? Macy hadn't seen her apply anything all morning, yet Brooke's lips were slick and shiny, full and pink... Macy cleared her throat, glanced over her shoulder at something else. *Anything* else.

"Okay, next time, I get this one." Brooke gestured at Macy's glass, then playfully took another sip before sliding the glass back to her. "Do you want to taste mine?"

You have no idea shot through Macy's head like an Olympian running the fifty-yard dash, but she somehow managed to simply nod and take a sip. "Tastes like breakfast."

"Right?" When Brooke reached for the glass Macy slid back to her, their fingers touched, and the sizzle that passed between them was palpable, at least for Macy.

"Tell me about your family," she said suddenly. It surprised her and apparently surprised Brooke as well, judging by the way her brows went up to visit her hairline. But Macy didn't care. She needed to focus on something other than how much she wanted to grab Brooke's face in her hands and kiss the bejesus out of her. "Parents, siblings, whattaya got?"

That smile again. "I have parents, yes, and a younger brother. Eddie."

"And they're all still in Ohio."

"Yes."

"I bet they're bummed you moved away." Macy sucked on her straw, tasted what she realized was apparently Brooke's cherry-flavored lip gloss, and watched the different emotions roll across Brooke's face in waves. It was interesting to her that she'd initially thought Brooke was stoic, an emotion hider. But you just needed to know how to look at her and her feelings were right there on her face. Right then, that meant a combination of hesitation, frustration, and a pretty big helping of sadness all made quick appearances before she caught them.

"Well." Another sip of her milkshake, which was almost gone now. "I'm not so sure about that. I mean, they miss me. Of course they do. But having me farther away is probably also a bit of a relief for them."

A tip of her head. "How so?" Macy asked.

"My parents..." Brooke gazed up into a high corner of the shop as if the words she was looking for were stenciled on the ceiling. "Their faith is very important to them. As is mine. But our views about it and our...adherence to it differ. Pretty significantly."

Macy waited patiently, as she suspected there was more explanation to come.

Brooke leaned forward, lowered her voice to just above a whisper. "They don't know what to do with my bisexuality." A puff of air left Brooke's lungs, and Macy wondered if talking about her sexuality was hard for her. Sure seemed like it, like she wasn't comfortable with people knowing.

"Ouch."

"Yeah. I mean, they're fine with it when I'm dating a guy because they can ignore it. But they don't like the girl aspect."

A disdain-filled snort. "Sounds like some lesbians I know."

Brooke's chuckle held a layer of bitterness. "Yeah, I've met some of them." She sighed and suddenly looked so sad that Macy wanted to wrap her up in her arms and protect her from everything bad in the world, even though Brooke Sullivan was not a woman who needed protecting. Still, the vulnerability in her eyes right then squeezed Macy's heart. "My last—well, my only, really—long-term relationship was with Michael. We met in college, hit it off, wanted the same things—or so I thought. We ended up kind of drifting apart until we finally realized we were barely more than friends."

Macy got the distinct impression there was more to that story, but she didn't push. Just listened.

"After he and I finally split, I met a woman through some friends. We went on a couple of dates, nothing serious, but I thought it was a good time to mention it to my parents. And when I finally told them, they kind of freaked. My mom told me she just wants me to be *normal*." She made air quotes around the last word.

She was trying to be strong, to act like it was no big deal, as if her mother had said something as harmless as not liking the shoes Brooke was wearing. But Macy could see it. The pain. The loneliness. The shame. She couldn't help it—she reached across the table and closed her hand over Brooke's. Squeezed.

"There is nothing wrong with you. You *are* normal. You know that, right?"

"Most of the time, yes." Brooke squeezed back, seemed to study their hands as she spoke. "Can I ask you a question?"

"Sure."

"Are you familiar with the local churches?"

It was an odd way to phrase the question, and it made Macy wonder if she was really asking something else. "I mean, I've lived here all my life, so I know of them. My parents...I wouldn't say they're regulars, but they attend fairly often. Why?"

Toying with the straw in her glass, turning it slowly in her long fingers, seemed to help Brooke find her words. "Well, as much as my parents use their religion as the reason they don't approve of my *lifestyle*"—again with the air quotes—"I still have my own faith. And I miss going to church."

That wasn't a feeling Macy had much experience with. She didn't mind church. And on Christmas Eve, one of the days the Carrs went as a family, she loved it. The hymns, the decorations, the sheer beauty of it. But missing it? That was unfamiliar to her. That being said, the soft sadness in Brooke's eyes made her want to help. "I could certainly send you to the church we go to. It's—okay, brace yourself for these two words in the same sentence—Catholic inclusive."

The way Brooke's face lit up right then? It was as if the sun had come out on what had been a gray and overcast day. Macy would swear the entire ice cream shop got brighter. "That would be amazing. You don't mind? Will your parents?"

"Why would they mind?" Macy waved off the question because the fact of the matter was, her parents would love it. It would give them an excuse to go, and they loved getting to meet and hang out with Macy's friends. That word again. She took out her phone and did a little surfing until she found what she was looking for. "There. I sent you the link. Take a look, see what you think, then let me know. I can go with you. I can talk to my mom. You can go on your own."

"This is amazing. Thank you so much. I'll probably check it out on my own at first, but maybe at some point, you can go with me?"

"Of course." There was no hesitation. Macy simply answered. Immediately. Honestly. This was obviously important to Brooke, so she would absolutely help out. Not to mention, the relief that washed over Brooke's gorgeous face was totally worth it.

The crowd had grown since they sat down, the hum of conversation a little bit louder now. Their glasses were empty, the shakes long gone, but Macy wasn't quite ready to say good-bye to Brooke—something that both bothered her and put that weird fluttering in her stomach.

"What's your plan for the rest of your Sunday?" Brooke asked, as if privy to Macy's thoughts.

A half-shrug. Super casual. No big deal. "It's nice out, so I was going to walk my dogs at some point, but then probably just watch a movie or something. Make some popcorn."

Brooke was thinking about something. Macy could see it in her eyes. She was rolling something around in her head. She nodded, glanced at the line of customers. "Yeah, me, too. Minus the dog walking." Her smile was soft.

Macy rolled her lips in. "Why don't you come over?" God. She said it. She actually said it.

The eyebrow raise again. "Yeah?"

"Yeah. We could find something we both want to see. And keep this under your hat, but…" Macy leaned forward, made a show of looking around, then stage-whispered, "I happen to make the world's most excellent popcorn."

"Seriously? I mean, this is a big claim. Not to be taken lightly."

Macy sat back up. "Not a claim, ma'am. A fact."

"I see. I see." Brooke nodded. "Well, obviously, there's only one way to prove this fact. I'll have to see—and taste—for myself."

"Then we should arrange that." The giddy excitement shooting through her was enough to make her knee jump up and down under the table.

"Definitely. And then I can report back to Popcorn Headquarters with my findings."

"I like this plan." And she did. More than she could possibly say.

"Me, too. Let's do it."

CHAPTER FIFTEEN

"J ust answer them. What can it hurt?" Lena was nothing if not practical. Logical. Two things that Brooke normally was as well. She was the epitome of logical, happy when things made sense. Her dating profile had gotten a couple of hits—okay, no, it had gotten numerous hits. She'd quickly waded through some of them and admitted to herself that there were two men who were appealing. She'd been scanning their profiles when she'd decided to give Lena a call.

"Yeah, okay. I will."

"Promise me." That meant more from Lena than it might have from somebody else. Brooke never made a promise to her that she didn't intend to keep.

"I promise."

"What are you doing with your Sunday?"

Brooke had left Macy so she could run home, take care of Rorschach, and change into more comfortable clothes. After googling the best wine to pair with popcorn, she'd pulled a full-bodied cab off her little wine rack and set it on the counter.

"I'm going to go visit my work friend, Macy. Have a little wine and munchies." She said nothing about the movie or the popcorn. Nothing about how drawn to Macy she was. She didn't let herself think about why.

"Oh, good. I'm glad you're meeting new people there. Just don't find a replacement for me, okay?" Lena did her best to play it off as teasing. Joking. But Brooke knew her friend well, could hear the tiny frisson of worry in her voice.

"Not possible. You're irreplaceable."

"You got that right." The relief was clear.

"When are you coming to visit me? I miss you." Brooke wasn't an emotional person. Vulnerability was not something she enjoyed, and the past few years had made that even more apparent to her. But Lena was different. She was the only person on the planet that Brooke had really opened up to, the only one who knew all her deepest, darkest secrets.

So why wasn't she telling her about Macy?

It didn't take much effort to answer her own question. Brooke knew why, she just didn't want to think about it. Didn't want to analyze it. Didn't want to even admit it.

Macy scared her.

And it wasn't even just Macy herself. It was everything that came with her, everything she caused in Brooke. Her feelings, her thoughts, and—yes—her desires. Her *desires*. Did she desire Macy?

God, yes.

With a groan and a vigorous shake of her head, Brooke did her best to focus on the evening that lay ahead instead of trying to overanalyze everything that was—or wasn't, but should've been—in her brain. She signed off with Lena, kissed Rorschach on the top of his furry head, gathered her purse and the wine, locked her place, and got in her car. All she wanted to do was enjoy herself. There wasn't anything wrong with that. When her mother's voice popped into her head to argue with her statement, Brooke turned on the radio and cranked up the volume, then began to sing along loudly, as Taylor Swift told her she needed to calm down. She so did.

The directions were simple, and Brooke was surprised to realize that Macy was only a quick fifteen-minute drive from her own place. She pulled into the driveway behind Macy's SUV, put her car in park, and took in the cute little bungalow. It had light brown siding the color of melted chocolate ice cream, and four low porch columns made of flat rock. It wasn't a big house, but looked expansive somehow, and the wooden front door with the mullioned window beckoned to her, invited her to enter. Empty pots populated the edges of the porch, and as she headed up the walk to the four steps, Brooke wondered what kinds of flowers Macy usually planted in them. What colors? Red geraniums? Pink and purple pansies? Yellow tulips?

The door opened before she could knock, startling her out of her flower imaginings and plopping her back in the present, right in front of the most adorable version of Macy yet. Through the barking of multiple dogs, Brooke saw that Macy had changed, too, and was now wearing soft-looking leggings and an oversized gray sweatshirt with the Under

Armour logo in a very faded navy-blue print across the front. Her hair was tousled, down, tucked behind her ears. Her brown eyes were soft and smiling, and it was clear to anybody who looked that she was happy to see Brooke.

"You found me."

"Wasn't hard." Brooke held up her phone, tipped it back and forth. "Siri knows everything."

"She thinks she does." Macy stepped aside. "Come on in. I've blocked the beasts in the kitchen for now so they don't tackle you."

"Tackling is a worry? This happens? You never said. I don't have my shoulder pads or mouth guard. I'm ill-prepared for dog tackles." At Macy's laugh, she held out the bottle of wine. "I am, however, prepared to have wine with popcorn."

"My dream woman," Macy said on a sigh and took the bottle. She closed the door behind Brooke, then gestured with a flourish. "Welcome to my humble abode. Please note that it never looks like this. I have been cleaning like a madwoman since I got here from the ice cream shop."

"So you're trying to impress me." Brooke heard the flirty tone of her own voice, wondered where the hell it had come from.

"Absolutely always."

"This is adorable," Brooke said as she looked around, and she wasn't kidding. The living room was a good size. Not huge, but not tiny. The gas fireplace on one wall was the focal point, its hearth and chimney made of river rock, the flames flickering invitingly. On either side of it were built-ins, sprinkled with an almost even number of books—twelve—and framed photos—ten. The hardwood was well-worn, but good quality oak. The small chocolate-brown sectional was likely leather—or a decent facsimile—and a beige area rug with a burgundy and deep green geometric design helped pull the sectional and wooden coffee table together. Near the window was a large cat tower, empty of felines. A round dog bed sat in a corner, another in front of the fireplace, a crate in another corner. There was also a basket filled with stuffed animals in various stages of deconstruction. Brooke's attention was drawn to the small whimpers and whines coming from the kitchen. "They stopped barking."

Macy gave a nod. "Yeah, that whimpering is them trying so hard to be patient." Her smile was radiant, and it was clear this was a woman who loved her pets.

"Will they remember me?"

"Shall we find out?"

"Release the hounds!" Brooke said in her best English accent. Which wasn't good but made Macy laugh.

In the next minute, dogs were all over her. Not literally, but almost. Pete, the golden, was a love. Brooke could tell that right away. He had the gentlest face, and he looked at Brooke as if he'd adored her his entire life, his big, fluffy tail sweeping back and forth nonstop as he pushed his snout against her thigh. Angus, being the terrier he was, sniffed every inch of her he could reach, which meant from the knees down. Every now and then, he would glance up at her, and she'd get a shot of his rich, soulful eyes, hard to see in all of his black hair. Priscilla, the dachshund, kept a bit of distance, watched as if unsure whether Brooke deserved her attention. Brooke pointed at her.

"She doesn't like me."

Macy shook her head. "No, she's just watching. This is how she does it. She *observes*." She drew the word out. "She takes in all the information before she makes a decision. Sometimes, it takes her a long time."

"She and I are a lot alike, then."

Macy picked the small dog up and brought her close to Brooke, who held a hand out to her nose.

"Hi there, pretty girl." Priscilla gave her a sniff, looked up at her. Sniffed again. Looked at Macy. "She's calculating." Another sniff and then, finally, a swipe of a pink tongue on Brooke's knuckle.

"There you go. Seal of approval. You're in." Macy handed the dog over, and Brooke took her long little body in her arms.

"Well, hello. I'm Brooke. It's nice to meet you." Priscilla touched her nose to Brooke's, then snuggled in to her. Brooke looked at Macy, wide-eyed with surprise.

Macy threw up her hands in mock defeat. "That's it. I've been replaced. You're in. I'm out. I'll go pack my things." She sighed dramatically, then laughed and pointed at the couch. "Have a seat. I'll pour some wine and get the popcorn started."

"What if I want to follow you into the kitchen and watch?"

"You can follow me anywhere you want to," came Macy's reply, and damn if she wasn't giving off a seriously sexy vibe.

Brooke followed her because she was no dummy.

The kitchen was a little more chaotic than the living room. It was obviously where Macy dropped things as she came through the door. Keys, mail, her purse were in a pile on one corner of the black speckled counter. A freestanding island on wheels was off in a corner and held two sets of small bowls of kibble and water. Brooke pointed at them.

"I almost forgot you had cats."

"Yeah, they're upstairs hiding." Macy's oven was on, and she opened a brown paper lunch bag. "They might venture down eventually."

"Something smells good." She squatted to peek in the oven window.

"S'mores popcorn."

Brooke snapped her head around to face Macy. "I'm sorry, did you say s'mores popcorn?"

A mischievous grin. "I did. I'm making us two kinds. Regular butter and s'mores. In fact"—a black oven mitt went onto her hand—"this is probably done. It just needed a couple minutes under the broiler."

The cookie sheet looked like it had been made by baby Jesus and all his angels. Popcorn, yes, big and white and fluffy. But on top and melted through was chocolate and the mini marshmallows had browned on the surface, just as if they'd been toasted over a campfire. Bite-size graham cracker pieces were sprinkled throughout.

Brooke watched as Macy poured popcorn kernels into a glass bowl, drizzled them with olive oil, then stirred them and dropped them into the paper bag. She folded the top twice, put it in the microwave, and hit some buttons. She met Brooke's eyes and gave a shrug.

"My own version of microwave popcorn. Way better." She lopped a hunk of butter off a stick and set it in the bowl, and when the popcorn was done, she switched the bag with the bowl and melted the butter. Five minutes later, they had two bowls of popcorn—one with butter and sea salt, the other with chocolate, marshmallows, and graham crackers.

Brooke offered to open the wine but realized she'd have to put Priscilla down to do so, and Macy must've caught her hesitation, and her eyes sparkled. She took care of it, poured them each a glass, and they adjourned to the living room.

It was about an hour later when it hit Brooke.

They were halfway into the rom-com they'd picked. Side by side on the couch, they had somehow inched closer to each other, with each reach for popcorn or shift to make room for a dog or cat. Now their hips and thighs were touching, they both had their feet on the coffee table, crossed at the ankles and skimming the other's. Snuggled under the same blanket. Lights off, only the TV and the fire fending off the darkness.

But she wasn't nervous. She didn't feel weird. She wasn't freaked. For the first time since she could remember, she felt completely, utterly peaceful and comfortable, and before she realized she was doing it, she tipped her head so it rested on Macy's shoulder. And as if she'd been waiting for a sign, as if that move had given her permission, Macy lifted one foot, crossed it over one of Brooke's, and pulled so that their legs entwined.

Neither spoke.

They kept watching the movie.

❖

Is it hot in here?

Macy was totally content. And also freaking the hell out. How was that even possible? To be in both those spaces at the same time?

She'd been struggling to pay attention to what had turned out to be a fairly mediocre movie because Brooke had gotten closer and closer—or had Macy done that?—until the only thing she was aware of was where their bodies touched. Thighs. Hips. Feet. Shoulders. God, Brooke smelled good. More than once, Macy had to physically prevent herself from turning her head to bury her nose in Brooke's sunset hair. Ball her hands into fists. Clench her jaw. But, strangely, on top of all that navigating and distraction?

Chill.

There was total chill and contentment. That was what she felt sitting on that couch next to Brooke. And that was what was freaking her out. Which made zero sense. She closed her eyes, tried to steady her breathing...

And felt Brooke's head rest on her shoulder.

Fuck.

It felt so good. Better than good. It felt *right.* It felt perfect.

She moved her foot—or rather, her foot seemed to move on its own—and crossed it over Brooke's. And the perfection she felt only increased.

All rational thought left her head then, flew out of it like a flock of swallows leaving a barn. Instinct took over. She turned her head, Brooke lifted hers, and their eye contact, there in the dim light, was so hotly intense, Macy was sure it would scorch both of them. Her gaze dropped to Brooke's full lips. She felt it happen, had no control over it, just like she had no control over how she leaned forward. Slowly... so very slowly. Until she and Brooke were breathing the same breath. Until she could *feel* her more than see her.

Caution went the way of the wind.

Macy pressed her lips to Brooke's. Tentatively at first. Gauging. Testing. Bracing for an adverse reaction—a horrified gasp, a push-off, hell, a slap. But none of those things happened. Instead, she felt Brooke's hand at the back of her neck, hooking it, pulling her in, and the kiss deepened.

It was so utterly cornball, but kissing Brooke felt *magical*. Truly. Like sparkles floated in the air. Like *she* was floating. They shifted their bodies, turned so they had better access to one another. Macy pressed her tongue between Brooke's lips, tentatively at first. She felt more than heard Brooke hum in approval, felt her tongue push back, and a sexy little battle was waged.

How much time had passed? Macy had no idea. And she didn't care. If lightning struck her house in that moment and fried her to a crisp, she'd die an incredibly happy woman because this? This kissing right here? Kissing this woman? Macy had no words to describe the level of sheer bliss.

Two things struck then. The first was that if they were that good at simply making out, how combustible would they be if they were actually naked in bed, having sex? That thought was so strong that it made Macy open her eyes so she could look at the gorgeous creature in her arms.

That's when the second thing struck, because her gaze landed on the framed photo of her and Michelle at the top of Whiteface Mountain in the Adirondacks. Bright winter sunshine, arms wrapped around each other, enormously happy smiles. It was all right there in the photo. To remind Macy what she'd had. To remind her what she'd lost. To remind her that she'd already had her one true love.

She broke the kiss. Ragged breaths were the only sound, and Macy absently realized that the movie had ended, and all the credits had rolled, and neither of them had noticed.

"Wow," Brooke said, then rolled her lips in, visibly swallowed. "That was...God."

Macy nodded, shot her a half smile, glanced away.

"You okay?" Brooke asked.

"Yeah, absolutely. Totally good. Fine." *Oh my God, way to be subtle, Mace.*

Brooke squinted at her, clearly not believing that she was totally good or fine. "You sure?"

More nodding.

More squinting.

Brooke seemed to choose her words carefully as she said, "I feel like we should be talking about something, but I'm not sure what. I mean, aside from the fact that we just made out and it was beyond amazing." She was trying for levity. For lighthearted. Macy could see that. But Michelle just kept staring at her from the photo over Brooke's shoulder, and she felt helpless.

"It really was." That was no lie, and it made Macy feel worse, as did her sudden inability to look Brooke in the eye.

Brooke's discomfort was growing. It was obvious in the way she shifted, put a little distance between their bodies. It was as if Macy could see her various doors and windows slowly closing, one by one. "I think maybe I should go?" Brooke posed it as a question, clearly looking for a little help from Macy. She didn't move for a moment, likely giving Macy time to stop her, but Macy couldn't, and she watched, sadly frustrated with herself, as Brooke freed her legs from the rest of the blanket and stood.

All three dogs also got up, curious as to what their company was doing, following her into the kitchen as she took her empty glass and popcorn bowl in, despite Macy's protests. Once she'd stepped into her shoes, donned her jacket, and shouldered her purse, Brooke turned to look at her. No, study her was a more accurate description. She did that thing where she narrowed her eyes—something Macy was beginning to understand was her thinking face. It occurred to Macy that Brooke had a whole lot to say.

"I had a really good time." She kept it simple. Still studying. Searching Macy's face.

"Me, too."

"Yeah?"

Nodding. Macy did a lot of nodding now, apparently. She groaned inwardly.

Another beat. Finally Brooke said, "Okay. I'll call you?"

The fact that it was a question made Macy's stomach clench. She'd done that. She'd placed that uncertainty into the voice of a woman who seemed almost always certain. Yet she couldn't seem to do anything to fix it. "Yes, please."

"All right." Brooke gave her a quick peck on the lips and then left.

It was weird how empty the house felt once Brooke was gone. How could that be? With Macy and five animals in it, how did the house suddenly feel so hollow? Lifting her fingertips to her lips and noticing that they still tingled, still tasted like Brooke didn't help answer that question.

Not even a little.

Chapter Sixteen

S leep had been elusive.

Brooke had slept for an hour, woken up. Drifted off for twenty-five minutes, woken up. All night. It was now 4:17 a.m., and she was pretty sure she was awake for the day, yet she couldn't seem to move. Haul herself out from under the warmth of the covers and get her day started.

Thoughts and memories were weighing her down. Holding her in place like a gravity blanket, on her back, staring at the ceiling. Rorschach purred away next to her, his sleeping kitty mind oblivious to her confusion.

So many mixed emotions about yesterday. So very many. They simmered in her brain, like homemade soup on the stove on a Sunday afternoon, just cooking, each ingredient getting its share of heat. First, foremost, and the bit she seemed to hold on to the tightest was that she'd had a fabulous time. *Fabulous.* From the antique shop to the ice cream place to Macy's home, Brooke had enjoyed every second. She couldn't remember the last time she'd felt like she'd been able to relax the way she had at Macy's. Be herself. She'd felt…safe. That was the word. And how was that even possible? She hadn't known Macy long. Hadn't spent a ton of time with her. How was it that in the past several years of her life—even in the time she'd spent with Michael, in the time that she'd loved him—she'd never felt quite as safe as she did with Macy? It made no sense to her, and that was a big part of what had kept her tossing and turning all night.

The other? That kiss.

Oh my God, that kiss.

She'd replayed it over and over and over. And over some more because why not? It was hot and sexy and erotic and *God*. She hadn't had that kind of physical chemistry with anyone, male or female, in her entire life. Never. And she was pretty sure Macy had felt it, too. You didn't kiss somebody like that if you weren't feeling it.

So what had happened?

Why had Macy pulled back? Oh, she'd tried to play it off, to be casual and nonchalant about it, but she'd definitely pulled back. Not that Brooke would've let things go—or taken things—much further, but Macy had not only put the brakes on, she had brought them to a screeching halt.

Maybe that was a good thing?

Because once she'd gotten home and gotten into bed where she'd gotten very little sleep, other things had entered her head. Her mother's voice was clear and loud, and Brooke could even picture her disapproving face, crystal clear in her mind. How could she ever mention a girl again, let alone bring her home for the family to meet? Her stomach churned sourly at the thought.

I need to talk to Macy. And then, immediately on the heels of that thought was *Maybe we just need some time.*

Next to her, Rorschach stretched out a paw and set it on her shoulder, as if reassuring her that it was all going to be okay somehow, and she couldn't help but smile. She scratched his head in acknowledgment. "Thanks, little man," she whispered.

She needed to get her ass out of bed. The sky was beginning to lighten behind the blinds, and she couldn't think about this anymore. She'd go nuts, she was reasonably sure. She'd be Kevin McCallister from the movie *Home Alone*, running through her house, waving her arms and screaming.

No, thanks.

She was much more in control than that. She was the boss of her own life, damn it. That was enough to propel her out of bed and into the shower.

Not quite an hour later, she was dressed and downstairs spooning what according to the tin was turkey in gravy onto a small saucer for Rorschach while she waited for her coffee mug to fill. Checking her schedule for the day on her phone had her stopped in her tracks, holding the saucer above the cat's head, as she stared at her day for a beat, then sighed.

Half her day was going to be spent at Whitney Gardens. She'd forgotten about that. There was also a message from Sasha.

Whitney wants another apartment staged in a completely different style. Got a call in to Stage One. I'll pop by at some point today to see how things are going.

That meant two things.

One, her boss could pop by at any given time during the day. No big deal. That didn't alarm Brooke at all.

Two, Macy would likely be there for much, if not all of the day. That was alarming in multiple ways, and Brooke found herself getting angry at all the warring feelings in her head.

An annoyed *meow* yanked her out of it, and she blinked rapidly, realizing she was still standing there, holding Rorschach's breakfast well out of his reach like a big, teasing meanie.

With an apologetic smile, she set it down. "Sorry, sweetie," she said softly and stroked the silky black fur. After a moment, she stood back up, grabbed her coffee, and straightened her posture. She tipped her head from one side to the other, hearing vertebrae pop into place.

Okay. She could do this.

She mentally put on her armor, even as she felt herself slump just the tiniest bit.

Mondays, man.

Brooke headed to work.

❖

"Someday, somebody is going to ask me to stage a house or an apartment with only antiques." Macy said it aloud, but not really to any specific person. One of the burly movers across the room set down his end of the slate blue sofa and chuckled.

"Maybe a retirement community or something?"

Macy pointed at him with a grin. "Hey, you never know. It could happen."

"It could." The guy looked toward the door, where his moving partners were carrying a rocking recliner between them. "Where do you want it?"

It was a weird day. The weather had been all over the map, going from rainy to sunny to overcast but warmish. Typical late-April weather in upstate New York, but the fluctuation in the atmosphere also had her mood fluctuating. She'd woken up feeling unsettled. That was the best word for it. Too many conflicting emotions rolling around for her to deal with. Thank God for her animals. They needed to be fed and let out and played with, and Captain Jack needed ear drops, which he protested loudly and with claws, and they were a fantastic distraction from the person she needed distracting from…who happened to be in the apartment next door, showing it to a client.

What the hell was she going to do about Brooke and the guilt that had buried her like an avalanche?

And right after that question, was there really anything she *could* do?

She had answers to neither.

Yesterday had been amazing. There was no arguing that. She'd had a blast, and she'd been so happy at how open Brooke was to just winging it. She was so organized and a little, well, rigid, for lack of a better word. Or was that just the assumption Macy had made? Because Brooke had absolutely gone with the flow yesterday and seemed to have fun doing it. She'd surprised Macy. In a big way.

Until Macy had pretty much chased her out of the house.

She sighed, frustrated with herself, and pointed out the perfect spot for the rocking recliner. She couldn't think about this right now. She needed to focus on her job.

As if the Universe was trying to help her out with that, her phone pinged an incoming text. Tyler.

Game tonight at 6.

Despite the ever-changing weather, Macy was relieved. She hadn't seen Tyler in a while and she was missing him. Plus, it would give her something to do other than sit around her house and overanalyze everything that had been done and said while she was with—

"Macy?"

Macy turned to face her. That voice. Those eyes. Brooke stood in the doorway dressed in a gorgeous deep green pantsuit that was the perfect complement to her auburn hair, which she wore down today. Hesitation was clear on her face, though it was also clear that she was fighting against it. Brooke Sullivan in business mode wasn't somebody Macy imagined being okay with hesitation.

"I have a client in the other apartment," she said, jerking her head in that direction. "Is it possible to show him this one as well? I know you're not finished setting it up, but…"

I had my tongue in her mouth yesterday.

The thought shot through Macy's head so unexpectedly that it made her face instantly warm, and she hoped it didn't actually turn as red as it felt like it did. She swallowed down the panic, gave herself a mental shake, then waved Brooke in. "Oh, sure. Of course. Bring him over." *It's all good here. I'm a professional. I'm not having sexy flashbacks of you at all. Nope. Not a one.*

Brooke nodded once and went back to get her client.

"Jesus Christ on a bike," she whispered as she glanced back down at her phone.

I'll be there! She typed the text and sent it off to Tyler just as Brooke returned with both the client and Sasha Wolfe.

"Macy." Sasha's heels clicked as she crossed the hardwood toward her, her pace quick like she had a million things to do, which she likely did, and wrapped her in a hug. "Good to see you."

"You, too." And it was true. Sasha was a blend, one that was thankfully becoming more common in women in small businesses. She could be cutthroat when necessary. She knew the business world, and you would be wise to remember that. But she was also warm and kind and generous. Her company sponsored many local charities and charity events. She was the best of business and human rolled into one tall, blond, very attractive real estate agent.

Sasha held out an arm toward Brooke and the gentleman standing with her. He was maybe forty, dressed in business casual attire of navy-blue pants and a light blue oxford. His dark hair was shiny with product, but stylish, his dark goatee trimmed to precision. "Macy Carr, this is Aidan Bush. He's interested in an apartment here at Whitney Gardens, so Brooke's been showing him the one next door."

Macy stepped forward, and it took effort to focus only on Aidan Bush and not on Brooke. "Nice to meet you."

"This is amazing," Aidan said as he slowly walked around the open space. The sun chose that moment to make another appearance and lit up the whole apartment beautifully, as if it was on Sasha's payroll. "I like this layout a little better." He turned to Brooke. "Can we look at the bedroom and bathroom?"

"Absolutely."

Macy watched them walk off just as two of the movers came in carrying some artwork for the walls. "You want me to keep going?" she asked Sasha.

"Well, you're pretty well finished, it looks like, and"—she lowered her voice—"this guy could fall through."

"True."

"Might as well finish it up."

"You got it." Macy directed the guys where to leave the art, glancing over her shoulder toward the bedroom, banging her knee on the edge of an end table as she did so. "Damn it," she muttered, clenching her teeth through the pain. When she looked up, Sasha was smiling knowingly. "What?"

Sasha shrugged. "Just that if you'd been watching where you were going instead of where she went, you might have avoided that."

"Listen, I'm a klutz. We both know it."

"This is true."

"Had nothing to do with…the other thing."

Sasha tsked. "And to think I *almost* believe you."

Macy felt heat in her cheeks. "Shut up," she muttered, making Sasha laugh.

Brooke and Aidan returned from the bedroom before Sasha could say more, but her wink only heightened Macy's embarrassment.

"All good?" Sasha asked, joining them as they headed toward the door.

"Fantastic," Aidan said. "I'd like to talk numbers."

"Let's head next door where Jasmine has the paperwork," Brooke said. As they left, she turned, gave Macy a wave and a mouthed "Thanks."

Macy lifted a hand, waved back, felt the crash of disappointment fall over her. And for the very first time since Michelle passed away, Macy felt anger toward her. Anger and confusion and wonder and more anger because…she liked Brooke. She really liked her. But any acknowledgment of that suddenly weighed her down with a thin veil of guilt, which was followed by a confusion so dense, she could barely handle it.

Slowly, she let herself drop to the couch, and she sat there with her elbows on her knees, hands clasped loosely as she stared at the open, empty doorway. "What the fuck?" she whispered into the room.

She had zero idea what to do with any of it.

Chapter Seventeen

How'd it go?" Sasha had her things packed up, her light trench on, as she popped her head into Brooke's office late Monday afternoon.

Brooke had been staring out the window at the approaching evening but spun her chair around to face front. "Great. He's got fantastic credit and no contingency. We're putting in an offer." Sasha had left right after they'd shown Aidan Bush the apartments, trusted Brooke to take care of the details.

"Fantastic. Seemed like a cool guy." Sasha knocked once on the doorjamb and turned to go.

"He asked me out." *Oh God. What are you doing?*

Sasha stopped. Turned back. "Yeah?"

Unable to believe she'd just blurted it out like that—*to my boss!*—she gave a nod and added, "I told him it would have to be after things are finalized, that it would be inappropriate to..." She hesitated, didn't like the next word, but couldn't find a replacement. "Date a client."

Sasha remained in the doorway, seemingly waiting for something.

Brooke met her eyes for a beat. Two. Shook her head slightly. "What?"

"I'm just waiting for you to tell me why you had such a weird look when you told me that."

"I did?" A scrub of a hand over her face. "I don't."

"You do. Still there."

Brooke made a sound between a groan and a growl.

Sasha stepped into the office and shut the door. Set down her things. Took off her coat. Sat. She crossed her legs, clasped her hands in her lap, and said, "Talk to me."

Her resistance lasted about five seconds, and then she spilled like a dam hit with explosives. Everything came pouring out. No. *Gushing* out. She told Sasha all of it. From her first date with a woman to her relationship with Michael to her nearly instant—and shockingly unexpected—attraction to Macy. She spilled about the weekend, about Sunday's make-out session, how Macy had gotten all weird and confusing, and about Aidan Bush's very kind invitation to have drinks with him. By the time she finished, she was breathing quicker than normal, like she'd just race-walked up and down the halls for a bit. She reached for the water bottle on her desk, drank deeply from it as Sasha watched her silently.

Finally, Sasha began to shake her head. Slowly. With obvious amusement.

"I'm glad I can entertain you," Brooke said, but there was only a little bit of bite to it because she really liked Sasha.

"I am *endlessly* entertained right now," Sasha said as she switched her legs.

"Terrific."

"You two. I swear to God."

"What two?" Brooke squinted at her.

"You and Macy. Two peas in a pod, the both of you. Trying so hard to resist what's right there in front of you. Stuck in place by weird rules and pasts and crap."

"I don't know what that means."

The look Sasha gave her then made her feel like she was back in elementary school and being lazy about learning the day's lesson.

"Listen," Sasha said, sitting forward and meeting Brooke's eyes. Hers were a light blue with a dark ring around the iris. Pretty. "As a woman currently not in a relationship, I can't say much. I'm no expert. But from where I sit, the biggest obstacle in the way of anything developing is baggage."

"I mean, duh. Thanks, Captain Obvious." Brooke's chuckle bubbled up, genuine, because of course there was baggage. Everybody had it. Didn't they?

"Do you want something to develop?" Sasha's voice had softened. "Because I think she does."

Brooke blew out a breath and sat back in her chair. "I don't know if that's true. I mean, we were pretty hot and heavy last night, and then she put the brakes on so fast, I got whiplash."

"And you said yes to a date with somebody else today."

A grimace. A slow nod. "I kinda did."

"I think maybe you're both dealing with some stuff, and maybe if you can focus on it, work through it, and—oh, I don't know—*talk to each other about it*, who knows what will happen?"

Dropping her head back against her chair, Brooke groaned. "Ugh. Why must you logic me to death?"

"That's how I roll, babe." Sasha stood, put her coat back on. "My work here is done." She picked up her bag and stood there for a moment, just looking at Brooke and smiling. "Everything will work out in the end. If it hasn't worked out, it's not the end." With a shrug, she headed for the door.

"Thank you, oh wise oracle. Did you steal that from your grandmother?"

The door shut behind Sasha and Brooke was alone once again, the hazy remnants of the conversation still hanging in the air like a vapor.

Aidan Bush was nice. She found him attractive. He was successful and smart. He'd made her laugh a few times, always let her walk ahead of him, held the door. His mama had raised him right. Why wouldn't she go out with him?

As if the Universe just wanted to toy with her some more, her phone pinged. A text. She glanced at it and felt two opposite reactions at the exact same time when her brain told her it was from Macy—giddy excitement and dread.

Whatcha doin'? I'm watching Tyler play soccer.

Ambiguous enough. Apparently, Macy wasn't up for discussing the previous night either, and Brooke was okay with that. Sort of. She typed a response.

Just thinking about leaving work. Long day.

A moment went by, the bouncing gray dots teasing her. Then, *Could I entice you to join me? It's a decent night out and I have an extra Gatorade...*

Brooke smiled and replied without even an ounce of hesitation, *Tell me it's blue and I'm there.*

IT IS SO BLUE, came the response, and she laughed out loud at the all-caps of it.

She told Macy to send her the address so she knew where to go, packed up her things, and didn't stop to think twice about what she was doing. She wanted to see Macy. It really was that simple.

❖

Macy tried, rather unsuccessfully, not to constantly crane her neck as she sat in the folding chair, soccer field in front of her, parking lot behind her. It was obvious to anybody who saw her that she was waiting for somebody. That included Eva.

"She here yet?" Eva asked in a stage whisper, like it was a big secret that Brooke was going to stop by.

Macy hadn't quite thought it through that far, to the point where she was going to have to introduce Brooke to Eva. Who was her family. She was going to introduce Brooke to her family. Already.

Crap.

But then she saw her. Still in the green pantsuit, Brooke sauntered through the parking lot, across the grass—how she managed to navigate the squishiness in her heels, Macy had no idea—and Brooke's face lit up when she saw Macy. Lit up. Like the proverbial Christmas tree.

Okay, that was nice. More than nice. That was awesome.

Brooke was happy to see her.

"You made it." Macy stood, offered her chair, as she unfolded the extra one Eva always brought.

"Listen, blue Gatorade is my weakness." Brooke sat, her big brown eyes soft, tiny crinkles in the corners barely visible but endearing, and it occurred to Macy how gorgeously Brooke would age. Which was a weird damn thing to think, and she shook it the hell out of her head.

"Hi. I'm Eva, sister of that rude chick right there." Eva stuck her hand out in Brooke's direction as she gestured toward Macy with her chin. In her other hand, she held a small bottle of Gatorade. Blue. She gave it to Brooke, who smiled so widely and genuinely that Macy's knees went a little weak.

"I was getting to it," Macy said, trying to laugh off her embarrassment. "Eva is Tyler's mother." She watched Brooke shake her sister's hand, smile warmly, tell her it was nice to meet her, open the bottle, and take a sip. Then she looked out at the field.

"Where is he?" Brooke asked, squinting. "I can't find him."

Macy squatted next to her chair, arm along the back, close enough to smell the perfume that still lingered, even after the long day. Stretched out her arm. Pointed so Brooke could follow her trajectory. "He's right there, number nineteen."

"Oh, I see him."

As they watched, Tyler's teammate, Jeremy, passed him the ball. He took the shot and scored. The crowd burst into cheers as Macy threw her arms into the air, then double high-fived Eva. On the other side of Eva's chair were a handful of teenage girls, one of whom was the cute little blonde from the last game Macy watched. Kelsey, wasn't it? Macy nudged Eva, gestured to the girl with her eyes.

Eva smiled widely, then whispered, "I think he's going to ask her to the Spring Fling next week."

"What? How did I not know this?" Macy was kidding. Sort of. Tyler usually told her everything. How was it she didn't know he was thinking about asking a girl to the dance? A glance down at Brooke reminded her that she had been a bit…preoccupied. A mental note to text Tyler later went into her files.

Eva shrugged, typing out a text on her phone. "Harlan's gonna be so bummed he had to work late."

"Charlie at Mom's?" Macy asked, to which Eva nodded.

"So, Eva. What do you do?" Brooke asked, and Macy gave her points for engaging Eva in conversation.

"I'm a dentist." And they were off.

Macy watched in awe as her sister and her—what the hell should she call Brooke? her date? girl she was interested in? chick she'd made out with?—fell deep into conversation, discussing career paths for women, the challenges they faced, the extra work they always had to put in. Macy, too, could speak to all of this, but she found herself both amused and freaked enough that keeping her mouth shut and pretending to watch the game when she was really eavesdropping was just fine.

When the game ended not long after that, and the sidelines became crowded with players and parents and friends all at once, Tyler came over and threw his arms around Macy.

"Ew! You're all sweaty and gross, get off me!" It was her standard reaction, complete with disgusted faces to go with it, whenever he hugged her after a game. Which, of course, was why he did it. His laugh and the feel of his arms tightening around her brought her some relief from her guilt about being preoccupied lately. Over his shoulder, she saw Brooke watching. Smiling. And when he let go of her, he saw Brooke, too.

"Oh, hey," he said, always with the manners. "It's nice to see you again."

"You, too." Brooke held out a fist for him to bump. "Good game."

He didn't hesitate, and if his face hadn't already been flushed from the game, Macy was pretty sure he'd have blushed.

"Ty, you coming?" It was Kelsey, and she had that look of a girl who was definitely smitten. *Smitten? Is this 1957?* Macy chuckled quietly at her own thoughts, but then noticed that Ty had the same look on his face. And then Jeremy was there, too.

"Dude, let's go. I'm starving." He gave Tyler a playful shove, and that expression on Tyler's face didn't change in the least. At first. Then a cloud passed over it. Quickly. If Macy didn't know him so well, she never would have seen it. He looked to Eva.

"Mom, we're gonna get pizza, okay?"

"Be home by nine, please. You've got homework." Eva handed him a twenty.

Ty thanked her, kissed Macy on the cheek, waved to Brooke, and bounced away to be with his friends.

"Ah, to have one quarter of that energy," Brooke said, suddenly much closer to Macy's ear than expected.

"God, right? To play an entire soccer game, which—let's be honest—is basically running up and down a field for an hour, and still have the energy to bounce off like that? I would pay cash money."

"Hell, I would bottle and sell it." Brooke folded up the chair she'd been sitting in, and Macy took it from her. "Make a fortune. Buy a mansion. And a Ferrari. Never have to work again."

"You've certainly got it all planned out," Macy said with a laugh. "E, where's your car?" Eva led the way to her SUV, and they loaded the chairs in.

"I'm meeting Harlan for dinner before we pick up Charlie. Wanna join?" she asked as she opened the driver's side.

"You go ahead," Macy said and waved her off. "Next time."

Eva's eyes held a sparkle, her smile was knowing, and Macy prayed to God that Brooke didn't know her well enough yet to see those things.

"I'm starving," Brooke said as they watched Eva drive off.

"Me, too."

"Not a fan of your brother-in-law?"

Macy glanced down at her feet. "I mean, he's okay. But sometimes"—she lifted her gaze—"I'm just not in the mood for him."

"Are you in the mood for me?"

Had everybody in the parking lot disappeared? All the cars? All the people? All the sound? The entire rest of the world? "I haven't not been in the mood for you yet."

"Are your animals taken care of?"

"I stopped home before I came here."

"Good. Take me someplace to eat." Brooke held out her hand. Macy grasped it, because why wouldn't she?

Macy tugged Brooke to her car. Happily. *I mean, what else can I do, right?* "I got you. Let's go eat."

❖

"Man, they are not kidding about the name of this place." Brooke grinned as she had to set down her burger for a second time so she could wipe the juice off her hands.

"It's a staple around here. Founded in the early seventies, 'cause you can imagine how nobody in their right mind is going to name their restaurant business Hot N Juicy today." Macy picked up her cup, took a sip of her Diet Coke. "Piece of advice for you—don't google it. Ever. You'll be sorry."

Brooke laughed and Macy let the sound settle over her. It was like glitter in the air, that laugh, and Macy loved being the cause of it. "Believe me, I am very careful with my googling. Ever since my brother was thinking about getting a dog and had me looking up poodle mixes for him. Piece of advice for *you*—don't google anything where part of the name is *p-o-o*. Just don't do it."

It was Macy's turn to burst out laughing. She popped a fry into her mouth as Brooke picked up her burger and tried again.

"As a vegetarian, does it bother you when other people eat meat?" Brooke dabbed the corner of her mouth with a napkin. "I probably should've asked that before I ordered." She clenched her teeth, made an adorable *oops* face.

"Only if they're dicks about it like my brother-in-law."

"Oh no. He is?"

"He just acts like the whole thing is ludicrous, because meat is delicious and why wouldn't I want a big juicy steak, what's wrong with me?" A grimace. "He can be kind of a caveman."

Brooke's face was hesitant. "Is my burger bothering you?"

"Please." Macy scoffed. "Of course not. I wouldn't have brought you here if it was going to be an issue for me. You do you. I never push it on anybody. I never expect anybody to go out of their way to make a special meal for me. This is my choice, just for me."

"How long has it been?"

"I started after Michelle died." It shocked her how quickly she just blurted that out.

"Oh." Clearly, Brooke didn't know what to say to that, and Macy rushed to explain.

"I've always loved animals, and that's why I don't eat meat, but I'm not even sure why I started then. I've analyzed it a lot." A bitter chuckle. "I think because I didn't want to feel like I was contributing to more death. You know? It sounds kind of ridiculous, but it's all I could come up with." She shrugged, took a bite of her veggie burger.

"That makes total sense to me." It was somehow all Macy needed to hear. Because it came from Brooke. "And I'm sorry your brother-in-law is a dick about it."

"He can be a dick about a lot of things." Tyler was on her mind, and almost before she realized she probably needed to talk about it, she did. "I think my nephew might be gay."

Brooke's brows rose toward her hairline. "Tyler?"

Macy nodded, chewed a French fry.

The fact that Brooke tipped her head to the side and seemed to think about it for a moment told Macy it had already crossed her mind. "Could be?"

"You think?"

"I mean, I don't really know him. At all." Brooke shrugged, sipped her soda.

"Yeah, true." Macy inhaled, let it out slowly. "It's just…I really thought he had a thing for his buddy, Jeremy. But Eva says he's taking Kelsey to the Spring Fling dance and he's all excited about it, and he seemed to kind of light up around her."

"The little blonde? I saw that."

"So I started to think maybe I'd gotten it wrong, but then he was still extra chummy with Jeremy and he gets this look on his face…"

"I saw that, too."

Macy kept going, couldn't seem to stop herself from talking, from laying out all the things she'd been analyzing around her nephew for the past six months or so. "He loves musicals. When he comes over to my place, he wants to watch *Rent* or *Chicago* or *Les Mis*, and he asks me to keep it our secret so his dad doesn't give him a hard time."

Brooke nodded. She didn't say anything, but Macy had her attention. Every ounce of it, and it was something that made Macy relax. Knowing Brooke was listening intently was somehow…freeing.

"He's a crazy good athlete. And he's not great with the hygiene—Eva has to remind him to shower. And yes, I realize I'm being horrifically stereotypical, but I don't know what else to go on."

"Maybe he likes them both." Brooke said it as if it was the simplest thing in the world. Then she took a bite of her burger and looked expectantly at Macy.

"Like, maybe he's bi?" Surprised didn't begin to cover it. "I never even thought about that. Never occurred to me." Macy wondered if she looked as ashamed as she felt. Brooke's expression said she was used to being overlooked or uncounted.

"Or maybe he just doesn't understand yet. He's what, fifteen? Sixteen?"

"Sixteen. He'll be seventeen in a couple months, yeah." Macy's mind was racing as she popped a fry into her mouth. "I hope he knows he can talk to me…"

"Are you kidding? That kid adores you."

They finished eating, cleared their table, and headed out to Macy's car. The silence wasn't uncomfortable or awkward or anything like that as they drove. It was perfect. Right. As if they occupied close quarters like that all the time, were used to being in each other's company.

The school parking lot was empty except for Brooke's black Audi sitting alone under one of the lights. Macy glided her SUV to a stop, put it in park, then turned slightly in her seat so she could face her passenger, and that's when the silence became charged. Like a slight electricity had filled the car, made the air crackle, and caused Macy's nerve endings to be hyperaware. Being in close proximity to Brooke seemed to do that now.

Brooke faced her, and their eyes locked, stayed that way. Then she set her hand, palm up, on the center console.

Macy didn't hesitate. She laid her hand in Brooke's and watched as their fingers entwined.

Time passed. Macy had no idea how much before Brooke finally spoke.

"What happened last night?" Even though her voice was barely above a whisper, it felt loud in the dim quiet of the car's interior.

Macy swallowed. "A valid question, for sure."

Brooke rolled her lips in, bit down on them, her gaze intense. Even when Macy looked away, she could feel those eyes on her. She waited Macy out.

"You scare me." There. She'd said it. Softly. Almost too softly—

she half expected Brooke to ask her to repeat herself. But she'd said it. And it was the truth.

"Right back atcha," Brooke said, one side of her mouth quirked up in what looked in the darkness to be part smile, part grimace. Brooke waited a beat before asking, "Why?"

"Why do you scare me?" She felt Brooke's nod more than saw it. "I…" Another hard swallow. She knew exactly why—it wasn't a difficult puzzle to solve. Putting it into words and saying it loud, though? A whole other story.

"Because of Michelle?" Brooke said, obviously trying to help.

All Macy could do was nod. She had so much more to say, but the words stayed infuriatingly lodged in her throat.

"Okay. Well, if you ever want to talk to me about it, I'm here, you know." She reached for the door handle and turned toward the door, but Macy held tightly to her hand, stopping her mid-exit.

Macy nodded. She did want to talk about it. With Brooke. She absolutely did. And yet…something kept her from doing so. Instead, she sat there, squeezing Brooke's hand, looking into her eyes in a silent plea for understanding. She did not want to lose whatever chance she might have with this woman. She knew that more solidly than she knew anything in the world in that moment. And it terrified her.

Terrified her.

Before she could fully drown in her own fear, Brooke leaned toward her. No warning, no words. She simply leaned in, pressed her lips softly against Macy's. More comfort than demand. At least at first. But then…

Good Lord, it escalated quickly. No. *Macy* escalated it quickly. Deliciously so. Mouths opened. Tongues came into play. Hands grasped at clothing, dug into hair, tightened on shoulders. Brooke whispered Macy's name, which ratcheted everything up even higher until Macy was sure she would simply burst into flames.

So good…God, so amazingly good…

It was the only thought running through Macy's mind. How was it possible that she and Brooke kissed this well together? Brooke wasn't the first person since Michelle who she'd kissed, but she was the first one Macy was tempted to go any further with, the first one who didn't feel all kinds of wrong. And not just go further with sexually, but in general. Overall. In life. Despite the fear those things instilled in her, Brooke's lips kept her riveted in the moment, shoved those thoughts into a corner to be dealt with later. Maybe they could stay like this forever, just kiss like this until the end of time…

Tap, tap, tap!

They jumped apart, startled at the sound of insistent rapping on the driver's side window, to find a flashlight working hard to light up the interior of what had become a very fogged-up SUV. Macy used her sleeve and wiped a spot so she could see what turned out to be a police officer standing next to her vehicle, flashlight in one hand, the other hand parked casually on his hip.

"Oh, crap," she whispered as she powered down her window. In addition to what she could already feel were very swollen lips, she felt heat rushing to her face, which went from warm to on fire when the cop lowered his flashlight and she looked up into his weathered, close-to-retirement-age face. She cleared her throat as her entire body flushed with embarrassment. "Hi, Uncle Frank."

CHAPTER EIGHTEEN

Macy's mortification was adorable.

Brooke couldn't help it. That thought was the main one running through her head, and it was all she could do not to burst into laughter—yet—as they watched Macy's uncle Frank get in his squad car and drive away. It wasn't until he had turned out of the parking lot and his taillights were no longer visible that Macy blew out a huge breath, hung her head, and finally spoke.

"I cannot believe that just happened." Slowly, she shook her head back and forth. "I am so sorry, Brooke." Eye contact was apparently something she was avoiding, but Brooke reached over, fingers under Macy's chin, and turned her so they faced each other.

"I'm not," she whispered and pressed her lips to Macy's once more.

Macy pulled away just enough to look her in the eye, and she could see the relief on Macy's face. Relief and more. Surprise. A glimmer of joy. And the biggest one, the one that was the clearest: desire. Macy wanted her as much as she wanted Macy. She'd bet her entire financial portfolio on it.

It was time to do something about it.

"Take me home with you." She said it softly, a command rather than a question, and watched with satisfaction as Macy's brows rose in surprise. Then her eyes darkened. She could see them even in the dim light of the parking lot.

Macy glanced over her shoulder at Brooke's car, sitting empty and alone.

"I can get it tomorrow."

Apparently, that was all the convincing Macy needed. She turned a heated gaze back toward her and shifted the car into drive.

The ride was quick and silent. Brooke kept her hand on Macy's thigh as they drove, could feel the tightening of her muscle, and squeezed it in acknowledgment. They both kept their eyes forward. Brooke could feel her own heart pounding in her chest and wondered if Macy could hear it, too.

Still no words were spoken as they exited the SUV in Macy's driveway and headed into her house. The cacophony of dogs welcoming them in was unfamiliar to Brooke, but it made her smile, as did the look of love and happiness that fell over Macy's face as she squatted and greeted each of her animals. When she turned back to Brooke, though, that dark look of arousal still sat in her eyes, and Brooke swallowed hard. God, she wanted her. So badly it was making her entire body ache.

"I just need to let them out," Macy said quietly. When she stood, she reached a hand out, touched her fingertips to Brooke's face, and it was like a sizzle of electricity buzzed along her skin.

"Hurry," she whispered.

Macy's bedroom was so very Macy. If Brooke's mind and—more urgently—her body hadn't been preoccupied, she'd have taken time to wander, explore things, pick them up and examine them, get to know Macy better through the items that were important enough to her to be kept in her bedroom.

But now wasn't the time.

Macy had led her into the room by the hand, told the dogs to settle—shockingly, they did—and then she turned, and the wait was over. Brooke yanked her closer, crushed their mouths together in a flurry of want and need and impatience. They kissed. They'd kissed deeply before, but this? This was as deep and as thorough as it got. So incredibly sexy. Tongues danced, the soft sounds of their lips filled the room, and Brooke could not get enough. A soft moan sounded, and she wasn't sure if it came from Macy or her own throat, but she didn't care. Her hands found their way under Macy's shirt, and then she *was* the one who moaned because the feel of that soft warm skin against her fingers was undeniable bliss. She wrapped her arms around Macy more tightly, her hands splayed across her back where her fingers found the clasp of Macy's bra, and she didn't think twice before unfastening it.

Macy gave a surprised little gasp and pulled back long enough to catch Brooke's eye.

"You okay?" Brooke asked.

Macy nodded and with a mischievous glint in her eyes said, "I'm just impressed by how quickly you undid my bra."

"Listen, so am I," Brooke said, and they both laughed, still close enough to breathe the same air. Their laughter died down, and Brooke studied Macy's face. While she hesitated to ask the question because she didn't want to derail something that felt this good, she knew she had to. Inhaling a quiet breath, she bolstered herself for whatever the answer might be. "You're sure about this?"

Macy's entire expression softened, her smile was tender, and she reached her hand up, touched her fingertips to Brooke's lips. Her answer was to slip that hand around to the back of Brooke's neck, dig her fingers into her hair, and pull her head down, resuming their kiss, but increasing the heat by a hundred. The jacket of her pantsuit was tugged over her shoulders and off, and then Macy's hands were pulling her silk tank over her head. The lace bra followed right behind, and it occurred to Brooke that she'd unleashed a monster. A sexy, demanding, dominant monster. A monster in the best of ways. And then Macy closed her mouth over Brooke's nipple, and all creative wording was driven out of her head by sensation.

Colors exploded behind Brooke's eyelids. She'd never, ever felt this way with someone. This hot. This sexy. This *wanted*. It was all consuming. The only description that came to her sex-addled brain, the only coherent thought she could hold on to. It was all consuming. The good kind of all consuming. Sizzling pleasure shot from her nipple to her center and back, controlled solely by Macy's mouth.

Was she walking backward? Dimly aware of movement, she was only clear on it when the backs of her legs hit Macy's bed. Abandoning her breasts for a moment, Macy looked up at her as she unfastened her pants, let them drop in a puddle of green around her ankles. Brooke swallowed hard at the things she saw in those eyes. Confidence. Dominance. Depth. Want.

So much confidence.

So much want.

Brooke was used to being the person in control of things, but that was not the case in that moment. She felt like a puddle of arousal as she watched Macy hook her fingers into the waistband of her bikinis. Macy's gorgeous dark eyes never left hers, and she squatted slowly, sliding the underwear down Brooke's legs—which were now trembling, by the way, actually *trembling*. Macy stood again and took a step back. Two. Three. Stood there looking at her, and that gaze was like nothing

Brooke had ever experienced. It was like Macy was touching her with her mind, with her eyes, pinning her in place like a butterfly on a board. She could feel it, she swore to God, her entire body flushing with heat as her thighs continued to quake.

"Macy," she whispered. "Please."

"My God, you're beautiful," came Macy's reply as her eyes kept roaming. Stopping on a breast, a leg, the smooth apex of her thighs. Macy undressed herself the rest of the way, her gaze staying on Brooke's, holding her there, waiting. Wanting. God, the wanting.

And then they were both naked.

There in Macy's moonlit bedroom, they stood quietly, the only sound that of their ragged breathing. Macy was gorgeous, curvier than Brooke had expected, with rounded hips and breasts that her palms and fingers suddenly itched to touch. Shoulders she wanted to lick.

"Macy." Brooke tried again, certain she was about to burst into flame, but still somehow held in place.

Macy covered the distance between them, and they stood face-to-face. Macy was slightly shorter, and she lifted her chin to compensate.

"Please," Brooke repeated. Macy's closeness seemed to have freed her to move, and she did, setting her hands on Macy's bare hips, digging her fingers into the flesh there, then sliding them up Macy's sides and around to those breasts. As predicted, they fit perfectly in her hands, and Macy's breath hitched when Brooke ran her thumbs slowly over the prominent nipples.

As if things had been moving in slow motion—and it had kind of felt that way to her—they now switched back to regular speed, and Macy pushed into her, forcing her back onto the bed.

And they were kissing again. Hard. Deep. Like there was nobody else in the world, and they had until the end of time. Macy's weight was on her, and nothing had ever felt more spectacular than that. Brooke wrapped herself around Macy, her legs around her waist, hand in her hair, tongue in her mouth, until they were almost one entity, moving together in a gentle rhythm. Brooke couldn't get enough. Her hands were everywhere on Macy, and still she wanted more. And she wanted Macy's hands everywhere on her. And just as she had that thought, she felt Macy's fingers between her legs, felt them slick through the hot wetness there. Her back arched as a gasp was pulled from her throat.

"Oh God, Macy..." She felt Macy trailing down her body, using her tongue to lead the way, down the side of her neck, along her collarbone, between her breasts—with a slight detour to suck quickly on each nipple, which tugged more gasping from her—down her stomach, and around her belly button. Macy's hands were on the backs of her thighs as she lifted, positioned her legs on either side of her head, and gave Brooke no time to brace before Macy used the flat of her tongue in one long swipe, from bottom to top, that had Brooke grappling for something, anything to hold on to. Blankets, pillows, the headboard, anything to keep her from flying off into oblivion as Macy worshipped her body using her mouth, filled her with waves of pleasure she'd never experienced before, pushing fingers into her, setting up a rhythm that was merciless in its perfection, sending her to heights beyond anything she'd imagined—and then toppling her over the edge into the most beautiful explosion of sensation. She arched like a bow, every muscle taut, sounds forced out of her that she knew would embarrass her later. Macy had switched to only fingers by then, and the entire time, quietly in the background, she could hear Macy's voice, endlessly, softly coaxing her.

"Come on. Come for me, baby. That's it. I've got you. Let go. Let it go. You're so beautiful…"

Had she blacked out? She honestly wasn't sure as she finally came back to herself, a gentle tingling running through her limbs, a fluttering in her belly, and a warm, wonderful weight to her body as she settled back down into the comforter. When she finally opened her eyes, Macy was looking at her from between her thighs, smiling like the cat that ate the canary and then told the canary's parents about it. Brooke reached toward her, wiggled her fingers.

"Come up here."

Macy obeyed, taking her time working her way up Brooke's body again, using her tongue, her fingers, causing twitches and leaving goose bumps in her wake, until she was lying on her side, head propped in her hand, looking down at Brooke with the darkest, sexiest eyes she'd ever seen.

She thought she'd had so much to say, but the words seemed to evaporate like morning dew in the summer sun as she got lost in those eyes. Maybe she didn't need to say anything at all. Instead, she reached up, laid her palm against the warmth of Macy's smooth cheek, and held those eyes with her own. She did her best to channel everything she was thinking, everything she was feeling, into that one gaze.

Macy rested her hand over Brooke's, pressed her cheek closer, and her eyes became wet. Brooke could only tell because the moon chose that moment to peek out from behind a cloud, and she could see the unshed tears glistening.

"I know," Macy said.

It was all Brooke needed.

❖

Deep blue to indigo to magenta to…

Macy watched the color of the sky change as dawn tiptoed closer. She was warm. Sated. Comfortable. The soundtrack of the early morning around her was familiar—Jellybean purring from the foot of the bed, Pete snuffling in his sleep on his dog bed, the soft scraping of Angus running in his dreams where he slept under the bed. But there was a new addition. It was soft. Rhythmic. Made her go all mushy and warm inside. She turned her head just slightly.

Brooke was sleeping deeply—unsurprising, given the physical workout they'd finished only a couple hours ago. Her deep, even breaths blended seamlessly with the rest of the room's soothing sounds.

She turned her whole body so she was lying on her side, could get an eyeful even in the predawn light. Brooke was just as beautiful asleep as she was in the midst of an orgasm. There was no arguing that. Macy had never felt skin so smooth, had never experienced such response. Brooke was her perfect match in bed. Her brain tossed her several images, memories of their night, Brooke's hands on her, her mouth doing indescribably erotic things to Macy's nipples, fingers pushing inside her, stretching her, claiming her, owning her. It was the sexiest, most sensual night of her life. There wasn't a doubt in her mind as she lay there and watched Brooke sleep, her lips slightly parted, her red hair tousled and sexy, her cheeks still a little bit flushed from the last time she came. She reached out and brushed some hair off Brooke's forehead.

Peaceful.

An elusive concept and not a word Macy had much experience with over the past couple of years, but it was what she felt in that moment. The irony that her surprise about feeling peaceful overrode the peace only made her smile widen. This woman…

The sky had pinkened up, and Pete began to stir. He stretched his long golden legs, and when he saw that Macy was awake, his tail—which not only had broom qualities, but also had drumstick qualities—

began to wag, tapping a gentle rhythm against the floor. As it happened every morning, one by one, her animals awakened. To prevent them from waking Brooke, she slipped quietly, reluctantly, from under the covers, stepped into leggings and a baggy sweatshirt, and herded them all out of the room, closed the door behind her, and followed them down the stairs.

Preparing breakfast for her zoo was such a routine that she could do it without much focus, which was a good thing because the only thing on her mind was Brooke. Their night, this morning, what happened now. All things that rolled and turned and swirled in her head. She examined each emotion, each feeling, mentally held them in her hands even as her actual hands scooped kibble and shredded chicken and added sweet potatoes for the dogs. The cats got kibble and a little salmon. Once all bowls were down on the floor and the house was filled with the sounds of breakfast being gobbled, she put the coffee on.

Did Brooke eat breakfast?

When Macy realized she didn't know, she felt herself smile, knew it was one of the many things she wanted to learn about Brooke. Empty mug in hand, halfway out of the cabinet, she stopped. Held the mug in midair as something hit her. Not an emotion she had, but one she didn't, one that was missing.

Guilt. Where was the guilt?

What the hell?

It took a soft whine from Pete to yank her out of her trance, and she blinked rapidly, gave her head a quick shake, and opened the back door, and all three dogs trooped out to the backyard.

She didn't feel guilty, and when that sentence ran clearly through her head, she moved quickly into the living room, picked up the photo that had stopped her first make-out session with Brooke, and stared at it. She and Michelle kept smiling, kept looking stupidly happy, yet the guilt didn't come surging in, didn't wash over her like an ocean wave.

Gently, tenderly, she ran her fingertips over Michelle's face, then set the photo frame back down.

Lucas would call this progress.

She grinned, knowing she'd need to call him later, tell him what had happened, how it felt, ask if she should be worried. But for now...a huge inhale of breath, filling her lungs to capacity before letting it out slowly, then walking to the door to let in her animal menagerie. After breakfast and a trip outside, they were wide-awake and ready for the day, which meant Pete galloped through the house with his favorite stuffed squirrel in his mouth—and gallop he did, sounding more like a horse than a dog—Angus close on his heels, while Priscilla watched them with distaste, too prim and proper and regal to stoop to such menial things as playing. Jellybean had retreated to her cat tree to guard the front yard from the very real dangers of birds and squirrels. Captain Jack looked up at Macy with his one good eye, still at his bowl, where he slowly chewed. He took his time, was always the last one finished eating. Macy liked to think he savored his food.

The quiet, soothing soundtrack of her early morning had morphed, as it did every day, into the energetic, playful soundtrack of the daytime, and Macy loved it. She'd never really understood the concept of a heart warming until the first time she'd watched all of her animals at once, just after breakfast. Yes, it could be chaotic. Yes, when one animal was sick or off their game, it affected the others and worried her. But it was worth it to her. She loved them all, would take a bullet for any of them. Michelle had always rolled her eyes at that, not in a mean-spirited way, but in an *Isn't my girlfriend adorable?* way. They'd only had Pete and Captain Jack then. When Michelle was gone, Macy had needed more life in her house. She understood that now, but then? When she brought home another dog? And then another cat? And then one more dog? She wasn't quite as clear.

Pete shot by her and slid on the hardwood as he cornered, knocking a dining room chair up against the table leg with a loud *thwack*. Macy shook her head with affection, then set to work doctoring two cups of coffee. If Brooke hadn't been awakened by the door opening and closing, the table crashing probably did it. She headed upstairs and shut the gate at the bottom behind her—the one she'd installed to keep Angus from going upstairs during the day and wreaking havoc, which he'd done more than once—leaving the animals downstairs. Unhappy whines followed her up the stairs and into the hall, and she pushed the door to the bedroom open gently with her foot.

Brooke was awake. On her back, arms up and hands behind her head, looking out the window as the new day dawned. Macy had the sudden need to swallow hard at the sight. Morning-after Brooke was nothing short of downright fucking sexy, and when she turned her head, her dark eyes met Macy's, and Macy found herself bracing. For what, she wasn't sure. But she was ready.

"Hi," Brooke said softly, and the smile that lit up her face...Macy felt like it actually lit up the entire room. She felt everything in her relax and unbrace. Just like that.

"Hey." She stepped to the bed, sat on the edge, held out a cup. "I come bearing gifts."

"Oh my God, you're amazing." Brooke pushed herself to a sitting position, self-consciously pulling the sheet up to cover her breasts. She seemed to realize the silliness of the gesture and blushed prettily.

"Yeah, I've seen all those already," Macy said, waving her hand in front of Brooke's torso. "You don't have to cover them up. In fact, I insist that you don't."

"Listen, I'm a lady," Brooke replied. She sipped from her cup, her eyes smiling over the rim. "Gotta leave something to the imagination."

Oh, early morning sexy flirting was *good*.

"I will be doing nothing *but* imagining today. Remembering. Flashing back…" Heat coursed through her body even as she watched Brooke's blush deepen. She sipped her coffee, felt the warmth and the caffeine enter her system, her gaze never leaving Brooke's face. "You're so beautiful." The words were out before she thought about them, before she even realized she was going to say them. And that was okay. Nothing had ever been truer.

Brooke smiled, cast her eyes downward for a moment before glancing back up. "You're one to talk. My God."

And those words went straight into her, warmed her from the inside, wrapped themselves around her heart, and made themselves a home there. She shifted so she was on the bed, sitting next to Brooke with her back against the headboard, and slipped her legs under the covers. Without missing a beat, Brooke put her leg over Macy's, and they sat there together, sipping coffee and watching the sunrise. Macy tipped her head, rested it on Brooke's shoulder, and felt her press a kiss to the top of it.

The sheer perfection of the moment was not lost on Macy, and she absently wondered if there was a way to stay right there, just like that, for the rest of her life.

CHAPTER NINETEEN

B rooke was never late.

She just wasn't. Her father had instilled in her at a very young age that being late to a meeting of any kind showed you had little respect for the other person. That had wormed its way into her brain and set up camp there. Built a house. Moved in permanently.

There was no meeting that morning. It was true. And she had no set time she had to be in the office. But she had her own set of rules, one of which was to be at her desk and working by nine. Of course, when a beautiful woman kept you up most of the night, taking your body to heights of pleasure you didn't even know existed, chances were, you were going to be a little late. Besides, the sex hangover was overshadowing any stress about tardiness, and she was pretty sure she floated into the building and down the hall to her office without actually touching feet to floor.

She hadn't expected this. Any of it. Her head was so full, her heart even fuller, and she wasn't sure what came next. Order was her thing. Order. Organization. Control. The night with Macy? Not only unexpected, but all on her. Yeah, that was a thing she was going to need to revisit because, wow, she'd had no idea she had it in her to make such a bold move as to demand to be taken home by somebody. She glanced at the vague reflection of herself in the window of her office as she approached the door. Who was she? Who was this woman? Where had she come from?

"Hey there." Sasha must have been right on her heels, because she spoke before Brooke even set down her things.

"Good morning," Brooke said and wondered if she sounded overly cheery. Because that's how she felt. There was a smile on her face—she could feel it. It had been there all morning. It was new. She liked it.

"I need a favor." Sasha took a seat and gave Brooke time to shed her jacket, wake up her computer, everything but get coffee, which she really wanted, but could wait on for now.

"Of course. What's up?"

"Can you cover an open house for me this weekend? Just from two to four?" Sasha sighed. "It's residential, and I know that's not really your thing, but I'm in a bind. The agent taking care of it just had an emergency appendectomy, and I asked Brennan, but he made an excuse, because of course he did." She rolled her eyes to show how that had gone over, then immediately seemed to catch herself. "You know what? Forget I said that, and pretend you didn't notice my eye roll. That was terribly unprofessional of me." She groaned and stood, and Brooke wondered if she had something going on at home, wondered if she should ask.

"Of course. It's no problem at all. This Sunday?" With a nod, Sasha rattled off the details, and Brooke put them into her phone.

"You may not see much traffic. It has promise, but it's in a less-than-desirable neighborhood, and it needs some work. The owners are out of town, so you can take your time getting in and out, so there's that. If you could just man it for the two hours, I'll owe you."

"You owe me nothing. It's my job." Brooke was happy to help out her boss. Small businesses couldn't succeed if their employees weren't team players. Sasha thanked her and turned to go. Catching her at the door, Brooke asked, "Sasha? Everything okay?"

For a split second, Brooke was sure Sasha was going to turn around, sit back down, and unload. For a split second, it really looked like she wanted to. Instead, she smiled softly. "Totally fine."

Brooke wasn't sure whether to believe her, didn't know her well enough to decide one way or the other, but let it go. Alone again, her good mood was still there, and Brooke still felt like she might be floating. She got herself situated and sat down at her desk. Just as she opened her email, her phone pinged an incoming text.

I miss you already.

Macy. Good Lord, how was it possible that a simple four words could set her heart to pounding, her stomach to fluttering, and make her wet? In an instant.

Same. So much same. She sent it back.

Dinner tonight?

What she wanted to type was *Yes! Yes! Yes!* But she also realized she needed to at least try to play it somewhat cool. "Yeah, it's way too late for that," she muttered to herself with a grin as she shook her head and typed out *I'd love to.*

Come here? I'll cook.

That fluttering wave hit her in an instant, low in her body. What the hell had happened to her? She almost didn't recognize herself. Sex wasn't a thing that had ever moved to the forefront of her mind, that dominated every waking moment, but right now? That's exactly what was happening. All she could think about was being in bed with Macy again. Kissing her. Undressing her. Whispering naughty words in her ear. How the hell was she going to get through her workday?

Sounds perfect.

They ironed out the time. Macy had a house to stage that day and a couple client meetings, and their paths weren't set to cross at all. Probably a good thing, since she needed to find a way to cool down her body and quiet her mind. This weird, wonderful feeling that was sitting in the pit of her stomach, coursing out through her body, along her limbs, out to her extremities, like a gentle tingling? It was strange. New. Something she hadn't felt in a long time.

She was pretty sure it might be happiness.

❖

"What's going on with you?" Lucas eyed Macy suspiciously. Squinted. Tilted his head one way, then the other as if examining a puzzle. "You're different. Something's different."

"I don't know what you mean," she replied with a shrug as she walked through Everything Old Is New Again and stopped at the counter where he stood. "Where's the table? Sounds like it'd be perfect for the house I'm staging next week."

He didn't respond. Instead, he kept looking at her. No. Scrutinizing. Studying.

She squirmed. "Stop that."

A gasp. Sudden and loud. Lucas pressed a hand to his chest as his eyes went comically wide, and he pointed at her, said loudly, "You got laid!"

The flood of heat rushed through her body so fast, Macy thought she might faint. She looked around in panic to see who else might have heard, but saw nobody within earshot. Then she turned back to him, shock all over her face, she was sure. "Oh my God, how the hell could you possibly know that?"

"Why do you bother questioning my abilities?"

"I just don't understand how you could possibly know that. Are you stalking me, Creepy McCreeperson?"

"Stop trying to change the subject. Spill."

He waited.

She waited.

He waited longer.

"Damn it." She shook her head, unable to stop the soft laugh, wondering if she'd ever understand how Lucas knew her so well.

"Was it Brooke? Please say yes." He held his hands together in prayer. "Oh please, oh please, oh please."

She sighed in defeat. "It was Brooke."

He clapped like a delighted child and squealed with glee. "Sam owes me ten dollars."

"Wait, what? You guys bet on my sex life?" Macy blinked at him, torn between humorous surprise and insult.

"Bitch, please. We've been betting on your sex life for months now."

"Well, it's a good thing for you that I'm too damn happy to be pissed off right now." It was true. She pointed at him. "But we're gonna revisit this, mister."

"Then you'd better bring Eva. She owes me twenty."

Macy gasped. "You all suck."

"You got laid."

Her sigh was downright dreamy. "I really, really did."

Lucas propped his elbows on the counter, his chin in his hands. "Tell me all about it."

She did. She started with the soccer game, the way Brooke had looked walking toward her, still dressed in work clothes, how they'd gone to get burgers, all the talking and getting to know each other, the make-out session.

"Oh my God, it's like a teen movie," Lucas said with delight when Macy mentioned getting caught by her uncle. "Also, you know your whole family likely knows now, right?"

A grimace because yeah, she'd thought the same thing. "It's not like I'd hide it, but I would've liked to tell my family a little slower. On my terms."

"Yeah, you gotta let that go, honey. I'm surprised you haven't heard from your mom yet."

Macy grinned, despite the embarrassment. "I fully expect a text by noon."

They laughed about that, but then Lucas seemed to sober a bit, grow serious. "And? How was it?" He was her best friend, her confidant, and he knew things about her that nobody else did. He also knew that this had been the first time she'd had sex since Michelle died. It was a big deal. A really big one.

"Oh, Lucas…" She sighed, joined him in the elbow propping, and just gazed off. "It was…" She shook her head as she recalled her night with Brooke. The passion of it. The perfection. *My God, the orgasms…* "It was amazing." She looked at him with intensity. "I don't know if I'd have had the balls to ask her to come home with me. I mean, I wanted her to, but getting those words out? I don't know."

"So it was her suggestion?"

Macy nodded.

"What did she say?"

Recalling how dark Brooke's eyes had gotten, the sexy catch in her throat, the words she said just turned Macy on all over again, and she swallowed down the sudden surge of arousal. "She said, *Take me home with you.*"

Lucas made a growling sound and let his head fall to the surface of the counter. "Oh my *God*, that is so fucking sexy."

Heat washed through her system. Again. Seemed like her body had some kind of inner thermostat that was triggered by her flashbacks of the previous night. "It really, really was."

"And it was…good?" With this question, Lucas seemed more gentle. Sensitive. His eyes were soft with concern and an underlying seriousness that Macy could clearly see.

Time to lighten the mood. She moaned, let herself go boneless, and humorously collapsed to the ground in a damn good impression of a puddle of goo.

Lucas's laugh cut through the air. "I'll take that as a yes."

"Yes," Macy said as she hauled herself back to her feet. "So much yes."

"It's the stoic ones you gotta watch out for," he said, pointing at her. "Still waters and all that." He held her gaze as they smiled at each other. Then he reached across and tapped his forefinger against her temple. "And how are you doing here?"

"Shockingly well." It was true. Surprisingly so. "I half expected to wake up this morning racked with guilt, but..."

"You weren't."

"I wasn't." She scratched at a spot on the counter with her thumbnail. "And I want to delve in and way overthink it."

"Because that's what you do."

"Exactly. But I haven't." She looked up at him then. "Is that weird?"

"That you've been alone for more than three years, finally let yourself enjoy a night with somebody, and don't feel guilty about it? Hell, no."

She needed to hear that, and she didn't realize how much until Lucas had actually said the words. Unexpected tears sprang up in her eyes. The second Lucas saw them, his breath hitched, and he hurried around the counter to wrap her in his arms. Another thing she didn't realize she needed until it was happening.

"You're the best, Lucas." She meant it.

"I know."

"I'm keeping you."

"You should." He held her for another beat before letting go and returning to his spot behind the counter. "When do you see her again?"

Macy couldn't hide her smile. Didn't want to. "Tonight. I'm cooking her dinner at my place."

Lucas clapped his hands in quiet applause, his gaze traveling to the two women walking along the wall of the shop, apparently browsing. He looked back at Macy with a sparkle in his eye and asked, "Do you need help figuring out what to make?"

"Why do you think I'm here?"

The way his face lit up was totally worth the price of admission. "Let's knock the socks—and hopefully other articles of clothing—off that girl, shall we?"

CHAPTER TWENTY

The day was gorgeous—sunny, breezy, warm for May—so Macy allowed the dogs to linger out in the backyard. Angus, always the terrier, was nose-to-the-ground, giving the perimeter a good once-over. Pete was in the center of the lawn, and it was thankfully dry because he was on his back and rolling like it was the only thing he ever wanted to do in life. Priscilla lounged on the deck in the early evening sun, surveying her kingdom.

Inside the house, in the kitchen particularly, the atmosphere was slightly less relaxed but smelled delicious, the mouthwatering combination of garlic and basil lingering in the air. Lucas had suggested a meal of linguini with fresh ingredients: parsley, basil, garlic, tomatoes, parmesan, olive oil. He said it was a dish that tasted amazing, seemed complicated, but wasn't. A loaf of fresh Italian bread and a bottle of sauvignon blanc topped off the menu.

Macy had everything ready to go so that all she had to do was some quick cooking when her phone pinged. For a split second, dejection filled her because she was certain it must be Brooke canceling. But it wasn't. It was Eva.

Fogging up the car windows in the high school parking lot? What are you, 17? A laughing emoji followed. And then five more.

Macy winced, then pressed her lips together and nodded because she'd been waiting for this, totally expecting it. Uncle Frank had apparently filed his report, likely with her parents. She sent back no words, just an emoji of a woman face-palming herself.

Heard from Mom yet?

Blissfully, no. A wink emoji.

It was Brooke, right? Like Eva didn't know this already.

Yep. A blushing emoji.

You should know that Ty overheard and told me to send you this. A fist-bump emoji appeared, and Macy couldn't help but laugh.

They went back and forth a couple times, the tone staying light and fun. She was glad about that. Deep and emotional weren't things she was prepared to deal with at the moment, and when the dogs began barking and there was a knock on the side door, she sighed in relief and signed off, trying to ignore that her heart rate had kicked up to triple time.

A deep steadying breath, a smooth of her hands down her sides, and Macy opened the door.

"Hi." Brooke stood there, smiling and looking nothing short of breathtaking. She must've gone home after work because she was dressed much more casually than her office attire. Faded jeans with a rip in one knee, a ribbed black Henley under a light jacket, unbuttoned to a spot that made Macy thank the stars above for the peek of cleavage it afforded her. Hair pulled back into a ponytail, a few wisps framing her face. Bright eyes and cheeks with a soft pink blossom on each. "Can I come in, or do you just want to stare at me for a while?"

A few weeks ago, those words would've mortified Macy, flushed her a deep red, and sent her scurrying off to pull herself together. Now? They did things to her. Low in her body. Really low. "Shh. I'm staring."

Brooke snorted a laugh and gently pushed her way in, handing Macy a bottle of wine and placing a quick kiss on her lips as she did so. "Step aside, ogler. I'm starving and it smells absolutely *divine* in here." She took off her jacket, draped it over a dining room chair, and went straight for the back door like she'd done it a thousand times before. Suddenly, dogs were happily surrounding her, and Macy felt her heart squeeze in her chest when Brooke sat right down on the floor and let Angus bring her a tennis ball to throw while Pete circled around her and around her and around her some more, his huge, fluffy tail whacking her in the head on the regular. Priscilla sniffed carefully, stood, and seemed to study her for a moment, then made a decision and hopped into Brooke's lap.

She looks good like that.

The thought echoed through Macy's head, and it made her grin so widely, she assumed she looked either goofy or slightly insane. But Brooke on her floor, covered by Macy's beloved animals, was almost more than her heart could take. It was perfect.

And it didn't scare her.

What the hell was that about?

Opting not to dwell on it, she clapped her hands once. "Okay, guys, don't smother her." When Brooke looked up at her, eyes shining, she asked, "Wine?"

"Is that a real question?" No moves to get up off the floor were made.

"I will take that as an *I would love some wine, Macy, you're the best, thank you so much.*" She winked, opened the chilled bottle of sauvignon blanc, poured two glasses, and delivered one to the dining room table. "Pete's tail has been known to clear a room, so I'm putting your wine up here." She looked down again at the gorgeous woman on the floor being piled on by her dogs and just shook her head. In the best of ways.

A few moments later, she was in the kitchen sautéing garlic in olive oil, and the water was close to boiling when Brooke's arms encircled her from behind. "Hi," she said quietly in Macy's ear.

"Well, hello there. Have the dogs finished monopolizing you?"

"For now." A gentle kiss to the side of her neck made Macy's skin erupt in goose bumps. Apparently, Brooke noticed. "Are you cold?" she teased. Another kiss to the other side.

"No." Macy's voice was a croak, and it amused them both.

"Can I help with dinner?" Brooke asked, still wrapping her up.

"Nope. You're the guest. You can sit there and look pretty while I cook." With her chin, she indicated the small bistro table for two tucked in the corner.

"Don't tell me what to do." The humorous twinkle in her eye emphasized the playfulness of the words.

Macy felt the absence of Brooke's body heat immediately as she let go, stepped back against the counter opposite the stove, and slid herself up so her butt settled on it. Wineglass in hand, she casually swung her feet and watched Macy, and nothing had ever been sexier. "Because you do what you want?"

"Exactly."

Macy dropped linguini into the water, set the timer, added diced tomatoes and a tiny bit of vegetable broth to the sauté pan. She swore to God she could feel Brooke's eyes on her. "And what do you want to do?" she asked quietly, not daring to look.

"Well, I am currently entertaining a very sensual fantasy of undressing you and having my way with you right here on the kitchen counter."

The shock of arousal electrified Macy's body. Her stomach

tightened, a pleasant shiver ran down the back of her neck, and her bikinis became instantly damp. "God," she whispered.

"But dinner smells so good, and I'm really enjoying the view from where I am, so I think I'll bide my time."

This time, Macy did turn to look at Brooke, whose eyes were darker than normal and focused directly on hers as she lifted her wineglass to her lips and took a sip. "You're killing me," Macy said very softly.

"Not yet I'm not. But give me time."

Sweet Lord in heaven, how was she going to get through this dinner without spontaneously combusting?

❖

"How do you feel about sitting by a fire?" Macy asked. She had no idea how attractive she was. Brooke was sure of it. It wasn't the first time she'd thought it, and it seemed even more prominent in her brain now as they stood there in the kitchen. The dishes were done, the dishwasher loaded, the counters clean. Macy, in soft-washed jeans and a long-sleeved T-shirt with a print of Pooh and Piglet that was so faded, it was almost indistinguishable, her brown hair caught up in a messy ponytail, wiped her hands on a dish towel as she looked at Brooke and waited.

"I mean, what kind of fire are we talking about? A campfire? A fireplace fire? A house burning down? I need specifics."

Macy tossed the dish towel onto the counter as she headed toward the sliding glass door. "I have a fire pit out there. It's best on chilly nights. We can stoke up the fire and sit on the love seat there with blankets, and we can talk and have hot chocolate for dessert…" Her voice trailed off as if she was second-guessing her suggestion, but Brooke rushed to reassure her, hated the uncertainty that clouded her face just then.

"I think that sounds fabulous. Let's do that." She held up a finger. "Though I have one request."

"What's that?" Macy gave her her full attention.

"Let's go dancing this weekend."

"Like, to a club?"

"Exactly like that. I would take you, but I have no idea where to go…" She shrugged. "Take me to a club."

"Okay." Macy's blush surprised Brooke, but then Macy added

softly, a little shyly even, "I'd like to be out in public with you," and Brooke blushed, too, she was pretty sure.

Yeah. That was the exact right thing to say.

Fifteen minutes later, the fire was burning cheerfully, and Angus and Pete were stretched out in the grass, Priscilla opting to stay inside like the princess she was. Macy's outdoor love seat was wrought iron with surprisingly comfortable cushions, and Macy brought out a fleecy blanket that covered them nicely as long as they sat close.

"This is a pretty subtle trick you've got going here with the blanket." Brooke scootched closer so that they were touching from hip to knee, and her shoulder was snug against Macy's.

"Why, whatever do you mean?" Macy's exaggerated slow blinks made her laugh. She liked this version of Macy, this flirty side. It had taken Macy a little while to relax, to enjoy the game. At first, she just seemed shocked and uncertain what to say back, which was actually super charming, Brooke thought. Once she'd had a glass of wine, though, she'd loosened up, played along, and now? In the dark by the fire drinking big mugs of hot chocolate and pressed up against each other? Brooke felt like her whole body was on fire, and it had nothing at all to do with the fire pit.

"Can I ask you something?" The question was out before Brooke even examined whether or not she should ask it or take them down the path she was facing.

Macy turned to her, brown eyes reflecting the firelight. "Of course you can."

"How are you? Around this? Around us?" One finger moved between them, and she squinted at her own vagueness. It was something she'd been wondering, had wanted to touch on, but hadn't known how. Tonight, apparently, she just blurted things out.

Macy stared at the flames, and Brooke watched as they flickered over her face, bathing her creamy skin in warm tones of orange. She took a long time to answer, and Brooke wasn't sure if she was organizing her thoughts or just wasn't going to say anything at all. But finally, she shifted her gaze, met Brooke's eyes, and smiled. "I'm actually doing great around us. Really, really great."

Her words warmed Brooke more than any fire could. "Yeah?"

"Yeah."

"Good. That's good." She leaned toward Macy until their lips met, and this particular kiss wasn't passion. It wasn't sex. It was warmth and joy and… No, Brooke wasn't ready to go *there* yet, but it was just around the corner and she knew it. Felt it coming like a train in the distance. She liked Macy. She liked Macy a lot. *A lot*, but she wasn't quite ready to verbalize it. She'd settle for the kissing. Because kissing Macy was so many things. It was blissful and soft and wet and hot and dripping…

Dripping?

She pulled away just as Macy muttered, "What the—? Oh, for God's sake…" and righted her tipped mug, groaning at the small splashes of hot chocolate on the ground that Pete and Angus had both discovered and were cleaning up with their tongues before Macy shooed them away. With a glance up at Brooke, she lifted one shoulder and said, "Evidently, kissing you makes me spill stuff."

"Oh no, don't blame me. I've seen you spill plenty of stuff when *not* kissing me."

Macy stood, seemingly to assess how much spillage there was and to keep the dogs from licking up any more chocolate. A good-sized puddle was visible on the ground, a little more on the blanket, and she sighed. "You make a fine point, my friend."

Brooke stood, too, gathered up the blanket. "I'll toss this in the wash."

"Boys. Leave it." Macy shooed the dogs back into the house, and Brooke followed her. Once inside, the blanket tossed down the basement stairs to be washed, Macy turned to her and frowned. "Well, that was an unfortunate end to something lovely."

Brooke gathered her things, then reached out, tucked some hair behind Macy's ear. "It's perfectly okay. It's a school night anyway, and we both know if things had gone further, neither of us would get much sleep tonight." Just the thought sent the fluttering through her belly and made her thighs tighten.

"Another good point." Macy stepped closer. "We've both got busy weeks, but we also have a date."

"For dancing."

"For dancing." The smile lit up Macy's entire face.

"There will be plenty of time for more kissing." She hoped that was true because she was making some assumptions, and she knew it. But the warmth in Macy's eyes right then told her they were most definitely on the same page, and she leaned in.

How was it that kissing Macy was so easy? So comfortable and so hot at the same time. They kissed softly, gently at first, and when things deepened, it happened slowly. Lips parted a little bit. The tip of a tongue made an appearance. And then time didn't exist, and they were making out at Macy's side door, in each other's space, tongues exploring, breaths ragged. Brooke finally wrenched herself away, knowing that they could easily end up naked on Macy's couch. It wasn't that she didn't want that, but she wanted more than sex from Macy, and she wasn't sure Macy was ready to hear that.

Fingertips to Macy's lips. Foreheads touching. Breathing. Calming.

"Text me tomorrow?" she whispered.

Macy nodded, as if not trusting her brain to make actual words.

Brooke gave her one more quick peck on the lips, then headed out to her car. Once inside, she keyed the ignition and let her head drop back against the headrest. "Oh my God," she said to the empty interior. It was not at all what she'd expected when she moved, and in less than two months? But a smile broke out on her face—she felt it appear, then grow as the warmth spread through her. She glanced at her silly, smitten face in the rearview mirror. Because that's what she was: smitten. It was a corny word. She could hear Lena's voice in her head calling her a smitten kitten, something she'd heard her own mother say once, and it was true. She was smitten with Macy. And more…

The goofy grin stayed as she shifted the car into reverse, backed out of Macy's driveway, and headed home. The rest of the week was busy for her, but that was okay because she had something to look forward to.

A date.

With Macy.

Oh, this was bad. She was in trouble with this one. So much trouble.

The goofy grin stayed.

CHAPTER TWENTY-ONE

The club scene wasn't really Macy's thing—she preferred to stay home with her animals and watch Netflix, thank you very much. But once some time had passed after losing Michelle, she realized it was important for her to get out and be with people every so often. For her own sanity. Lucas had been great about tugging her out of her comfort zone here and there, and this time, Brooke was doing it.

For Brooke? Macy would happily step out of that zone. She'd be thrilled to. Hell, she'd *jump* out of it with great enthusiasm. Hop up and down. Dance the night away. Because it was Brooke. Brooke had asked to go dancing, so goddamn it, Macy was going to take her dancing. She was ready. She'd spent her Saturday at home with her animals so she wouldn't feel guilty about leaving them to go out. She'd gotten herself dressed up in a nice outfit—black pants, a red short-sleeved top because she knew she'd get hot dancing, and black ankle boots with a slight heel. The calendar said spring, but the evenings were still chilly, and she wasn't ready to put her boots away yet. A quick once-over in the mirror had her giving herself one nod of approval just as the doorbell rang. She was prepared.

What she was *not* prepared for was Brooke in her dancing attire.

"Holy shit." The words popped out before she could catch them.

Brooke looked over her own shoulder. "What?"

"You." Macy's eyes wanted to roam over Brooke's body. Slowly. She let them. They lingered. Dark jeans, skinny ones that conformed to her legs. Clingy white T-shirt with a line drawing of a martini glass on it. Olive-green army jacket with the sleeves pushed up to her elbows, and several bracelets on her wrist. Brown booties with enough of a heel to make her a good two inches taller than Macy. Her hair was partly pulled back, the rest hanging in bouncy waves the color of fall, and she smelled like glamour and beauty and sensuality, if that was even possible. "You," she said again. "That's what."

Brooke stepped through the door, and the dogs greeted her with their usual enthusiasm. She squatted to their level and gave them back as much as she got. "What did I do?" Brooke asked as she looked up at her.

"You showed up at my door looking like that."

"You're one to talk." Brooke stood, pointed at her, moved her finger up and down. "Red looks amazing on you. I realized that the first time you wore the V-neck sweater."

"You noticed that?"

"I did."

There was a beat of silence, and Macy could feel Brooke's eyes on her. It was delicious, like fingertips moving along her spine. "Ready to dance?" she asked softly.

"Are you kidding? I've been looking forward to this all day."

"Me, too. Let's do this." She ordered them an Uber and they headed out.

Glam was a fairly new gay club in the city, but word of mouth on it was strong. Owned by gay men, it was LGBTQ+, but not exclusively. Anybody and everybody was welcome, and that's what Macy liked most about it. She'd been a handful of times with Lucas for drag shows, and she really liked the atmosphere. They arrived, Macy paid the cover charge for both of them, to Brooke's protest, and they headed in. It was dark, like most clubs, with a thumping bass beat and lots of flashing purple lights. There was always a cocktail du jour, something invented by the bartender on duty that night. The music was a great mix of house music, current tunes, and classic dance music. And tonight, it was crowded, even as early as they were.

"I can't believe how busy it is." Brooke raised her voice to be heard over the music and commented as if reading Macy's mind. "It's not even ten yet."

"What do you want to drink?"

One Sex on the Beach later, and Macy was in her glory. Dancing with Brooke was an incredible thing. How to describe it? Sexy, no doubt. But it went deeper than that. When they moved together, their hips swaying in tandem, it was perfect. When Brooke tucked her knee between Macy's legs, wrapped an arm around the small of her back, and picked up the beat? Macy thought that if she died right there, if a rafter fell on her and killed her instantly, she'd die the happiest of women.

The music kept pumping, morphing from Zedd to Lizzo to Marshmello so seamlessly, it was as if the DJ was playing one continuous track. At one point, they found themselves dancing in a group, three other women forming a sort of dance circle with them, and they laughed and taught each other moves and it was amazing.

Macy stepped out of the group to get herself a refill and take a much-needed break—it was eye-opening to realize the dancing stamina she used to have had left her, apparently for more dedicated dancers—placed her order with the sexy butch behind the bar, then turned to watch. Brooke threw her head back and laughed as one of the other girls in the group twerked like her life depended on it, and Macy couldn't help but grin. Seeing Brooke having so much fun made Macy go all mushy inside.

"Macy?"

She turned toward the voice, recognized Shannon, an old friend of Michelle's from her work. "Oh my God, hi," Macy said and accepted the warm hug.

"It *is* you. Holy crap, how long has it been?" Shannon asked, then a shadow passed over her eyes, as they both knew exactly how long it had been. "You look terrific," she quickly added, probably in the hopes of zipping past the *I haven't seen you since your girlfriend's funeral* discomfort.

"Thanks, so do you. How've you been?" Conversation wasn't easy with the music at such a high volume, so Macy did a lot of smiling and nodding as Shannon talked. At one point, she indicated the other side of the bar where her wife, Jo, stood with a handful of other women, some who looked vaguely familiar to Macy. Jo waved. Macy waved back.

"It's so good to see you out," Shannon said, just as Brooke made eye contact with Macy and waved. Shannon's gaze followed Macy's. "Is she with you?"

Is she with me? The question pinballed through Macy's head before she felt everything in her relax. "She is."

"That's fantastic, Mace," Shannon said, and she really sounded like she meant it. "It really is great to see you." Another hug and Shannon returned to her group.

She picked up her drink, turned to lean her back against the bar, and just watched.

It had never occurred to her that Brooke could dance. Like, *dance*.

She was usually so buttoned-up that this version of Brooke, the one with her arms above her head, the one whose hip movements could give Shakira a run for her money, wasn't one who had ever even crossed Macy's mind. But wow.

And then something interesting happened. One of the other women in their dancing group grabbed Brooke by the hips, pulled her close, and pushed her knee between Brooke's legs just as Brooke had done with Macy. As Macy watched over the rim of her glass, Brooke's expression never changed. But she subtly removed the other woman's hands from her hips and put enough distance between them so the woman's knee was no longer in places it wasn't welcome. The woman took it well, bowed her head, and danced her way back a foot or so. When Brooke's gaze met Macy's, she smiled widely and beckoned for Macy to join her. Not needing to be asked twice, she set her drink down, danced her way back onto the dance floor. Brooke watched her approach and, when she was close enough, reached out and grabbed *her* by the hips, pulled her close, tucked her knee back between Macy's legs.

If that wasn't possession, Macy didn't know what was. But she loved it. Relished it. It had been so long since she felt like she might belong to someone, and she wanted to fill a tub up with the feeling and submerge herself in it, bathe in it. She pulled Brooke's head down so her lips were near her ear.

"I think we should go home." She moved her head back so she could see those big brown eyes, which had gone even darker and slightly hooded.

Brooke quirked one eyebrow. "I think we should."

❖

It was a wonder they managed to keep their hands off each other in the Uber ride home, but they caved at Macy's side door, practically falling through it. Their lips fused in a blistering kiss, their hands groping at clothing and the bodies underneath, they stumbled through the entrance and up the stairs to the loud greeting of excited barking and the *tick-tick* of canine nails on the hardwood floor.

"Let me take care of them," Macy whispered when she was able to extricate herself from Brooke's mouth. Brooke simply shifted gears and ran her tongue down the side of Macy's neck. She groaned. "You... you head upstairs." Brooke tugged the red shirt's neckline to the side, fastened her mouth on to the soft flesh of a shoulder, and sucked. Macy heard a whimper, recognized it as her own. *That's gonna leave a mark.* The thought made her wet.

"Hurry," Brooke said, then kissed her quickly and headed for the stairs.

Macy herded the dogs to the back door, slid it open. "Do your fastest peeing ever," she ordered them. "I have a very hot, hopefully very naked woman upstairs in my bed, and I need to join her ASAP!"

It was like they understood. Well, it was like Pete and Priscilla understood. Angus, being a terrier, might have wanted to understand, but his nose had other plans, and he walked the perimeter of the backyard twice before Macy went out to physically urge him back inside. Doors locked, lights off, treats handed out to both canines and felines, and she took the stairs two at a time, stopping in the doorway of her bedroom to take in the sight.

Was Brooke naked? Yes. But that didn't even begin to describe the vision before her. The room was lit only with candles. Brooke must've found the ones in the bathroom, added them to the two already in the bedroom, and turned off any other light. She sat upright—no, *lounged* was a better word. She lounged on Macy's bed, one leg bent, one straight, and Macy's eyes traveled their length, noted the blue polish on her toenails. The candlelight flickered, causing a sexy movement of shadows and light to play over Brooke's breasts, her hair loose now and trailing down, one end wrapped around a finger that twisted and untwisted, twisted and untwisted.

Her eyes tracked up, locked on Brooke's, held.

She swallowed.

"Come here," Brooke whispered, and it was plea and command both at once.

Macy had never stripped off her clothes so fast in her life, but in the next moment, she was naked, too, and she crossed the room, put a knee up on the foot of the bed, and crawled up Brooke's body to her mouth.

This kiss was different somehow, and Macy was vaguely aware of it. It was deeper, slower, and it meant more. That was the big thing—it meant more. She let herself sink in, so it was hard to tell where she ended and Brooke began. And just as she lifted a hand to touch one of those gorgeous breasts, Brooke flipped them around and she was suddenly on her back. She lay there for a moment, blinking, as Brooke looked down at her with unmistakable triumph in her eyes.

"You had the upper hand last time. My turn."

Before Macy could form a coherent thought, Brooke's mouth crashed down on hers. Captured hers. Owned hers. She tried her best to pay attention to what Brooke did to her. Where she touched her. How she touched her. How fast or slow or hard or soft, but it all morphed together into one giant wave of pleasure. She had no idea what were Brooke's hands, what was her mouth, where her fingers were. All she knew was that Brooke took her to heights she hadn't even known existed, and all she could do was hold on for dear life.

So she did.

As the orgasm ripped through her, washed over her like a tsunami of sensual bliss, she held on.

As sounds were torn from her throat, sounds she'd never heard herself make in her life, she held on.

As the words that had been growing within her for the past few weeks formed, bubbled up, and parked themselves on the tip of her tongue, she held on.

It was all she could do.

She held on to Brooke with everything she had.

❖

The clock said it was 3:12 a.m.

Pete snuffled from his dog bed on the floor. Angus snored from under the bed. Captain Jack purred quietly at Macy's feet, Jellybean at her head. And as she lay in her bed on her back, Brooke's deep, even breathing from where she was snuggled up in her arms comforted her, kept her feeling safe and warm and loved.

Yes. Loved.

A scary word. And a true one.

A true one.

They'd made love until nearly two in the morning, and then Macy had drifted off to sleep. The dream she'd had was the reason she was lying awake now, and she recalled it like it had just happened, as if it hadn't been a dream at all, but absolutely real.

She'd dreamed of Michelle. No particular setting. No setting at all, really. It had just been sort of…foggy. Ethereal, almost. And there stood Michelle. Not far away, but not terribly close. She simply stood there. Macy couldn't speak, couldn't move to reach out to her, to touch her, to ask her to stay. They stood, face-to-face, and looked at each other.

And the thing that had struck Macy the most, the thing that had actually woken her up from a sound sleep, was the expression on Michelle's face. She was smiling. Macy recognized it, that smile. It was the one she used to get when she was exceedingly content with everything and everyone around her. When she was completely relaxed and happy. She'd remained for…Macy had no idea how much time had passed. It was a dream, after all. Then Michelle's smile had widened, and she'd brought her fingers to her lips, kissed them, and sent it Macy's way before she turned and walked into that glowing fog, had disappeared.

Michelle was happy. She'd blown her a kiss, and she'd looked so happy.

It's what had popped Macy's eyes open and left her staring at the ceiling of her bedroom, Brooke sleeping soundly in her arms. The message couldn't really be any clearer, could it?

Michelle had given her permission to move on.

With Brooke.

CHAPTER TWENTY-TWO

Had Brooke turned into Snow White?
And if she had, was that such a bad thing?

She swam up to the surface of the morning slowly, the sunshine beaming in through Macy's bedroom window and warmly caressing her face as if wanting to wake her up in the most gentle way possible. Out from under the covers came her arms, and she stretched them over her head, felt that pleasant soreness in her muscles that only came after a night of intense passion, and relished it.

It wasn't lost on her that she slept more soundly in Macy's bed than she ever remembered sleeping in anybody else's, her own included, and she took some time to just breathe in the quiet of the morning.

One cat—Jellybean, she knew, because it had both eyes—was the only other living creature in the room with her, and she was curled up in a ball next to Brooke's hip. She couldn't hear the cat's purr so much as feel it, a gentle buzz, comforting and pleasant, and she reached down and gently scratched the soft striped fur.

Last night had been something.

Something hot. Something fun. Something intense. Something special...

Yeah, that last one.

Last night had lifted them to another level, and she was pretty sure they'd both been aware of it. The weirdest part? It didn't scare her. Not anymore, not even a little bit. She wasn't quite sure what to do with that, and before she could think about it further, she heard footsteps coming up the stairs. *Six, seven, eight, nine, ten.* Two more steps in the hall and the bedroom door was pushed open slowly. Only the top of Macy's head and her eyes peeked in, and Brooke grinned at the sight.

"Good morning," she said.

"You're awake," Macy said and came all the way into the room, mug of coffee in hand.

"I could get used to this in-bed coffee delivery, you know. Watch out. I'll start making demands."

Macy sat on the edge of the bed. "You can make all the demands you want." She leaned in, kissed her softly. Then, "What's your Sunday look like?"

She sat up, pulled the sheet up to cover her breasts, and grinned at the dejected look on Macy's face. "Stop pouting and hand over that coffee."

"Those should never be covered," Macy said, giving her the mug.

Holding it in both hands, she brought it to her nose and inhaled. "God, does anything smell better?" A tentative sip to gauge temperature, and she was sure she could feel the caffeine hitting her bloodstream. "Okay. My Sunday. Well, I was thinking of going to that church you mentioned. Then I told Sasha I'd cover an open house for her. But I'm free after that." She looked at Macy over the rim of her mug and used her best sexy voice. "Whyever do you ask?"

"I thought maybe we could do something."

"What kind of something?"

"I can't tell you."

"Ooh. A secret, huh?"

Macy nodded. "Something fun. I promise."

"I mean, since you promised…" She shrugged like it was a done deal. Because it was. She'd do anything with Macy, something she only realized in that very moment.

"Text me the address of the open house. Bring comfy clothes with you to change into, and I'll come by and meet you, and then you can follow me to where we're going."

"So mysterious." But she loved it. Michael had been a sweet guy, but he wasn't even close to spontaneous. He never would've planned a surprise date for them. It just wasn't his thing. This? This had her excited already.

"Gotta keep you on your toes." Macy sat more fully on the bed, her back against the headboard like Brooke's.

"I love it."

"I'll remember that."

They sat quietly, contentedly, and that was the part that warmed Brooke from the inside. The part that made her sappy and mushy and all those silly emotional clichés. That she had no need to talk. She felt no pressure with Macy. No urge to fill the silence. They sat for a long moment like that, just as they had the last time, gazing out the window at the big oak tree in Macy's side yard and enjoying being close to each other.

"Last night was..." Macy gave an exaggerated shiver as she grinned.

"It was pretty awesome." She pressed herself sideways so her shoulder pushed into Macy's.

Macy turned to her, wide-eyed. "And who knew you could dance like that? I mean, wow!"

Brooke laughed at the expression on Macy's face. God, she was cute. "Listen, Sex on the Beach is about the only thing that loosens me up enough to dance in front of other people."

"Really? Well, that's a damn shame because you were a sight to see. I noticed that one chick getting a little possessive..." *Ah.* Brooke had wondered if Macy'd seen that. She obviously had, and it had apparently bothered her.

"I think I made it pretty clear to Ms. Handsy who I was there with."

The vague shadow that had passed over Macy's face at the memory vanished, and she did that all-over shiver thing again. "Oh, you did, and it was awesome."

"Good." She studied Macy's face for a moment, gauging whether or not to say the words in her head, and decided—yes. "Macy." When Macy rolled her head to meet her gaze, she said, "When I'm with you, I'm *with you*. And I am with you." A raised hand, a stroke of Macy's cheek. "Okay?"

Macy's smile rivaled the sun in its brightness. "Okay."

"I'm glad we got that settled." She grinned back, pressed into Macy again. "Now let me enjoy my coffee and being this close to you before the dogs steal you away, and I have to go home to change."

"Deal." Macy laid her head on Brooke's shoulder, and right then? That very second? The most perfect moment in time that she'd ever experienced.

❖

The sermon that Sunday had been about being true to yourself. Apropos, Brooke thought as she'd sat in the back row and listened as best she could, given all the thoughts swirling around in her mind like fruit in a blender.

It had been her first time in a Catholic inclusive church, and she still marveled at those two words in the same sentence: Catholic and inclusive. Not a pairing she'd grown up with, that was for sure. It was a gorgeous building, not an actual church, but an auditorium used by a music school. Apparently, the church held Mass there on Sunday mornings because the actual church was very small and wouldn't hold the sizable crowd Brooke was currently a part of. She didn't mind that it wasn't an actual church because between the prayers and the hymns, it felt like one. She'd told only Macy she was going, and she'd asked if Brooke wanted her company, but it was really something she wanted to do alone the first time. Macy had understood completely, yet another point in her win column. She'd hesitated at the door—it had been way too long since she'd been to Mass. Simply setting foot in church again filled her with emotion. Relief, joy, and guilt—always with the guilt, thanks to Catholicism—rolled around inside her as she crossed herself and took a seat. And the first time the reverend, not a priest, said, "The Lord be with you," and the congregation had replied, Brooke's eyes filled with tears.

She was home.

That's how she'd felt. And the fact that there was a rainbow banner and that she noted several same-sex couples made her feel even more comfortable. Macy hadn't been kidding.

Macy…

As she sat now at the top of the sixteen steps in the park, which had become her thinking spot, and tipped her face toward the sun, one thought ran through her head on a loop. Good Lord, what was she going to do about Macy?

And then she smiled. Big. She felt it bloom across her face, and she sat there like that. Smiling like an idiot falling in love.

Oh my God.

Was that true? Was she falling in love with Macy?

As if on cue, her phone pinged and she slid it out of her pocket. A text from the object of her thoughts.

I was just having flashbacks from last night. A heart emoji.

Then another ping. *And from the middle of the night.* A heart emoji.

Another ping. *And from this morning.* A heart emoji.

Brooke held the phone. Stared at the screen. Went all soft and warm inside. When was the last time she'd felt like this when hearing from somebody she'd dated? Somebody she'd spent the night with? Again, the thought crossed her mind that Michael had been a super sweet guy, and she'd loved him, but he'd never instilled such…She tipped her head back, searching the bright blue of the sky for the right word.

Passion.

It didn't strike her so much as settle firmly in her lap, like a fall leaf drifting down from a branch. It was passion. Macy had so much of it, and she brought it out in Brooke. Macy made her feel soul-searing passion. Macy made her *crave*.

Another perfect word. Crave. Macy showed her passion and then made her crave it when they were apart. Nobody, male or female, had ever made her feel like that before. Ever. And it was like a drug. She wanted to feel it every minute of every day.

Her thumbs hovered over the keyboard of her phone as she auditioned, then cut several sentences before keeping it simple. *I miss you, too.* And she added her own heart emoji.

Is it 4 yet? came Macy's next text.

That flutter in her belly. That tightening of her thighs. *Almost…*

See you soon. Then too many happy emojis for Brooke to count, the sheer amount of them making her laugh into the park air.

It was time. She stood, slid her phone back into her pocket, and began the walk home, passing other walkers, joggers, dog walkers, and folks just enjoying the lovely spring Sunday. Rain was forecast for much of the upcoming week, so people were obviously taking advantage. Smiling to herself, she made a mental note to call home later and tell her parents about church. At last, something they could discuss without there being underlying discomfort, disappointment, disapproval.

Once home, her phone rang. Expecting it to be Macy, she was surprised to see Lena's name on the screen.

"Hey, you," she said, putting the phone on speaker so she could change her clothes.

"Hi! I was just thinking about you," Lena said. "Thought I'd call instead of text."

"Well, I'm glad you did. Texting is convenient, but it's not the same as hearing somebody's voice, you know?" It was true, Brooke realized as she said it. "I've missed you."

"I miss you, too."

"Is everything okay? You sound weird."

"Yeah." A beat went by. "Am I on speaker?"

"You are. Sorry. I have an open house and need to get ready."

"*Oh,*" Lena said, drawing out the word. "I knew that." More quiet.

"Lee. What's wrong?" Brooke stopped what she was doing, picked up the phone, put it to her ear. "Talk to me."

Lena sighed, and Brooke could picture her cute, round face, her bouncy brown hair and expressive blue eyes, could picture her waving her hand dismissively as she said, "Nothing. It's nothing. I just... dreamed about you and woke up with a weird feeling, but now that I hear your voice, I feel better."

"Well, good." Brooke's heart swelled.

"Things are good there?"

"Things are great."

"I'm so glad to hear that." Lena's tone changed so that her smile was apparent in her voice. "And I'm just being a nervous Nellie. Go. Do what you do best, and I'll call you later tonight."

They signed off, and Brooke finished changing out of her churchgoing outfit and into a business suit. With all her supplies packed into her car, she headed out. She knew where the house was, had driven past it the day Sasha had asked her to cover, so that she could get a feel for the neighborhood, and so she wouldn't get lost the day of the open house. It was a small Cape Cod that had been very close to foreclosure in a slightly downtrodden section of town. The owners were gone, and it was being sold as-is. Sasha had said it needed some work, so she was not expecting shiny new appliances or a remodeled bathroom or kitchen. But she'd sat through dozens of open houses in her years as a Realtor before she'd focused on business real estate, and it was something she could do in her sleep.

After setting up a couple of *Open House* signs at the ends of the street and one out front, she used the lockbox on the front door and let herself in. She was early—it was only one fifteen—but that was intentional, and she got to work, pulling out the cookie sheet and break-and-bake chocolate chip cookies she'd brought with her. Nothing helped to make a house feel like a home more than the scent of freshly baked cookies. Brooke had learned the trick from the very first Realtor she'd ever worked with, and she'd used it ever since. She fiddled with the gas oven and wondered if it was older than her as she set it to preheat.

The instructions on the cookie package warned her not to eat the raw dough, and she snorted. "Please," she said to the empty kitchen. "If you people had any idea how much raw cookie dough, pie crust, and brownie batter I've eaten in my life, you'd be horrified." To punctuate the statement, she popped one of the squares of cookie dough into her mouth and chewed happily.

By the time two o'clock rolled around, she had a plate of warm cookies and some bottled water on the counter, and sell sheets for the house fanned out on the table. She was a little less enthusiastic, as a dull headache had set in behind her eyes, but there was Advil in her purse, and she downed a couple tablets just as the first ring of the doorbell sounded. She pulled herself together, pasted on a smile, and opened the front door.

Five people came through in the first half hour, but that was it, and by three o'clock, Brooke felt awful. She was nauseous, a little dizzy, and sure she was coming down with something. The Advil hadn't touched the headache, and she tried not to look at her watch every five minutes, but the two hours she had to be there were starting to feel like seven.

At three forty-five, she breathed a sigh of relief that she was almost finished. As she gathered her things together, she tried to figure out the best way to tell Macy she probably couldn't go to her surprise location tonight.

She didn't get any farther than that before her knees gave out, she dropped everything in her hands, and followed it all down to the floor. The last thought she was aware of as she lay on the linoleum was that the kickboard under the cupboards could use a coat of paint.

CHAPTER TWENTY-THREE

Somehow, Macy had managed to keep herself busy all day.

It hadn't been easy. All she'd wanted was for time to speed up so she could pick up Brooke and take her out. She had such a fun evening planned for them that she could hardly keep herself from bouncing around on the balls of her feet like a ten-year-old waiting to open Christmas presents.

At noon, she'd received a Snapchat from Tyler that showed him lying on the floor with Charlie sitting on his head. He hashtagged it #BigBrotherLife, and it was all kinds of adorable. She'd texted him.

So? Spring Fling? Taking Kelsey?

The bouncing gray dots bounced. Stopped. Bounced some more. Then came, *Nah, gonna go with a bunch of friends instead.*

Oh. Your mom thought you might be asking her.

Changed my mind, came the immediate response.

She'd squinted at the phone for a beat before typing, *Everything okay?*

Totally good. A smiling emoji wearing Ray-Bans followed.

Okay. All right. He seemed okay about it. She wondered if Jeremy was going to be in that bunch of friends. Thinking about her own school dances reminded her that, while she did go with Michelle, it was because they'd gone with a group of friends. For prom, seven of them had rented a limo, gone to dinner, and ended up back at Michelle's house after the dance. They'd had a blast. Every dance. Every time.

She busied herself with puttering around the house for the rest of the afternoon, running the vacuum, throwing in a load of laundry, taking the dogs for a walk. The whole time, all she could think about was whether it was time to go pick up Brooke yet. Honestly, it was like she was seventeen again.

When a glance at her watch finally told her it was 3:45, she shot off a quick text to Brooke asking if she was almost ready. When she didn't hear back after a few minutes, she assumed Brooke was busy answering the endless potential-buyer questions that usually came with an open house, so she didn't text again.

The address wasn't all that far, so she got into her car at 3:55 and began to drive, figuring her drive time would give Brooke an extra fifteen minutes or so to clean up and get all her stuff together, shoo out stragglers if necessary. When she didn't get a text back by 4:05, she pointed her car in the direction of the open house. Five minutes later, she was parking out front. Brooke's Audi sat in the driveway. Simply seeing her car sent butterflies fluttering through Macy's stomach, and she couldn't help the grin that spread out over her face as she checked herself in the visor mirror. She was closing in on giddy. *Giddy*, for God's sake. The thought of seeing Brooke made her positively giddy. Not even a word she ever used, but it was the most appropriate in this situation as she shook her head at her own smiling-like-a-dope reflection.

"You're ridiculous," she said to it. She yanked on the door handle and headed up the front walk to the house.

The doorbell went unanswered, though she could hear it echo inside, so she knocked. No answer. Since Brooke's was the only car in the driveway, it didn't concern her that she might be walking in on the people who lived there, and she pushed the door slowly open.

"Hello? Brooke?" she called. The house was silent, and she stood and listened before just wandering in.

Nothing.

"Brooke? Hello?" she called again. Again, nothing. "Brooke?" This was weird. Something was off. The hair on the back of her neck stood up, and she said, "Brooke," again. Not a question this time. A demand. She could smell the remnants of cookies, remembered Brooke telling her it was a trick she used when she sold residential properties. She headed for the kitchen.

And time stopped.

Brooke was on her back on the floor, unconscious by the look of it. A cookie sheet lay near her feet, several cookies and papers scattered about.

Macy froze. The rush of blood in her ears was as loud as the howl of a tornado, drowning out any other sound. She closed her eyes as the past threatened—no, it didn't threaten, it literally *tried* to suck her back in time, it pulled at her, tugged at her clothes, showed her images of the last time she found somebody on the floor. She fought. She fought hard, clawed her way free of the memories long enough to move, to run, to drop to her knees and slide to a stop next to Brooke's unmoving form.

"Brooke! Oh my God, Brooke, wake up." There was no blood, she noticed, and Brooke was breathing, thank Christ. Shallowly, but she was breathing. Macy slid her phone out of her pocket and dialed 911.

❖

Had her head ever hurt this badly before? Like, in her entire life? She didn't think so.

Afraid to open her eyes, lest any kind of light at all lance through her eyeballs and render her blind and make her headache worse— which didn't seem possible at this point, but probably was—Brooke lay still and listened as she swam up from the depths of…wherever the hell she'd been.

The first thing she noticed was the smell. Sterile. Medicinal. Not at all helping with the headache. Then the feel of the bed she was in. Unfamiliar. Softer than her own bed, the sheet a little stiffer, scratchier. Then she let the sounds filter in, and once she did that, she confirmed to herself that she was in the hospital. Far-off conversations, likely in the hallway, were like background noise. She could hear voices, knew people were talking, but couldn't understand what was being said. With no desire to concentrate on that for fear of increasing the pounding in her head, she left them to hum along, the soundtrack to her slow waking up.

"And you say you've known her how long?" That was her mother, her voice a combination of authority and worry, the way she almost always sounded. She knew a lot, liked to be in control, but was always braced for the next bad thing in life to happen. Brooke always thought it must be an exhausting way to live.

"A couple months?" That was Macy, and Brooke felt everything in her relax at the sound of her voice. Thank God she was there.

"Well, we're very grateful for you finding her, calling an ambulance. We can take it from here." Not dismissive enough to come off as dismissive, but dismissive enough to think you'd *maybe* been politely asked to go. Typical of her mother.

"I appreciate that," Macy said, her voice also polite and also firm. "But I'm going to stay for a while."

Brooke wasn't sure if she was visibly smiling on the outside, but she sure felt like she was on the inside. Not many people stood up to Nancy Sullivan and her polite rudeness, but Macy had.

It was time to open her eyes.

Which ended up being a struggle she wasn't expecting. Come on, they were just eyelids. *Lift!* It took longer than it should have, but she finally managed to crack one open. Then the other. Light. Bright light. God, so much light. She squeezed them shut again as her mother let out a soft cry.

"Is she waking up?" Suddenly, she was closer, her voice near Brooke's ear. "I think she's waking up. Brooke? Honey? Can you hear me?"

She tried to answer. Was sure she did. But no sound happened. She swallowed—something that was much harder than it should've been—and tried again. This time, she croaked. Literally croaked because that was apparently the only sound she could make aside from a raspy whisper. So she shot for that. "Hi, Mom." She wanted to ask what she was doing there, how she'd gotten there so fast, but just couldn't summon the energy.

"Oh, my girl," her mother said and laid a warm hand on her forehead. "There you are."

"What happened?" The whisper got stronger. She swallowed again.

"They think it was carbon monoxide." Macy this time, and she was standing on the other side of the bed as if she'd materialized out of thin air. And she was gorgeous. "The stove in that house had some faulty connection or something."

Details filtered back into her brain slowly. The open house. The cookies. The weird dizzy feeling. That was about it. "I don't remember passing out."

"I came to pick you up, and you were on the floor. I mean, I could be wrong, but I don't know that Sasha approves of her agents napping during open houses." Macy went for lighthearted. She went for joking. Brooke could tell by her casual smile, the easy tone of voice. But there was something in her eyes. Behind them. Something more than concern. Beyond fear. She couldn't pinpoint it, but it was there, and it worried her. Still, she did her best to play along for the sake of her parents. For Macy.

"Listen, I was tired. I work hard." Chuckles went around the room, and Brooke noticed her father for the first time, sitting in a chair in the corner, watching and grinning. Even from where she lay, she could see remnants of redness around his eyes. He'd been worried. "Hi, Daddy," she said softly.

"Hi, Brook-a-look." His use of his pet name for her when she was a child warmed her, hit all the right emotional buttons to cause a prickling behind her eyes.

"Don't make me cry," she admonished him. "My head is already killing me." A squeeze to her forearm brought her eyes to Macy's.

"The doctor said you'd have a headache for a while. I'll tell the nurse on my way out that you could use another dose of painkillers." She smiled down at her, and Brooke was pretty sure everything inside her melted.

"You're leaving?"

"Soon. I have animals."

"Oh my God, so do I."

"You do?" The surprise in her mother's voice was apparent. She'd obviously forgotten about Rorschach, but Brooke kept her eyes on Macy.

"You've done so much already, but…" She swallowed down her worry when she realized she had no idea how long she'd been there. "Could you check on Rorsh? Please?"

Another squeeze. "Of course. Keys?"

Once she'd gone over the location of the spare key and instructions for feeding Rorschach, she watched as Macy got her things together. For the first time, she noticed how tired she looked. Lines creased her forehead. Darkness underscored her eyes. She looked like she'd aged twenty years in one evening. As Macy bent and pressed a kiss to her forehead, Brooke whispered a thank you and held those eyes with her own.

"You're welcome. Get some rest, and I'll come by tomorrow." She smiled, and that something was still parked behind her eyes. Brooke made a mental note to ask her about it the next day.

"She seems nice," her mother said once Macy was gone. Again, that special talent she had kicked in because she sounded judgy even though the words were not.

"She is. She's amazing." Brooke sighed, not about to get into any type of discussion about exactly who Macy was to her. She was too tired to explain it to her mother. She was too tired to explain it to herself. Her eyelids were already growing heavy when the nurse appeared, all cheerful demeanor and soft, inviting curves. Brooke wanted to curl up in the woman's lap and go to sleep.

"Heard you could use something more for that headache, honey. Yeah?"

Macy had remembered.

❖

The spare key to Brooke's town house was right where she said it was, under a rock out front the size of a small cantaloupe. Macy made a mental note to scold her for putting it in such an obvious place as she let herself in.

She felt like she was sneaking into a place she shouldn't be. The first thing she noticed was the smell. Fresh. Clean. A little citrusy. And that scent of almonds and vanilla that smelled like Brooke. Just like her. She stood still, closed her eyes, and inhaled deeply, took it in, let it fill her.

A small squeak caught her attention and tugged her out of her aromatic fantasies. Rorschach trotted toward her, sat down at her feet, and looked up at her expectantly. She wondered if cats had eyebrows because she was pretty sure he quirked one at her in disapproval.

"I bet you're hungry, aren't you, buddy?" she said quietly as she squatted down to meet his gaze. She reached out to scratch behind his ears, and he moved closer, between her knees, rubbed against her jeans. "Okay, let's get you something to eat."

Being there alone, without Brooke's presence, felt weird. She'd only been there the one time, so that probably contributed to the feeling of trespassing that sat on her shoulders, but she pushed it aside and headed for the kitchen. Everything was right where Brooke had said, and she scooped some dry food and a little wet into the small cat dish, then added a little extra wet because he'd be spending the night alone. Then she set the dish on the floor, let herself slide down so she was sitting next to it, and ran her hand along Rorschach's silky black back as he ate.

Closing her eyes did nothing to rid her brain of the image of Brooke, unconscious, oxygen mask over her mouth and nose, being loaded onto a stretcher and into an ambulance. And the sight of her on the floor, unmoving, was seared into her memory forever, just like the image of Michelle lying at the bottom of the basement stairs. She could still remember everything about that sight when she'd come home from work and found her…Michelle's gray sweats and blue T-shirt, the colorful spray of laundry scattered all around her, just like the cookies and papers had been scattered around Brooke.

Pushing her fingers into her eyelids sometimes helped, but now all that did was hurry the tears along, and in the next ten seconds, she was sobbing openly on Brooke's kitchen floor. All the fear, all the worry, all the horror that came with finding a woman she cared about—cared deeply about—unmoving, unconscious, possibly dead washed over her like an ocean wave, and she let it come. She had no choice.

With no idea how long she'd sat there, Macy finally took a deep breath. She wiped at her cheeks, used a fingertip to swipe under each eye, understanding that her makeup was likely gone after so much crying, and stood up. There was a napkin holder on the counter, and she took one to blow her nose. Rorschach was nowhere to be found, and she wondered exactly when he'd gotten fed up with the sobbing human and gone to find something more entertaining. A glance down told her he'd eaten every last bite of his food, so she tossed a little more dry into the dish to tide him over. Brooke would be discharged and sent home tomorrow, but what time was a mystery.

Intent on giving the cat a bit more love, she found him curled up in a ball in the corner of the couch, sleeping soundly, letting out a tiny whistle from his nose as he breathed. She smiled but didn't want to disturb him.

At the front door, she turned back and looked into the living space, inhaled deeply once again, taking in the scent that *was* Brooke, then headed outside, closing the door with a click behind her.

CHAPTER TWENTY-FOUR

That's two...
       Brooke waited, watched the second hand on the wall clock, then heard a sigh come from the kitchen.

That's three...

She had barely been home from the hospital for two hours, but her mother was already driving her crazy. Currently puttering in the kitchen, her mother sighed every time she found something either missing or not in the location she thought it should be.

It was nearly noon. Her father had gone to pick up something for lunch. Brooke was all set up on the couch, blanket around her legs—was she eighty-seven?—remote in hand, Rorschach curled up in her lap and watching the kitchen with obvious suspicion. Brooke kissed his head and whispered, "It's okay, sweetie. She's not staying forever." They watched together for a moment before she added, "I hope."

Pulling out her phone, she sent a text to Macy. *My mother is rearranging my cupboards. Send help!*

No bouncing dots. Macy had said she was staging a house that morning, so she was likely busy with that. Swallowing her disappointment, she set the phone down and reached for the remote as her mother arrived with a steaming mug of coffee.

"Oh, thank you so much." She meant it. Her stomach hadn't quite recovered from the nausea the carbon monoxide had caused, but the delicious smell of the freshly brewed coffee made almost everything better. Her phone pinged as she held the mug, and she saw her mother glance at it.

"Macy," she said, looking away quickly because she knew it was none of her business, but unable to hide the shadow of disapproval in her voice as she handed the phone to Brooke and took the mug back.

"She saved my life, Mom. You get that, right?"

Her mother set the mug on a coaster on the coffee table and nodded. "I do. And I'm eternally grateful."

"You don't sound eternally grateful." She had told her parents on the phone that she was dating a woman, and Macy had introduced herself as that woman in the hospital. Brooke supposed she should be thankful they'd even allowed her in the room. As her parents, they could have easily put up a stink about that while she'd been unconscious, but they hadn't. She had to take the little victories when she could. She glanced at the phone.

She's scared. Let her baby you. And a smiley.

A small, quiet sigh. *I want you to baby me* was what she wanted to text back. But that sounded so needy and clingy, and she wasn't that person, and she didn't want to be that person. Her mother lifted her feet, sat down, and rested them in her lap, then uncovered them and began to rub, just like she always had when Brooke was little. It was heaven. "Thanks for being here," she said softly, and when her mother met her gaze, there were unshed tears.

"I'm just glad you're okay," she said, her voice cracking slightly. She reached one hand out and Brooke took it. "Thank God."

Brooke squeezed it and knew that, despite everything they'd been through and everything they likely still had to go through, she was thankful to have her mom there with her.

The day floated by as Brooke drifted in and out of short naps, amazed by how much a shortage of oxygen could wipe out your energy. She sipped water off and on. Her mother switched her from coffee to tea, delivered it regularly, and Brooke watched daytime television with her parents. They were going to stay one more night, then head home tomorrow. Brooke had been ordered by both of them—and Sasha— to stay home for the rest of the week, but she knew she was rapidly approaching stir crazy as it was. She would wait for her parents to leave, and then she'd at least pop in to the office to assess the damage her absence had caused to her workload.

Texts and phone calls had come from Sasha, Lena, Eddie, Jazz, her grandmother, and even Aidan Bush, the client who'd asked her out for drinks—she'd put him off more than once. She got a text or two from Macy, but they were short and felt almost obligatory to her. She reminded herself several times that Macy was very busy that day, that she was staging and then had an appointment with a client, and she couldn't expect her to text constantly. But by four that afternoon, it had been almost two and a half hours since the last text, and she was feeling antsy, like her fingers itched, so she picked up her phone. She wanted to call, but the proximity of her parents made that feel impossible, so she sent a text.

How's your afternoon? You coming by? She reread it a couple times, reminding herself to keep it light, not demanding or expectant. Or needy or clingy. Man, she was afraid of those two words the most. She read it again, and with a little nod, she sent it. And waited for the bouncing dots. When they didn't come right away, she set the phone on her thigh next to Rorsh and turned her attention to the TV and whichever judge her parents were watching.

When the doorbell rang, Brooke sprang awake, having apparently drifted off. A glance at her phone told her she'd been asleep for nearly two hours. Yikes. She heard her mother's greeting, then the absolutely wonderful sound of Macy's voice in reply. When she came into view, everything in Brooke relaxed.

"Hi," she said softly as Macy approached. She pushed herself up so she wasn't so slumped on the couch, but Macy held out a hand.

"No, no. Be comfortable. I can't stay long. Tyler's got a game." She perched on the edge of the coffee table, the physical equivalent of *I'm not staying*, and Brooke tried to ignore the prick of wetness behind her own eyes.

"Oh," was all she could manage to say.

"How are you feeling? You look better. You have more color in your face." Macy's voice was extra cheerful, something her parents likely didn't pick up on, but she did. Forced cheerfulness. Something was definitely up, and she wanted so badly to ask about it, but her parents clearly had no intention of leaving the room so the two of them could have some privacy, and she didn't want to get into a personal, possibly uncomfortable conversation in front of them.

"I've been very tired," she replied, having no choice but to play along.

"She's been drifting in and out all day," her mother chimed in. "The doctor said rest was the best thing for her, so we've kept things quiet."

"That's great," Macy said. "I'm so glad you guys are here for her."

She hated being talked about like she wasn't there, so she shifted the topic. "How did the staging go? Where was it?"

Macy told her all about the home, the client—not Wolfe this time—and what style she'd used. She was animated, talked with her hands, knocked a thankfully empty mug off the table as she did, and it was almost easy for Brooke to tuck away the uneasiness and put it on a shelf.

And after fifteen minutes, Macy pushed herself to her feet.

"Okay, I need to get to the game." Her eye contact was off, Brooke noticed. As in, was hardly there. And that worry she'd put on a shelf fell right off and spilled all over the floor of her brain. Macy squeezed her hand. "Talk to you later?"

Brooke swallowed hard and squeezed back. Then she nodded. It was all she could do.

❖

You suck.

The thought came through loud and way more fucking clear than Macy needed it to. Because she knew it. She absolutely, one hundred percent, without a doubt knew it.

Letting out a growl over the self-accusation, she redirected her ire to the idiot who'd parked a good three inches over the white line, making the parking spot she was trying to slide into much narrower than it should've been. But Tyler's game was against their biggest rival, and the crowd of spectators was much larger than usual. The next open spot was way down at the end, and Macy was too pissed off at the world to deal with the distance and the walking. *And* she could almost see Lucas in her mind, rolling his eyes at her, calling her a drama queen.

If he only knew.

Shaking off the anger as best she could, she slid sideways out of her car, grabbed a chair out of the back, and headed for the soccer field where the game was already in progress. The sidelines were lined with spectators, some in chairs, some standing, the small set of bleachers to the right completely filled, a large group of teenage girls watching and cheering, when they weren't taking selfies. Kelsey was there again, and Macy wondered if she was one of those going to the dance in the bunch of friends Tyler mentioned. She finally found Eva sitting in her usual red fold-up chair, Harlan pacing behind her, as he always did during Tyler's games.

Eva did a double-take when Macy unfolded her own chair and sat next to her. "Oh, hey. I didn't expect to see you here tonight. How's Brooke?"

Macy scanned the field until she found Ty, his sandy hair flying as he ran. "She's good. Tired. Her parents are there."

"Is that why you're here?" There was no accusation in her voice. How could there be? She didn't know what a coward her sister was. But Macy felt guilty anyway.

"I didn't want to impose. They want to spend time with their daughter." She punctuated that fib with a shrug. *Yup, nonchalant about it all. That's me.* She felt Eva's eyes on her.

"What about spending time with their daughter's girlfriend who saved her life? They're that bad, huh?"

Another shrug. Apparently, she'd developed a tic in her shoulder. "They seem nice enough."

"Are they staying long?" Eva asked.

"Come on, Ty!" Harlan's shout made her flinch, a reminder of why she did not enjoy watching the games with him. "Damn it! You shoulda had that!"

Macy gave herself a couple seconds to make sure he was done criticizing his son before answering Eva. "I don't know."

"You didn't ask?"

"What's with the third degree? Huh?" There was enough snark in her tone to cause Eva's eyes to widen slightly, but she recovered.

"Sorry. I was just curious."

Macy sighed and squeezed her sister's forearm. "No, I'm sorry. I'm just tired." She couldn't bring herself to look Eva in the eye, sure that she'd see how much more was actually rolling around in her brain. Eva knew her too well—she couldn't risk it. But Eva studied her for what felt like a really, really long time before she finally spoke.

"No worries." Eva asked no more questions, and Macy felt both relieved and guilty. Yeah, apparently her best friend now, the guilt, was hanging around, wanting to do everything together. Doing her best to focus on the game, she shouted, "Go, Tyler!"

Ty's team won by a last-minute goal scored by Jeremy, and the crowd went nuts, jumping to its collective feet, arms thrown in the air. It was a good distraction from the current state of her overly taxed emotions, and she high-fived Tyler as he came off the field and grabbed a bottle of Gatorade from Eva. The overall atmosphere was of excitement and joy, and she let herself be surrounded by it, sank into the hum of it.

"Ty. Dude. What happened on that one shot in the first half? That was all you."

A shadow passed over Tyler's face, and Macy hated seeing that. He shrugged, the universal move of teenagers everywhere when they don't know what to say.

"You dribbled left when you should've gone right. Around that scrawny kid." Harlan pointed toward the field as if *that scrawny kid* was still there and available for demonstration.

"Yeah," Ty said, looking down at his feet.

Harlan laid a big hand on his son's shoulder. "You gotta watch for those things. You're better than that. You could've scored right there."

"They won," Macy said, trying hard not to grit her teeth. "You saw that, right?"

Harlan turned his gaze to her. Held it. It was his method of intimidation, and she'd seen him use it many times. And it was definitely intimidating. He never looked angry when he did it, never raised his voice or glared. It was simply…a look. And because of that simplicity, it could be a little nerve-racking. But not to her. She stared right back at him and—she would give herself credit for this later, she promised—instead of saying *So back the fuck off*, which was what she really wanted to say, she calmly said, "He should be celebrating that win with his teammates." She injected an overload of cheer into her tone. "Shouldn't he?" She held Harlan's gaze the whole time.

Harlan finally lifted his hand and waved his son away. He didn't say anything at all, just picked up Eva's chair and collapsed it in his meaty hands.

Ty didn't stick around. Jeremy came by right on cue, and the two of them trotted over to the bleachers, arms around each other, and stopped at the gaggle of girls.

It wasn't the first time she and Harlan had had a standoff of sorts, though it didn't happen often. Macy let a lot slide because Eva loved him and he loved Eva. He was never abusive. But he had his opinions and was pretty sure they were always the ones that mattered. As she once said to Eva after one of their stare downs, "It's good for him to know that he is, in fact, *not* always right." Eva had appreciated it then. Not so much now.

"What the hell, Mace?" she hissed when Harlan had headed to the car with the chairs and was out of earshot.

"What?" Macy asked, momentarily surprised by Eva's tone, the hardness in her eyes.

"You had to do that in front of Tyler?"

"What?"

"Please. Just because you're going through something doesn't mean you can take it out on everybody else."

Ouch.

Okay. She was right about that. Macy watched as Eva angry-packed, shoving Tupperware containers and empty bottles into her oversized tote bag.

"I'm sorry," she said and looked off at the now empty field. "You're right. I'm sorry."

Eva sighed. "It's okay. Just...maybe give it some thought before you embarrass somebody in front of his kid next time. Okay?" Her tone was less harsh, almost soft, but the words were not.

"Yeah. Fair enough." She picked up her own chair. Collapsed it. Grabbed the handle of Eva's small cooler. They walked toward the parking lot together, and when they got to Eva's car where Harlan was loading things into the back, she bumped her brother-in-law with a shoulder. "I'm sorry, Harlan. That was out of line. Won't happen again." It absolutely would if she caught him browbeating Tyler again, but for now, she needed to make peace for her sister's sake.

Harlan looked down at her. "I appreciate that." With a nod, he went around to the driver's side and got in.

"Thank you," Eva said quietly. "And if you need to talk about whatever's on your mind, I'm here." She surprised Macy by hugging her quickly. Then she turned to go around and get in the car.

Macy lifted one hand in a wave, then turned and headed to her own car. Everything in her head that had been held at bay by the game now came crashing back to the forefront. The sight of Brooke's unconscious form on the floor of that house was an image she couldn't shake, no matter how hard she tried. Her mind juxtaposed it with Michelle's body until they practically morphed into one figure.

In her car, she squeezed her eyes shut, tried to will the memories away as her heart hammered in her chest and her breaths came in short bursts. Dots appeared in the sides of her vision, and a whooshing sound filled her head.

She hadn't had a panic attack in more than a year, but she was having one now.

She was definitely having one now.

CHAPTER TWENTY-FIVE

"Mom. I'm fine. I'm good. I promise."

Brooke's parents had required more reassurance to be convinced that she'd be fine on her own than if she'd been deployed to war-torn parts of the world. She'd woken up from a night on the couch—she'd fallen asleep there immediately after dinner, and her parents apparently hadn't wanted to wake her up—on her side with Rorschach purring against her stomach, feeling three hundred times better than she had the previous day. All she wanted to do now was go for a long, leisurely walk. See the beauty of spring. Breathe in as much fresh air as she could, fill her battered lungs with it. Without her mother glued to her side, watching over her like she was a toddler.

"You're sure?" her mother asked for the dozenth time, then pulled her into a hug.

"I promise," Brooke said again, hearing her neighbor's front door open.

Once they'd parted, her mother got into the car, rolled down the window. "Remember the Parkers down the street? Their son James is back in town and I hear he's single. Maybe I'll get his number—"

"Mom." Brooke said it firmly, surprising even herself as she held up a hand. "Stop."

At least having the good sense to look sheepish, her mother said, "I just want you to be happy, honey."

"I'm happy. I love my job. I found a church. And I'm dating a wonderful woman. I'm happy. I love you guys so much, but you're going to have to accept that sooner or later." She stood and took a step back from the car, feeling a sudden mix of emotions—shock that she'd actually said that to her mother, relief that she'd actually said that to her mother, panic that she'd actually said that to her mother.

To her mom's credit, though, she didn't argue. Instead, she gave one nod and attempted a smile as her father backed the car out of the driveway, then waved as they drove away. Brooke followed the car down to her mailbox at the end of the driveway and grabbed yesterday's mail.

"I can't believe you're doing this." The voice came from the open door of her neighbors' place. The guy came stomping out, duffel bag over his shoulder, suitcase in his hand. "I was just joking around."

The woman followed him down the walk. It was the first time Brooke had seen her. Blond, slightly plump, pretty, she stopped at his car where he was angrily throwing his stuff into the back seat. Brooke pretended to sift through her mail as she strolled back up her driveway. "You know what's not joking around, Kevin? Telling me I'm stupid. Telling me I'm fat. Telling me I'm dumb, that I don't listen, that I never know what I'm talking about."

Wow, Brooke thought. *Somebody has had enough. Good for her!*

"You take everything so personally," Kevin said, but there wasn't the usual venom in his voice. He actually sounded unsure.

"Telling me I'm oversensitive. Another good one." She waved her hand like she was shooing a fly, then folded her arms. "Just go, Kev. Please? I'm done."

He stood there for a moment, hand on the driver's side door handle, and the only word Brooke could find to describe him was defeated. All his bluster apparently dissipated like fog. He hung his head for a moment, then got in his car and was gone.

Brooke watched his car go the way of her parents', then turned to meet the gaze of her neighbor. "You okay?" she asked.

The woman laughed through her nose. "Surprisingly. I can't believe I ever let him move in here."

"Well, that was impressive."

"Thanks. You were, too." The woman indicated the road with her chin. "Your parents?"

"Yeah." She sighed. "I guess we've both learned a little bit about standing up for ourselves, huh?" She stuck her hand out over the slice of lawn that separated their driveways. "Brooke Sullivan."

"Chrissy Burns." They shook. "Welcome to the neighborhood."

"It's nice to meet you."

"Likewise." Chrissy turned toward her house, then looked back over her shoulder. "You drink wine, Brooke Sullivan?"

"I do."

"We should have backyard wine time one day soon."

"I'd love that." With a smile, she went back into her own house. It had been quite a morning, and she was feeling a little antsy to walk. While she got ready, she recalled her text conversation with Lena earlier.

I'm so thankful they came, she'd typed. *Truly. But I'm so ready for them to go.*

I get it. Any opinions about Macy? Lena asked *Judgments? Fire and brimstone?* She added a witch's caldron in what was likely an attempt to keep it light.

At that, Brooke sighed, felt her heart grow a little heavy, and she replied honestly. *She hasn't been around much.*

Seriously? Lena sent a line of wide-eyed emoji. *WTF?*

She'd been trying not to dwell on that very thing. What the fuck? No, they hadn't talked exclusivity. They hadn't had the *Are we girlfriends now?* discussion. So she really had no right to put demands and expectations on Macy.

Or did she?

They'd slept together. Twice. They'd made out a lot. They'd *seemed* like a thing, at least to her. Weren't they a thing? She'd certainly wanted them to be, and she was pretty sure Macy had felt the same way. But once it had been made clear in the hospital that she was going to be okay, Macy had stepped back faster than if the floor of her room had turned to quicksand.

It was likely her parents. Yeah. That made sense. They could be intimidating. She nodded to herself as she began her walk, headed toward Ridgecrest Park. She'd text Lena later and tell her that was the going theory, that Macy was put off by the intensity of Brooke's parents—after all, she had no idea what might have been said while she was unconscious, right? And she wouldn't put it past her mother to have made her opinions clear about Macy's relationship with Brooke, but now that they'd headed back to Ohio, things would get back to normal. Yes, they'd have to have a discussion about how to handle things in the future. Because frankly, her parents weren't going anywhere, and they were important to Brooke, despite some of their misguided beliefs. But they'd work it out. Definitely. They had something, the two of them. And they were worth fighting for.

At least she thought so.

Did Macy?

That was the big question. The one she really needed an answer to and also the one she kind of wanted to push into a dark corner, because the reality was, it scared her. Either answer scared her. She was terrified of what it could mean to her relationship with her family to have a future with a woman. It terrified her more to think about *not* having a future with Macy. It was soon, she knew. So early in their relationship, but she'd never felt like this before.

She went around to the front end of the park, saw the stairs in the distance, and pulled out her phone.

Parents have gone home. I'm getting some fresh air. I miss you. How's work? She sent the text, then forced herself to put the phone away rather than stare in drooling expectation of bouncing gray dots like Pavlov's dog. *Those damn dots are brutal.*

It was late morning, and the park was sparsely populated. It was finally starting to be warm on a somewhat regular basis, April and its uncertain weather long gone, May and its lovely spring weather hanging out for a while, setting the stage for June. She trekked to the bottom of the staircase, counted them as she climbed, the way she always did, until she got to number sixteen and took a seat. It was amusing to her that she'd found this perfect thinking spot so soon after her move to town. She'd had one—a thinking spot—in every neighborhood she'd lived in. There was the bench near the dog park at home. There was the fountain outside the library where she'd gone to college. And now, there was the top step at Ridgecrest Park. She never really went looking for a thinking spot, but she always knew when she'd found one, could feel it in her bones. Her head would settle, her thoughts would organize, and she could sit there for a long while, just rolling things around, examining them from all angles.

Today, she didn't want to think. She wanted to sit. To breathe. To relax. But thoughts of Macy had her uncertain. Even more so when she ventured a look at her phone and saw no reply from her.

She's working.

Her heart told her that even as her head had far less positive things to say.

Sitting quietly, she tried her best to ignore her head.

❖

Twitchy.

That's how Macy felt. It was the best description. Like her nerves were all on red alert, jangling against her bones at the slightest provocation. It wasn't a constant panic attack, but it was damn close. Way closer than she'd like. She was exhausted and confused and on edge.

Despite what would seem to be an overabundance of energy in her system, she couldn't really get herself to *do* anything. Any semblance of concentration or focus was avoiding her like she had some contagious disease, until all she could do was sit at her desk in Stage One and stare. Out the window. At her computer monitor. At her own hands. Staring. It was apparently all she was capable of.

What the hell was she going to do? She couldn't live like this. Her brain felt like a blender that never turned off, whirling and swirling all of her thoughts into a thick mess of a smoothie that she couldn't sort out no matter how hard she tried.

Brooke had texted her over an hour ago, and she hadn't responded. She was horrible. She was a horrible person. There was no other explanation. Phone in hand, she typed, deleted, typed, deleted, typed, hesitated. She had to answer. She might be a horrible person, but she was not about to ghost Brooke. God. She wasn't that horrible.

Fresh air is a great idea! Glad you're feeling better! Work is super busy! And then a smile emoji. Sent.

Oh my God with the exclamation points. That was her first thought as she reread her own words. If there was one way to tell the other person you were forcing your cheer, it was to overdo the exclamation points. She tossed her phone onto her desk with a clatter, rubbed her forehead with her fingers. She could feel Emily's eyes on her from her desk across the room, but thank God the phone rang then, saving her from any inquiries. Because honestly? She had no desire to answer them and no idea how she would.

As Emily discussed details with a client, Macy's phone chimed an incoming text. Sure it was Brooke, she braced herself for the likelihood of more over-exclamation-pointed responses and was surprised to see it was from Tyler.

At Dunkin by your office.

Macy couldn't help but grin. So many possibilities contained in those five words. Could be *meet me* or *I want a doughnut and have no money* or *my parents are driving me crazy and I want to hang with my cool aunt.* She preferred the last one, of course, but needed to be responsible first.

Why aren't you in school?

His response came quickly. *Half day.*

Seeing his sweet face would help bring some much-needed cheer to her day. She made a series of hand gestures toward Emily that she hoped were read as *I'll be back soon* and headed out the front door. Dunkin' was literally a block away, so she took the opportunity to soak up a little sun on the beautiful May afternoon and walked.

Tyler was seated at a table by the window with a cup and a doughnut on the table in front of him. His face lit up when he saw her, just like it had ever since Macy could remember, and it was something that never failed to lift her spirits, no matter how low they were. In the weeks after Michelle had died, Tyler was the only person in the world who came close to cheering her up. Her bond with her nephew was something more special than she understood, and she was forever grateful.

"Hey," she said as she crossed to him. "I thought maybe you texted because you were out of cash and wanted a doughnut."

He gave his head a toss to get the hair out of his eyes. "No, but I *am* out of cash and I *do* want another doughnut."

She grinned and shook her head. "Of course you do. Hang on." At the counter, she ordered coffee and three glazed doughnuts. Back at the table, she gave two to Tyler and took one for herself.

"Aw, you're the best," he said, then took an enormous bite of one, and not for the first time, she wondered how on earth Eva afforded enough groceries to feed him. Their mother affectionately referred to him as a bottomless pit, and she was not wrong.

"What's new?" she asked as she sat. "Why the half day?"

"Some teacher thing or superintendent's day or something." He shrugged and polished off the first—his second—doughnut.

She took a bite of hers, and good God, was there anything more divine than a big blast of sugar in the afternoon of a workday? "Are you ready for the spring dance thingy? It's this weekend, right?"

Tyler nodded, tossed his head, started on the next doughnut.

"Can I ask you something?" She sipped her coffee, watched his face.

He nodded again, chewed.

"Your mom thought you were taking Kelsey to the dance. But then you decided to go with a group instead."

"Uh-huh."

She hesitated only a moment. She and Tyler had always been very open with each other, and while some might tiptoe around the subject of sexuality, they never had. "Did that have anything to do with Jeremy?"

Tyler pursed his lips, wrinkled his nose slightly. "Probably a little, yeah."

"You wanted to go with him?"

He lifted one shoulder. "I mean, yeah, I did, but I also kinda wanted to take Kelsey." He blew out a very teenager-like sigh. "And I didn't want either one of them to feel bad. Plus, taking Jeremy could've been"—his eyes shifted so he was looking at the ceiling—"risky. His parents aren't all that cool, and I didn't want to put him in a bad spot, you know?"

"I do know. I totally get it." She hadn't come here to broach the subject of her sister and brother-in-law but realized that was exactly what she was about to do. "What about your parents?"

He looked up, mid-chew, and seemed surprised. Which surprised Macy. "They're cool."

Macy squinted at him. "Yeah?"

Ty gave a teenager shrug, that one shoulder, half lift, tip of the head move. "Yeah."

"Do they know? That you…like boys, too?" That was the picture she was getting from him. "That you're bi?"

He shook his head, but with a smile. One that screamed of eternal patience. "I don't do the label thing, Aunt Mace. I mean, it's fine if you want to, but my generation tends to not like them so much. We're just us. We're just who we are."

Macy sat back. She suddenly felt super old. But she did her best to dodder around to where her nephew stood, in a much more progressive spot than she had been at his age. Hell, in a much more progressive spot than she was at her *current* age. "And you love who you love."

A nod. A bite of doughnut.

"And your parents are okay with it?"

Another shrug. "They love me and want me to be happy." Macy gave him a look that he seemed to read. "Yes, even Dad. He's a lot of talk, you know." The last of the doughnut went into his mouth. "He's kind of a teddy bear."

Macy's brain pulled up short. Harlan? A teddy bear? She let those words sink in. Was it possible she hadn't bothered to look any deeper at her brother-in-law? A sense of shame washed over her, and she nodded at her nephew. "Fair enough. Just know you can talk to me if you need to. About anything. Okay?"

"You think I don't know that?" Sweet Tyler was back. Young Tyler who needed and adored his aunt. The new, older, alarmingly mature Tyler scared the hell out of her in some ways. How had he become so much wiser than she even gave him credit for? So observant? The coolest sixteen-year-old she'd ever met?

"Well, good. And as for Jeremy, just know that sometimes—and maybe this wasn't the time, I trust your judgment—but sometimes, it's okay to take a risk. Go for what you want, to hell with the fear that holds you back. You know?"

Tyler nodded very slowly, picked up his cup. It was hot chocolate, she could smell it. Ty had yet to develop a taste for coffee. He watched her as he sipped, and she got the impression he was sorting his thoughts, figuring out how to say something he wanted to say. He set his cup back down, still looking at her. Pursed his lips. Squinted at her.

She circled a finger in front of him. "What's this? What's with this face?"

He took a deep breath, let it out slowly as he sat back in his chair and folded his arms across his chest. "I'm just wondering."

"Wondering what?"

"If you hear yourself."

Confused, she tipped her head. "What do you mean?"

He sat forward on his forearms. Looked her in the eye. Suddenly seemed forty instead of sixteen. "Mom thinks you're flaking on being with Brooke because you got scared by what happened."

She blinked at him. Blinked some more.

He took another sip as if completely unaware of the scab he'd ripped off her, the blood that was now seeping over her skin and onto the floor. Or maybe he *was* aware, referring back to her observations of a few moments before. Whatever, he was full of surprises today. He watched her and didn't seem the least bit uncomfortable.

"I—" She cleared her throat, took a sip of her coffee, and felt it land in her stomach like a rock. Was Eva right?

"Listen, I get it. Finding her the way you did? That must've sucked donkey balls. And Mom says it probs triggered you. Which makes sense." He lifted one shoulder in a half shrug.

There was a sudden lump in her throat. A lump of…what? Emotion? Realization? Shame? Whatever it was, it didn't want to be swallowed down, so she sat there helplessly, unable to form words. But that was okay because Tyler was doing just fine in that department.

"And she really seems to make you happy. You smiled a lot more once she showed up." A sip of his hot chocolate, casually, like he wasn't nudging at her heart with a red hot poker.

She nodded. He wasn't wrong. "She does."

"So, to be honest, I'm kinda surprised you're telling me to ignore my fears and take a risk when…" He glanced down at his hands and, for the first time since Macy took a seat, seemed like he might be trying to soften his words. "You're maybe afraid to do the same thing yourself."

❖

I was hoping I could see you tonight.

Brooke's text had been followed by a smiley emoji. Not a heart. Not a heart eyes emoji. Not even the big smiling emoji. Just the tentatively smiling emoji, which said a lot to Macy.

"I've pushed her into uncertainty, Pete," she said as she poured kibble into all her pets' dishes. They were gathered around her feet in the kitchen, waiting patiently—with the exception of Angus, who preferred to skitter around the kitchen and spin in circles and make little excited whiney sounds in anticipation of his meal. It was adorable and always made her smile, but tonight, she was glad to have Pete's soulful eyes and quiet disposition as he sat at her feet and looked at her as if he knew exactly what she was saying.

She had dinner with her parents tonight, and that's what she'd told Brooke. That it was a family thing, which was stretching the truth a bit because her mother would love to see Brooke, and Macy knew that. But she'd bowed out of seeing her, decided not to invite her. Took the coward's way out and she knew it.

She was stuck.

She knew that, too, was completely aware, but couldn't figure out how to unstick herself. She liked Brooke. She liked Brooke *a lot*. In fact, she might love her. She knew it was quick, only a couple months, but there was definitely more there than she'd felt in years. Also there? Sheer unadulterated terror. Literal *terror*. Every time she remembered the second her eyes had focused on Brooke's unmoving body on the floor, her muscles seized up, her stomach dropped, beads of sweat peppered her upper lip. Her brain toggled back and forth between Brooke's body and Michelle's, and it sped up until they blended, until they were one and the same in Macy's mind. It was a bone-deep, blood-chilling fear that she couldn't accurately explain to anybody, not even herself.

Tyler's words had reverberated through her mind all day like a pinball, bouncing around off her skull, through her brain to the other side, never quite leaving her alone. How the hell had a sixteen-year-old pegged her so perfectly? She was scared. She was terrified of starting something deeper with Brooke because…What if?

She carried the pet bowls to their designated spots in a flurry of barks and spins and meows. Once everybody was eating noisily, she inhaled deeply, filled her lungs.

She was stuck.

Reaching around her body, she pulled out her phone and punched a text off to her mother, bowing out of dinner completely. She couldn't face her parents because they'd surely want an update on Brooke. Facing Eva, knowing what she thought, was even more petrifying. She claimed she was just too tired to come over, that she wanted to take the evening and just be home with her animals, that she'd talk to her the next day. Then she turned her phone to silent and left it on the kitchen counter while she went into the living room to find something mindless on television.

She couldn't deal with anybody right now.

Not even herself.

CHAPTER TWENTY-SIX

R age.
　　　Brooke was pretty sure that's what was shooting through her bloodstream as if propelled by jet fuel and had been since last night. There was also sorrow, humiliation, and hurt, but the rage was much easier to grab on to than the other things, and boy did she grab on. With both hands. She let it drown out all those other feelings, which was safer, for sure. Right?

　　　She'd hardly gotten any sleep. Getting a text from Macy's mom, who was sweetly checking in to see how she was feeling, had started the ball rolling because she'd texted Mrs. Carr back to give her an update and also asked her to say hello to Macy for her. Macy, who, Mrs. Carr texted back, was apparently home, too tired from her day to come to dinner. Wait, what? So she couldn't go to dinner at her parents' house because she was too tired, but she couldn't hang out with Brooke because she was going to dinner at her parents' house—which was a family thing that she didn't feel right including Brooke in, apparently?

　　　Wasn't that interesting?

　　　Ideas for snotty texts ran through her mind like the ticker at the bottom of a news broadcast, an endless stream of not-so-nice words. She thought about calling but was pretty sure Macy would avoid her call. Besides, she was a person who believed in face-to-face conversation in an age of texting and emailing, even when it was hard. She'd come out to her parents face-to-face. To Michael, as well. Unlike so many people in her age group who thought a quick electronic note was enough, she went to her old boss and resigned in person. It was the respectful thing to do, and she'd been brought up to be respectful.

　　　In this case, respect be damned. She wanted her thoughts and feelings to be clear to Macy. Absolutely clear. Because exactly what kind of bullshit was this? Did she not know Macy at all? How was it possible that she didn't? The woman she was falling for?

Yeah, that had stopped her in her tracks.

Because…was that true? Was she falling for Macy?

She'd snorted, a scoffing sound through her nose, due to its ridiculousness. No, she wasn't falling for Macy.

She already had.

And goddamn it, Macy had made her think she felt the same way.

She'd left her phone in the bathroom that night, so she wouldn't be tempted in the wee hours, when she was weakest and at her most vulnerable, to send a pathetic, pleading text. No, she wanted to save up her words until she was face-to-face with Macy.

Being a massive drama queen crossed her mind as she showered and dressed. She could storm through the door of Stage One and unload on Macy right there, right as she sat at her desk, blinking in surprise. Oh, she wanted to. But whatever glimmer of respect she had left told her that wasn't the way to do things, that she needed to confront Macy in private. So she'd set her alarm, got up early. It was Wednesday and Sasha had ordered her to stay home the rest of the week. She felt fine, but Sasha had insisted, told her to catch up on movies or reading or whatever and to just rest. She'd promised Sasha she'd take at least a little time off but might make an appearance toward the end of the week, and as she stood in front of her mirror now and pulled a slate-blue and white plaid shirt over her blue tank, she knew she'd be going back to work tomorrow. There was no way she could stay home another day with all of this on her mind and not go completely mad. They'd have to come haul her away. Probably in a straitjacket.

She sat on the bed next to a yawning Rorschach and pulled on her white tennis shoes, cuffed her jeans a bit. "I know I'm focusing on my anger, Rorsh, but the truth? I'm kinda crushed." She whispered the last three words, felt her heart squeeze. She took a moment, cleared her throat, and felt back around into the dark recesses for the anger.

So much easier, the anger.

Once she had it firmly in her grasp again, figuratively fisted in both hands, and the heartbreak tucked away in a box, she dropped a kiss on her cat's head, scratched behind his ears for a minute, whispered, "Here goes, Rorsh, wish me luck," and headed out.

Traffic was light, as it was still before rush hour. The sun was shining, and it made her unreasonably mad. What the hell? The weather should match her mood, damn it. Gray and stormy. Dark and twisty.

Thunder and lightning would be a plus. A tornado, perhaps? This sunshine was all wrong.

She made her way to Macy's street, stopped in front of her cute little house, and jammed the car into park. The sun was coming up, but she could see a few lights on inside, knew Macy was likely in the kitchen feeding the dogs and cats.

With every step up the front walk, she weirdly felt a little bit of the wind taken from her sails. Trying to ignore that, she took the two front steps up, swallowed hard, and rang the doorbell, inexplicably glad Macy didn't have a Ring camera there. As soon as she heard the dogs barking wildly, she understood that if anybody *didn't* need an outdoor camera, it was Macy. The barking got closer to the door. Brooke shook out her arms as they hung at her sides, like a boxer getting ready for a fight.

The door opened.

"Oh my God, hi." Macy looked surprised, confused, elated, and worried all at once as she used her feet and legs to keep the dogs—that obviously wanted to love on Brooke—from escaping out the door. "Come in."

She hadn't intended to enter, only to say her piece on the front stoop and leave, but she hadn't factored the dogs in to that equation, and the only way to calm them was to obey and step inside. But she wasn't going any farther in, damn it.

"It's good to see you," Macy said, then instantly grimaced, clearly realizing the ridiculousness of her statement, which Brooke seized on.

"Yeah, well, you could've seen me any time you wanted. I've been home for two days. Which you know because I've texted you." Pause for dramatic effect or whatever. "How was dinner?" It was obvious Macy knew she was busted because circles of red blossomed on her cheeks, and she looked down at her feet. "Yeah, I texted with your mom last night."

She'd made Macy feel bad, and while that had been her initial intention, now she hesitated. The looks that washed over Macy's face. Chagrin. Guilt. Apology. She hated seeing them. Catching herself, she again felt around her brain for the anger that had fueled her so hotly last night, this morning. She found it, but somehow, it felt more lukewarm now than raging and fiery.

"Listen, I don't know what's going on with you." She did her best to be firm, to keep an edge in her voice, and she was pretty sure she succeeded. "And evidently, you don't want to tell me or talk about it. Which is a damn shame. But I thought I'd let you know that I'm fine. I'm better. I see the doctor on Monday for a follow-up, but I'm good. And I have you to thank for that. I am forever grateful to you for saving me. And forever saddened that this is how you've chosen to handle things, by avoiding me. I kinda thought we were on the verge of having something here, but I guess that was just me." And the remainder of the wind was gone from her sails. Just like that. "Okay. Well. I'm fine. Just wanted you to know. Have a nice day."

Part of her wanted to wait and see how Macy responded, but she was also tired and hurt, and a larger part of her wanted to run, to be done. So that's what she did. She fled. She turned and opened the door behind her, leaving Macy standing in her own foyer looking chastised, ashamed, and a little shell-shocked. She stepped through the door, shut it, then walked briskly to her car.

It wasn't until she'd pulled away and was safely onto another street that the sob bubbled up from deep in her chest and burst out of her.

❖

Macy watched through the small, square window in her front door as Brooke pulled away. As somebody she cared deeply about pulled away. As a person she might've liked to build a future with pulled away.

She turned, back against the door, and slowly slid down to the floor where she sat silently for a moment.

"Well, well, well," she finally whispered. "If it isn't the consequences of my own actions."

The dogs, of course, loved that she was on the floor and let her know it by kissing her face—Pete—and dropping tennis balls into her lap—Angus. She gave the ball a half-hearted toss, and Angus charged after it, his little tank of a body moving with surprising speed. She was always amazed at how fast those little legs could carry him, built like a cinder block the way he was. Pete lay down next to her and set his chin on her thigh, emotionally attuned to her as always. She rested her hand on his head.

"I fucked up, Pete. Big-time." Her head fell back to the door with a quiet thump. "You know what the worst part is?" Pete's ears pricked up as if he was really listening. "I knew it. I *knew* it as I was doing it.

In the midst of fucking up, I knew I was fucking up, yet I continued to fuck up. What is wrong with me?"

Never one to be great at talking openly about things that were emotional, she'd once wondered aloud why that was. It had been after Michelle's death, and Eva was on her about something she couldn't recall. But Eva had theorized that maybe it was because she'd been with Michelle since they were teenagers. That they'd developed emotionally together and knew each other so well that they hadn't needed to explicitly deconstruct problems or emotions. And with Michelle gone, Macy no longer had somebody who could predict her thoughts and register her feelings without needing her to verbalize them.

It made a crazy kind of sense.

The hurt in Brooke's eyes had been as clear as if she'd worn a big sandwich board that said, *You hurt me badly, Macy Carr.* She'd tried to hide it with the edge in her voice, with the firmness in her tone, but Macy had seen it. Glaringly. Accusingly. Painfully. And Macy felt horrible about that. Terribly guilty. Rightfully so.

"Why didn't I just tell her?" Her eyes filled with tears, and Pete, ever the emotion dog, sat up and touched his cold, wet nose to her face, sniffed her tears, nuzzled her. "Oh, Petey, what am I gonna do?"

He tried to get closer to her, pushed every one of his sixty-five pounds into her body, and she wrapped her arms around him, eternally grateful for his unconditional love, just as Angus returned and dropped his ball expectantly next to her. Priscilla was watching. Macy would never understand somebody who claimed to not be a dog person. Pete's big, brown, soulful eyes stared back at her. How was it possible to not be a dog person?

Brooke hadn't given her a chance to respond. She'd come in, hit Macy with both barrels, then turned and left. Which was likely how she'd planned it, Macy realized, but still. She wished she'd been quicker with a response. God, *any* response.

She grabbed Pete's face, placed a kiss right between his eyes, and said, "I have to talk to her, don't I?" He continued to stare at her, and she sighed. "Yeah, I know. You're absolutely right. It's the only way. I have to try to…explain."

A groan born of so many things: frustration, worry, embarrassment, dread. Because the idea of having to tell Brooke the truth—that finding her lying there, unmoving, had terrified her so much she couldn't imagine putting herself in that position ever again—terrified her even more. She was caught in a vicious cycle of fear, and admitting to it was her only way out. She knew that. She *knew* it. And she fought it with everything she had.

She needed time. Because right now? There was no way. She'd broken out in a cold sweat just sitting there on the floor and thinking about admitting to her fears. Her stomach roiled sourly, and she tried to swallow it all down. Closing her eyes, she breathed in slowly through her nose, tried to calm herself.

Nope. It was coming.

She pushed herself to her feet and ran up the stairs to the bathroom, both Pete and Angus clambering after her, Priscilla taking her time judging by the slow clicking of her nails on the hardwood steps. Sliding into the bathroom on her knees, Macy emptied her stomach of the breakfast she'd had no more than half an hour ago. She continued to retch until there was nothing left and she was simply dry heaving over the toilet.

Flushed. Sat back. Pete watched her carefully as she sat there, her entire body covered in a sheen of sweat, eyes tearing as the sound of her ragged breathing filled the room.

Jesus Christ, she had to pull herself together. She had to get dressed. Go to work. Get things done. This was ridiculous.

When she tried to get up, her stomach cramped painfully, her body's way of telling her to sit the hell back down and breathe. So she did. Pete lay down next to her, and even Angus gave up trying to play ball, as if realizing his mom was sick. He sat on the other side of her, watched her carefully with his big, brown eyes. Priscilla lay down in the hall, also watching, and both Captain Jack and Jellybean took turns casually strolling by the doorway periodically, as if checking on her but not wanting her to know it. Eventually, Captain Jack wandered in and made his way onto her lap, where he curled into a warm ball and began to purr.

Sitting on the bathroom floor, all of her animals crammed into the tiny space with her, painted quite a picture. Made it very clear to her how lucky she was, what she had. It also shone a very bright light on what was missing.

When her back finally let her know that spending the day on the tile floor was something she'd pay for later, she managed to make her way back to her bedroom, wastebasket in hand, just in case. Suddenly feeling utterly and completely exhausted, she burrowed under the covers of her bed, and the animals all found their spots and settled, somehow understanding that quiet resting was needed. Sending a quick text off to Emily saying she was feeling under the weather and was taking a sick day, she set her phone on the nightstand and closed her eyes.

She wanted to forget all of this, and at the same time, she wanted to fix it, while simultaneously wondering if she'd ruined it for good. Brooke had reached her limit, that had been clear. She'd been hurt. She'd also been super angry. Macy wondered if she could come back from it.

God, she wanted to hide from the world and pulled the covers over her head in an attempt to do just that.

Please let me escape.

Chapter Twenty-seven

The trouble with unloading both barrels before eight a.m. was that Brooke had the rest of the day still laid out before her. She was definitely going to go to work tomorrow because there was no way on earth she could wander around aimlessly with nothing to do for the rest of the week. She'd throw herself off a roof.

Macy hadn't said a thing beyond it was nice to see her. Well, okay, to be fair, she hadn't really given her a chance to. But still. Why didn't Macy interrupt? Why hadn't she chased her down in the driveway? Apologized? Asked her forgiveness and begged her to stay?

Oh my God, you're not Meg Ryan in an eighties rom-com. Stop expecting to get her ridiculously happy endings.

She sighed quietly at the accuracy of her thoughts.

Beans & Batter was hopping, but since most customers were coming in, grabbing their morning coffee, and leaving, she was able to find a table by the window with no problem. She sat down with her vanilla latte and a bagel with honey walnut cream cheese and tried to relax. The morning already felt like an entire stressful week.

People watching was a favorite pastime of hers, and she sat there doing exactly that as she ate her breakfast. It was a weekday, but that damn sun was still shining, so people were out and about, walking to this place or that. She spent a few minutes counting passersby in black coats—twenty-three—but then switched to something less common so that she could actually blink once in a while: people with red hair like hers. Friends in warmer climes didn't quite get this behavior. How people would flock to be outdoors anytime the temperature reached something considered warm for the season. Even if it was a chilly forty-five degrees, if it was January or February or March, people in the Northeast would be outside in T-shirts, breathing in the fresh air like they'd just been let out of prison. Hell, she'd been known to do it herself if the winter had been particularly brutal. There was nothing like warm sunshine to make everything feel a little bit better.

Except for today. She was still mad at Mother Nature for not creating the right backdrop for her visit this morning.

And then she was right back to thinking about Macy.

Had she been too hard on her? She didn't think so, but after the fact was when all the wondering and second-guessing happened, so she was right on track. The look on Macy's face was... Brooke squeezed her eyes shut, then took a bite of her bagel to occupy herself. No, she'd gone there to make her displeasure and her hurt known, and she'd done that. She had nothing to feel bad about.

Her phone buzzed in her back pocket, and her entire body betrayed her in the hopes that it was Macy. Her heart rate kicked up. Anticipation tickled her belly. A tiny shot of adrenaline pushed through her blood. And yet, she took her time. Casually set down her bagel. Picked up her napkin and dabbed the corner of her mouth with it. Took a sip of her latte.

Oh my God, what are you waiting for? her brain shrieked at her.

She slid out the phone and looked.

Not Macy. Not Macy at all. The opposite of Macy.

Aidan.

Her client from Whitney Gardens. The one who had looked at the apartment. The handsome guy with the neat goatee and the kind eyes. The one who had asked her to drinks sometime.

He was asking again.

Hey there, it's Aidan Bush from a couple weeks ago. Wondering if you're free and if you'd like to meet for drinks tonight. And a smiling emoji.

She was impressed. No begging. No time or place. Just the simple question with no pressure to answer yes or no. To the point. She liked that.

For a moment, she let herself agonize over a response. But then she reminded herself that she didn't *have* to answer right away. One of the drawbacks of texting—it made you feel pressured to respond, radiated a sense of urgency that wasn't necessarily there. She set the phone down. She'd think about it for a while. Because while she'd liked Aidan, had initially had no reason *not* to grab a drink with him, she needed to make sure that if she accepted his invitation, it wasn't simply to spite Macy.

Right now, if she was being honest, that would be exactly the reason.

She was frustrated as she took another bite of her bagel and counted her fourth redhead. Disappointed. Sad. Hurt. And also? She didn't quite understand. Maybe she should've hung out this morning and waited for Macy to explain to her exactly why she'd evidently decided to simply fade out of her life. She hadn't ghosted her, but it felt damn close to that. Had she done something? Had her parents said something? Should she give them a call and ask? She closed her eyes and exhaled through her nose. Her energy might have been returning, but it wasn't back in full yet, and she was pretty sure dealing with her mother on that subject was not something she could handle. Yet.

Maybe tomorrow.

She sipped her latte and counted another redhead.

❖

The sun shone through the windows of Macy's bedroom. Angus wasn't under the bed like normal but, instead, was stretched out against her hip. Captain Jack and Jellybean were near her head, Jack with a protective paw on her shoulder. Pete was at the foot of the bed, his chin on her ankle, and Priscilla was in a ball between her knees. All of her animals were on the bed with her all at once, which had never, ever happened.

They were watching over her. She understood that, and her heart warmed in her chest at the unconditional love of her animals. She looked down her body at Pete, who—despite his relaxed position on her foot—was wide-awake and watching her with his big brown eyes. Tyler often commented about how human Pete's eyes seemed, and he was right.

Tyler.

And then Macy was replaying their conversation about being true to who you are and about taking risks in life once in a while. She could hear his voice in her head, repeating the one thing that really stuck with her.

And she really seems to make you happy. You smiled a lot more once she showed up.

He still wasn't wrong. Brooke did make her smile. Chuckle. Laugh outright. Crack up. How long had it been since she'd felt complete joy being with somebody?

About three years.

And something in her settled. Just like that.

As she inhaled a big breath and slowly let it out, she felt something she hadn't felt since finding Brooke on the floor at the open house: calm. Totally calm and surprisingly relaxed, which was rarely the case lately, and especially now, given the stress she'd put her brain and heart through. But she felt completely at peace. Which was kind of nuts considering how rarely she felt that way.

So. Weird.

A glance at the clock told her she'd only been in bed for about an hour since leaving her breakfast in the toilet. Which was strange because it felt like it had been a lot longer. *A lot* longer. Hours. She felt the need to get up and go find Brooke, explain it all to her, apologize, ask for another chance. At the same time, she just wanted to stay in bed, curled up and warm with her animals, and not deal with anything at all.

She groaned. Loudly. With frustration. And as she lay there, something odd happened. The animals got up. One by one, they each stood, stretched, and hopped off the bed. And then they sat on the floor and stared at her. None of them made a sound. Pete wagged his tail, because Pete always wagged his tail. But that was it. It was as if they were waiting for her to get up. Patiently waiting.

Then she felt it. An urgency. It started as a tingle in the tips of her toes, like it was building slowly, and then it shot through her body like she'd gotten a slight zap of electricity. She sat up quickly. Looked from dog to cat to dog. And like the sun being unveiled by clouds, she suddenly felt more clarity than she'd felt in years. Three of them, to be exact.

"I need to find Brooke, don't I, you guys?"

Pete barked once, and all five animals turned and scooted out of the bedroom. Macy watched them go, felt the smile as it burst into bloom across her face.

"I need to find Brooke," she said again.

She knew exactly where to look.

Chapter Twenty-eight

The crowd had thinned. People were at work now, and that included the four sitting at different tables with their laptops open in front of them. Brooke had had more than enough coffee, had used the restroom, and needed to get the hell out of Beans & Batter before she bought herself a scone or a muffin or another bagel or something else she didn't need but was seriously tempted by.

With a wave to the barista, she pushed out the door and slid her aviators on against the brilliance of the stupid sun.

Her phone pinged an incoming text, and she tamped down any excitement, prepared herself for disappointment. Again, not Macy. Lucas this time, which Brooke found herself smiling about. He was checking on her, and that warmed her heart.

How's it going over there? Doing okay? Macy said your parents were in town. They taking good care of you?

At least Macy was in touch with somebody. Brooke used Siri and dictated her responses as she walked. *Hi there! I'm good. Parents left yesterday.*

How's Macy holding up?

She stared at the screen. Well, that was an odd question to ask. She thought about dodging it, being a snarkypants about it, even outright ignoring it. Instead, she went with a gentle truth. *I haven't seen much of her, to be honest.*

The gray dots bounced for what seemed like a long time, but probably was only fifteen or twenty seconds. Lucas's reply stopped her in her tracks.

Just be patient. Finding you the way she did stirred up a lot of memories for her. Bad ones.

"Wait. What?" She literally stopped walking and stood still, the guy walking behind her making a sound of surprise as he barely avoided running smack into her. She stared hard at the words on her screen. Read them over and over again and was pretty sure she was missing something. *What does that mean?* she finally typed.

This time, there were dots, and then they disappeared, and then a long stretch of time went by. She started to wonder if Lucas had ended the conversation completely until he finally returned with a paragraph.

I'm gonna guess she didn't tell you the details. She tends not to bring them up, and I usually don't either because it's not my story to tell, but she's the one who found Michelle. She tried to revive her the entire time she waited for the ambulance but couldn't. It did a number on her...

He left the rest for her to fill in on her own, and it wasn't hard. Finding Brooke unconscious on the floor must have reopened horrific wounds for Macy and brought awful memories surging back.

"Oh my God," she whispered as she looked up, her eyes wet. "Oh God, poor Macy. Why didn't she tell me?" She typed back to Lucas, *I had no idea* and a crying emoji.

She resumed walking, her pace slower now, as she recalled the things she'd said to Macy not long ago, how harsh she'd been. She felt terrible. And guilty. And so, so sorry.

And then a little shot of anger filtered in. It was small, but it was there. Because, seriously, *why* hadn't Macy told her this? Why hadn't she told her about finding Michelle, and why hadn't she told her what finding Brooke had done to her?

God, this was crazy. She wanted to yell at Macy...and then she wanted to wrap her in a hug and protect her from any more pain for the rest of her life. Her mind was a jumble. Her heart ached. Her face was tight, and she could feel that she was scowling. What the hell was she supposed to do now?

Her body began walking in the right direction before she even realized where she was headed. It was a gorgeous day. She didn't have to work. It made the most sense because she was afraid her head might explode.

She picked up the pace. More than anything right then, she needed to sit, and she needed to think.

❖

Macy had thought about bringing the dogs with her, just in case Brooke wasn't at the park. They could at least get a walk in. But then she'd realized that she had no idea how long this would take, how it would feel, where it would go, and it would be difficult to keep Angus still while in the park because, as far as he was concerned, the park was for brisk walking and sniffing *everything*. No, she needed no distractions. She just needed Brooke.

Ridgecrest Park was nearly empty, she noticed as she entered from the sidewalk at the base of the hill, and it felt a little weird. Macy was used to being there on weekends or weeknights when it was at its most populated. But ten o'clock in the morning on a Wednesday in late May was apparently a great time to have the place to yourself.

It wasn't hard to find Brooke. She was exactly where Macy expected her to be, and she gave herself a little pat on the back for knowing her so well already. Perched on the top step, her auburn hair reflecting the bright sunshine, she sat with her forearms on her knees, her head down, and she didn't see Macy approach at first. Macy walked silently until she reached the base of the steps. There, she stopped, and as Brooke lifted her head and met her gaze, she said quietly, "Hey."

"Hi." There was a lot crammed into that one word. Pain. Relief. Sorrow. Joy. Brooke's big dark eyes were slightly pink, and Macy wondered if she'd been crying. The thought of that squeezed her heart in her chest. They stayed silent for what felt like a long time, Macy trying to find the right words to say next, but Brooke beat her to it. "Why didn't you tell me?"

"Tell you what?"

"That you found Michelle's body?"

Oh. Okay. That's the direction the conversation was going to go. And if she was going to be honest with herself, she had to admit that Brooke not having *all* the information wasn't fair. It was high time she did. "How do you know?"

Brooke sighed, looked off into the distance. "Lucas texted me this morning. When I told him I hadn't seen much of you, he mentioned how finding me the way you did must've triggered some awful memories for you, and I had no idea what he meant. So I asked."

"I should've. I should've told you."

Brooke laughed through her nose. "You think?"

"I'm sorry." And she was. Desperately. "But..." She looked around the park at the grass that had become lushly green in the past few weeks. At the leaves on the trees bursting into being. She swallowed because that goddamn lump was back. The truth lump, as she'd begun thinking of it. "I don't talk about it with anybody." When Brooke's eyes captured hers, silently calling bullshit, she held up a hand. "I know that's not good. I realize that now. I think I've just gotten so used to keeping that all hidden away in a dark corner to avoid the pain that it's become natural for me not to say anything except in extenuating circumstances."

"That was about as extenuating as it gets, don't you think?"

"I do." She nodded vigorously. "I do, and I'm so, so sorry. I've been so afraid of taking a risk, but I have realized—very recently, thanks to my disturbingly wise nephew—that risks are a part of life, and it's not really living if you never take them."

"Very true." A moment went by, Brooke on the top step looking at her hands, Macy standing at the bottom. Finally, Brooke glanced back up, and this time, there were definitely tears in her eyes. "And I'm sorry, too. I should've given you a chance to explain this morning instead of unloading on you like I did and then running away. I was just so"—she clenched her teeth and her fists—"angry. I've had enough people in my life turn their backs on me. I never thought you would, so when you did, it just made me so angry. And it hurt, Macy. It *hurt*. I was angry and I was hurt and the hurt made me angrier."

"You definitely were. Remind me to always stay on your good side from here on out." A small smile coupled with her attempt at some levity.

Another moment went by. "From here on out, huh?"

Macy shifted from one foot to the other and back. "I mean, yeah. I'm hoping we can try this again. If you think we can. Because I…" Again, she looked off into the distance and wondered if she expected somebody to come riding out of the trees and hand her a script with all the right things to say written down in an orderly fashion instead of the stuttering and long pauses she was using now. Without bringing her eyes back to Brooke, she said, "I haven't felt this way about somebody in a long time. Not since…" No. She couldn't just leave things for others to figure out. Not anymore. She cleared her throat and turned to look up the staircase, right into Brooke's beautiful eyes. "I haven't felt this way since Michelle died. I never thought I would again. But you…" She shook her head and said, "You make me happy. So happy. You make me laugh. You make me think. You make me look forward to *life*. I'm not sure if you know how much that means, Brooke, but you matter to me. In a very big way, you matter."

Brooke's tears had spilled over and tracked down her cheeks. Macy could see them even from the distance between them, wanted to brush them away. "Well. You matter to me, too. You more than matter." Her gaze was intense as she said quietly, "I love you, Macy."

Somehow—Macy couldn't put a finger on it—but somehow, those words broke through a dam. The dam of her own emotions, as if Brooke's words finally gave them permission to flow, to rush, to wash over. Her eyes welled up as she realized the words, felt them, embraced them, and tried to say them. They came out in a croak. "I love you, too."

Two bursts of laughter through tears. Relief, at least for Macy, but she was pretty sure she saw it on Brooke's face as well. "Can I come up there?"

"Listen, I've just been sitting here waiting."

Macy didn't take another second and counted in her head as she climbed. When finally at the top, she sat down next to Brooke. "Sixteen steps to love."

"Sixteen steps to a kiss," Brooke said and leaned in.

It had been less than a week since the last time she'd kissed Brooke's lips, but in that moment, it felt like it had been weeks. Months. Years, even, which was silly, as she'd only known Brooke for a couple of months. She knew right then that she never, ever wanted to hide anything from this woman again. She pulled back, looked deeply into those deep, dark eyes, and said the words one more time. "I love you." She never wanted to stop saying them.

"I love you, too." Brooke's voice was a whisper, and she leaned in.

This kiss was slow. It was soft. It was tender and filled with love and relief and desire and promise, and in that moment, it felt just like coming home.

Kissing Brooke felt like coming home.

The thought caught her, held her tightly as she pulled her lips from Brooke's and looked her in the eye. She tucked a lock of red hair behind Brooke's ear and whispered, "Sixteen steps to forever."

Brooke's arms were suddenly around her, wrapping her up, and as Macy hugged her back, she was struck by how safe she felt. How loved. They sat there for a long while, Macy's head on Brooke's shoulder. The day was gorgeous. The park was quiet. They were together, so they simply stayed there, side by side, holding each other, and soaked it in.

"Sixteen steps to forever," Brooke echoed, and no four words had ever been so perfect.

About the Author

Georgia Beers is an award-winning author of nearly thirty lesbian romance novels. She resides with her pets in upstate New York on the shores of Lake Ontario. Her goal in life is to drink all the wine, eat all the cheese, and pet all the dogs. She is currently hard at work on her next book. You can visit her and find out more at georgiabeers.com.

Books Available From Bold Strokes Books

16 Steps to Forever by Georgia Beers. Can Brooke Sullivan and Macy Carr find themselves by finding each other? (978-1-63555-762-6)

All I Want for Christmas by Georgia Beers, Maggie Cummings & Fiona Riley. The Christmas season sparks passion and love in these stories by award-winning authors Georgia Beers, Maggie Cummings, and Fiona Riley. (978-1-63555-764-0)

From the Woods by Charlotte Greene. When Fiona goes backpacking in a protected wilderness, the last thing she expects is to be fighting for her life. (978-1-63555-793-0)

Heart of the Storm by Nicole Stiling. For Juliet Mitchell and Sienna Bennett a forbidden attraction definitely isn't worth upending the life they've worked so hard for. Is it? (978-1-63555-789-3)

If You Dare by Sandy Lowe. For Lauren West and Emma Prescott, following their passions is easy. Following their hearts, though? That's almost impossible. (978-1-63555-654-4)

Love Changes Everything by Jaime Maddox. For Samantha Brooks and Kirby Fielding, no matter how careful their plans, love will change everything. (978-1-63555-835-7)

Not This Time by MA Binfield. Flung back into each other's lives, can former bandmates Sophia and Madison have a second chance at romance? (978-1-63555-798-5)

The Found Jar by Jaycie Morrison. Fear keeps Emily Harris trapped in her emotionally vacant life; can she find the courage to let Beck Reynolds guide her toward love? (978-1-63555-825-8)

Aurora by Emma L McGeown. After a traumatic accident, Elena Ricci is stricken with amnesia, leaving her with no recollection of the last eight years, including her wife and son. (978-1-63555-824-1)

Avenging Avery by Sheri Lewis Wohl. Revenge against a vengeful vampire unites Isa Meyer and Jeni Denton, but it's love that heals them. (978-1-63555-622-3)

Bulletproof by Maggie Cummings. For Dylan Prescott and Briana Logan, the complicated NYC criminal justice system doesn't leave room for love, but where the heart is concerned, no one is bulletproof. (978-1-63555-771-8)

Her Lady to Love by Jane Walsh. A shy wallflower joins forces with the most popular woman in Regency London on a quest to catch a husband, only to discover a wild passion for each other that far eclipses their interest for the Marriage Mart. (978-1-63555-809-8)

No Regrets by Joy Argento. For Jodi and Beth, the possibility of losing their future will force them to decide what is really important. (978-1-63555-751-0)

The Holiday Treatment by Elle Spencer. Who doesn't want a gay Christmas movie? Holly Hudson asks herself that question and discovers that happy endings aren't only for the movies. (978-1-63555-660-5)

Too Good to be True by Leigh Hays. Can the promise of love survive the realities of life for Madison and Jen, or is it too good to be true? (978-1-63555-715-2)

Treacherous Seas by Radclyffe. When the choice comes down to the lives of her officers against the promise she made to her wife, Reese Conlon puts everything she cares about on the line. (978-1-63555-778-7)

Two to Tangle by Melissa Brayden. Ryan Jacks has been a player all her life, but the new chef at Tangle Valley Vineyard changes every-thing. If only she wasn't off the menu. (978-1-63555-747-3)

When Sparks Fly by Annie McDonald. Will the devastating incident that first brought Dr. Daniella Waveny and hockey coach Luca McCaffrey together on frozen ice now force them apart, or will their secrets and fears thaw enough for them to create sparks? (978-1-63555-782-4)

Best Practice by Carsen Taite. When attorney Grace Maldonado agrees to mentor her best friend's little sister, she's prepared to confront Perry's rebellious nature, but she isn't prepared to fall in love. Legal

Affairs: one law firm, three best friends, three chances to fall in love. (978-1-63555-361-1)

Home by Kris Bryant. Natalie and Sarah discover that anything is possible when love takes the long way home. (978-1-63555-853-1)

Keeper by Sydney Quinne. With a new charge under her reluctant wing—feisty, highly intelligent math wizard Isabelle Templeton—Keeper Andy Bouchard has to prevent a murder or die trying. (978-1-63555-852-4)

One More Chance by Ali Vali. Harry Basantes planned a future with Desi Thompson until the day Desi disappeared without a word, only to walk back into her life sixteen years later. (978-1-63555-536-3)

Renegade's War by Gun Brooke. Freedom fighter Aurelia DeCallum regrets saving the woman called Blue. She fears it will jeopardize her mission, and secretly, Blue might end up breaking Aurelia's heart. (978-1-63555-484-7)

The Other Women by Erin Zak. What happens in Vegas should stay in Vegas, but what do you do when the love you find in Vegas changes your life forever? (978-1-63555-741-1)

The Sea Within by Missouri Vaun. Time is running out for Dr. Elle Graham to convince Captain Jackson Drake that the only thing that can save future Earth resides in the past, and rescue her broken heart in the process. (978-1-63555-568-4)

To Sleep With Reindeer Justine Saracen. In Norway under Nazi occupation, Maarit, an Indigenous woman, and Kirsten, a Norwegian resister, join forces to stop the development of an atomic weapon. (978-1-63555-735-0)

Twice Shy by Aurora Rey. Having an ex with benefits isn't all it's cracked up to be. Will Amanda Russo learn that lesson in time to take a chance on love with Quinn Sullivan? (978-1-63555-737-4)

Z-Town by Eden Darry. Forced to work together to stay alive, Meg and Lane must find the centuries-old treasure before the zombies find them first. (978-1-63555-743-5)

Bet Against Me by Fiona Riley. In the high-stakes luxury real estate market, everything has a price, and as rival Realtors Trina Lee and Kendall Yates find out, that means their hearts and souls, too. (978-1-63555-729-9)

Broken Reign by Sam Ledel. Together on an epic journey in search of a mysterious cure, a princess and a village outcast must overcome life-threatening challenges and their own prejudice if they want to survive. (978-1-63555-739-8)

Just One Taste by CJ Birch. For Lauren, it only took one taste to start trusting in love again. (978-1-63555-772-5)

Lady of Stone by Barbara Ann Wright. Sparks fly as a magical emergency forces a noble embarrassed by her ability to submit to a low-born teacher who resents everything about her. (978-1-63555-607-0)

Last Resort by Angie Williams. Katie and Rhys are about to find out what happens when you meet the girl of your dreams but you aren't looking for a happily ever after. (978-1-63555-774-9)

Longing for You by Jenny Frame. When Debrek housekeeper Katie Brekman is attacked amid a burgeoning vampire-witch war, Alexis Villiers must go against everything her clan believes in to save her. (978-1-63555-658-2)

Money Creek by Anne Laughlin. Clare Lehane is a troubled lawyer from Chicago who tries to make her way in a rural town full of secrets and deceptions. (978-1-63555-795-4)

Passion's Sweet Surrender by Ronica Black. Cam and Blake are unable to deny their passion for each other, but surrendering to love is a whole different matter. (978-1-63555-703-9)

The Holiday Detour by Jane Kolven. It will take everything going wrong to make Dana and Charlie see how right they are for each other. (978-1-63555-720-6)